THE BEGINNING of EVERYTHING

THE BEGINNING of EVERYTHING

ROBYN SCHNEIDER

KATHERINE TEGEN BOOKS
An Imprint of HarperCollins Publishers

Katherine Tegen Books is an imprint of HarperCollins Publishers.

The Beginning of Everything
Copyright © 2013 by Robyn Schneider

Library of Congress Cataloging-in-Publication Data
Schneider, Robyn.
The beginning of everything / Robyn Schneider. — 1st ed.
    p.   cm.
Summary: "Star athelete and prom king Ezra Faulkner's life is
irreparably transformed by a tragic accident and the arrival of eccentric
new girl Cassidy Thorpe."— Provided by publisher.
    ISBN 978-0-06-221713-4 (hardcover bdgs) — ISBN 978-0-06-227550-9 (int'l. ed.)
    [1. People with disabilities—Fiction.   2. Interpersonal relations—Fiction.
3. High schools—Fiction.   4. Schools—Fiction.   5. Debates and debating—
Fiction.   6. Family life—California—Fiction.   7. California—Fiction.]   I. Title.
PZ7.S36426Beg 2013   2012030976
[Fic]—dc23

Typography by Carla Weise

14 15 16 17 CG/RRDH   10 9 8 7 6 5 4
❖

First Edition

TO MY PARENTS,
who will no doubt try to find themselves in this book.
Don't worry, I made it easy for you—you're right here,
at the very front!

THE BEGINNING of EVERYTHING

I fell in love with her courage, her sincerity
and her flaming self respect and it's these things
I'd believe in even if the whole world indulged
in wild suspicions that she wasn't all that she should be. . . .
I love her and that's the beginning and end of everything.
—F. SCOTT FITZGERALD

The world breaks everyone, and afterward,
some are strong at the broken places.
—ERNEST HEMINGWAY

1

SOMETIMES I THINK that everyone has a tragedy waiting for them, that the people buying milk in their pajamas
or picking their noses at stoplights could be only moments
away from disaster. That everyone's life, no matter how
unremarkable, has a moment when it will become extraordi-
nary—a single encounter after which everything that really
matters will happen.

My friend Toby came down with a bad case of tragedy the week before we started seventh grade at Westlake
Middle School. We were fanatical about Ping-Pong that
summer, playing it barefoot in his backyard with aspirations
toward some sort of world championship. I was the better
player, because my parents had forced me into private tennis
lessons ever since I'd been given my own fork at the dinner
table. But sometimes, out of a sense of friendship, I let Toby
win. It was a game for me, figuring out how to lose just convincingly enough that he wouldn't figure I was doing it on

purpose. And so, while he practiced for the mythical Ping-Pong world championship, I practiced a quiet, well-meaning type of anarchy toward my father's conviction that winning was what mattered in life.

Even though Toby and I were the kind of best friends who rarely sought the company of other boys our age, his mother insisted on a birthday party, perhaps to insure his popularity in middle school—a popularity we had not enjoyed in elementary school.

She sent out *Pirates of the Caribbean*–themed invitations to a half dozen kids in our year with whom Toby and I shared a collective disinterest in socializing, and she took us all to Disneyland in the world's filthiest burgundy minivan the last Tuesday of the summer.

We lived only twenty minutes' drive south of Disneyland, and the magic of the place was well worn off by the end of sixth grade. We knew exactly which rides were good, and which were a waste of time. When Mrs. Ellicott suggested a visit to the Enchanted Tiki Room, the idea was met with such collective derision that you would have thought she'd told us to get lunch from the Pizza Port salad bar. In the end, the first—and only—ride we went on was the Thunder Mountain Railroad.

Toby and I chose the back row of the roller coaster, which everyone knows is the fastest. The rest of the birthday party was fighting for the front row, because, even though the back is the fastest, the front is inexplicably more popular.

And so Toby and I wound up divided from the rest of the party by a sea of eager Disneyland guests.

I suppose I remember that day with such enormous clarity because of what happened. Do you know those signs they have in the lines at theme parks, with those thick black lines where you have to be at least that tall to ride? Those signs also have a lot of stupid warnings, about how pregnant ladies or people with heart conditions shouldn't go on roller coasters, and you have to stow your backpacks, and everyone must stay seated at all times.

Well, it turns out those signs aren't so useless after all. There was this family directly in front of us, Japanese tourists with Mickey Mouse hats that had their names embroidered on the backs. As Toby and I sat there with the wind in our faces and the roller coaster rumbling so loudly over the rickety tracks that you could barely hear yourself scream, one of the boys in front of us stood up defiantly in his seat. He was laughing, and holding the Mickey Mouse hat onto his head, when the coaster raced into a low-ceilinged tunnel.

The news reports said that a fourteen-year-old boy from Japan was decapitated on the Thunder Mountain Railroad when he disregarded the posted safety warnings. What the news reports didn't say was how the kid's head sailed backward in its mouse-ear hat like some sort of grotesque helicopter, and how Toby Ellicott, on his twelfth birthday, caught the severed head and held on to it in shock for the duration of the ride.

There's no graceful way to recover from something like that, no magic response to the "getting head" jokes that everyone threw in Toby's direction in the hallways of Westlake Middle School. Toby's tragedy was the seat he chose on a roller-coaster ride on his twelfth birthday, and ever since, he has lived in the shadow of what happened.

It could have easily been me. If our seats had been reversed, or the kids in front of us had swapped places in line at the last minute, that head could have been my undoing rather than Toby's. I thought about it sometimes, as we drifted apart over the years, as Toby faded into obscurity and I became an inexplicable social success. Throughout middle and high school, my succession of girlfriends would laugh and wrinkle their noses. "Didn't you used to be friends with that kid?" they'd ask. "You know, the one who caught the severed head on the Disneyland ride?"

"We're still friends," I'd say, but that wasn't really true. We were still friendly enough and occasionally chatted online, but our friendship had somehow been decapitated that summer. Like the kid who'd sat in front of us on that fateful roller coaster, there was no weight on my shoulders.

Sorry. That was horrible of me. But honestly, it's been long enough since the seventh grade that the whole thing feels like a horrifying story I once heard. Because that tragedy belongs to Toby, and he has lived stoically in its aftermath while I escaped relatively unscathed.

My own tragedy held out. It waited to strike until I was

so used to my good-enough life in an unexceptional suburb that I'd stopped waiting for anything interesting to happen. Which is why, when my personal tragedy finally found me, it was nearly too late. I had just turned seventeen, was embarrassingly popular, earned good grades, and was threatening to become eternally unextraordinary.

Jonas Beidecker was a guy I knew peripherally, the same way you know if there's someone sitting in the desk next to you, or a huge van in the left lane. He was on my radar, but barely. It was his party, a house on North Lake with a backyard gazebo full of six packs and hard lemonade. There were tangles of Christmas lights strung across the yard, even though it was prom weekend, and they shimmered in reflection on the murky lake water. The street was haphazard with cars, and I'd parked all the way on Windhawk, two blocks over, because I was paranoid about getting a ding.

My girlfriend Charlotte and I had been fighting that afternoon, on the courts after off-season tennis. She'd accused me—let me see if I can get the phrasing exact—of "shirking class presidential responsibilities in regard to the Junior-Senior Luau." She said it in this particularly snotty way, as though I should have been ashamed. As though her predicted failure of the annual Junior-Senior Luau would galvanize me into calling an emergency SGA meeting that very second.

I was dripping sweat and chugging Gatorade when she'd sauntered onto the court in a strapless dress she'd been hiding beneath a cardigan all day. Mostly, as she talked, I thought about how sexy her bare shoulders looked. I suppose I deserved it when she told me that I sucked sometimes and that she was going to Jonas's party with her friend Jill, because she just couldn't deal with me when I was being impossible.

"Isn't that the definition of impossible?" I'd asked, wiping Gatorade off my chin.

Wrong answer. She'd given one of those little screams that was sort of a growl and flounced away. Which is why I showed up to the party late, and still wearing my mesh tennis shorts because I knew it would antagonize her.

I pocketed my key lanyard and nodded hey to a bunch of people. Because I was the junior class president, and also the captain of our tennis team, it felt like I was constantly nodding hello to people wherever I went, as though life was a stage and I was but a poor tennis player.

Sorry—puns. Sort of my thing, because it puts people at ease, being able to collectively roll their eyes at the guy in charge.

I grabbed a Solo cup I didn't plan on drinking from and joined the guys from tennis in the backyard. It was the usual crew, and they were all well on their way to being wasted. They greeted me far too enthusiastically, and I endured the back slapping with a good-natured grimace before sitting down on a proffered pool chair.

"Faulkner, you've gotta see this!" Evan called, wobbling

drunkenly as he stood on top of a planter. He was clutching an electric green pool noodle, trying to give it some heft, while Jimmy knelt on the ground, holding the other end to his face. They were attempting to make a beer funnel out of a foam pool noodle, which should give you an idea of how magnificently drunk they were.

"Pour it already," Jimmy complained, and the rest of the guys pounded on the patio furniture, drumrolling. I got up and officiated the event, because that was what I did—officiate things. So I stood there with my Solo cup, making some sarcastic speech about how this was one for *The Guinness Book of World Records*, but only because we were drinking Guinness. It was like a hundred other parties, a hundred other stupid stunts that never worked but at least kept everyone entertained.

The pool noodle funnel predictably failed, with Jimmy and Evan blaming each other, making up ridiculous excuses that had nothing to do with the glaringly poor physics of their whole setup. The conversation turned to the prom after-party—a bunch of us were going in on a suite at the Four Seasons—but I was only half listening. This was one of the last weekends before we'd be the seniors, and I was thinking about what that meant. About how these rituals of prom, the luau, and graduation that we'd watched for years were suddenly personal.

It was slightly cold out, and the girls shivered in their dresses. A couple of tennis-team girlfriends came over and sat down on their boyfriends' laps. They had their phones out, the way girls do at parties, creating little halos of light around their cupped hands.

"Where's Charlotte?" one of the girls asked, and it took me a while to realize this question was directed toward me. "Hello? Ezra?"

"Sorry," I said, running a hand through my hair. "Isn't she with Jill?"

"No she isn't," the girl said. "Jill is completely grounded. She had like this portfolio? On a modeling website? And her parents found it and went crazy because they mistakenly thought it was porn."

A couple of the guys perked up at the mention of porn, and Jimmy made an obscene gesture with the pool noodle.

"How can you mistakenly think something is porn?" I asked, halfway interested at this turn in the conversation.

"It's porn if you use a self-timer," she explained, as though it was obvious.

"Right," I said, wishing that she'd been smarter, and that her answer had impressed me.

Everyone laughed and began to joke about porn, but now that I thought about it, I had no idea where Charlotte had gone. I'd assumed I was meeting her at the party, that she was doing what she usually did when we had one of our fights: hanging out with Jill, rolling her eyes at me and acting annoyed from across the room until I went over and apologized profusely. But I hadn't seen her all night. I pulled out my phone and texted her to see what was going on.

Five minutes later, she still hadn't replied when Heath, an enormous senior from the football team, sauntered over to our table. He'd stacked his Solo cups, and had about six of them. I suppose he meant it to be impressive, but mostly it just hit me as wasteful.

"Faulkner," he grunted.

"Yeah?" I said.

He told me to get up, and I shrugged and followed him over to the little slope of dirt near the lake.

"You should go upstairs," he said, with such solemnity that I didn't question it.

Jonas's house was large, probably six bedrooms if I had to guess. But luck, if you can call it that, was on my side.

My prize was behind door number one: Charlotte, some guy I didn't know, and a scene which, if I'd captured it via camera phone, could have been mistaken for porn, although that wouldn't have been my artistic intention.

I cleared my throat. Charlotte cleared hers, though this required quite a bit of effort on her part. She looked horrified to see me there, in the doorway. Neither of us said anything. And then the guy cursed and zipped his jeans and demanded, "What the hell?"

"Ezra, I—I—," Charlotte babbled. "I didn't think you were coming."

"I think he was about to," I muttered sourly.

No one laughed.

"Who's this?" The guy demanded, looking back and forth between Charlotte and me. He didn't go to our school, and he gave the impression of being older, a college kid slumming it at a high-school party.

"I'm the boyfriend," I said, but it came out uncertain, like a question.

"This is the guy?" he asked, squinting at me. "I could take him."

So she'd been talking about me to this douche-canoodler? I supposed, if it came down to it, he probably could take me. I had a helluva backhand, but only with my racquet, not my fist.

"How about you take her instead?" I suggested, and then I turned and walked back down the hallway.

It might have been fine if Charlotte hadn't come after me, insisting that I still had to take her to prom on Saturday. It might have been all right if she hadn't proceeded to do so in the middle of the crowded living room. And it might have been different if I hadn't babied my car, parking all the way over on Windhawk to avoid the scourge of drunk drivers.

Maybe, if one of those things hadn't happened, I wouldn't have inched out onto the curve of Princeton Boulevard the exact moment a black SUV barreled around the blind turn and blew through the stop sign.

I don't know why people say "hit by a car," as though the other vehicle physically lashes out like some sort of champion boxer. What hit me first was my airbag, and then my steering wheel, and I suppose the driver's side door and whatever that part is called that your knee jams up against.

The impact was deafening, and everything just seemed to slam toward me and crunch. There was the stink of my engine dying under the front hood, like burnt rubber, but salty and metallic. Everyone rushed out onto the Beideckers' lawn, which was two houses down, and through the engine smoke, I could see an army of girls in strapless dresses, their phones raised, solemnly snapping pictures of the wreck.

But I just sat there laughing and unscathed because I'm an immortal, hundred-year-old vampire.

All right, I'm screwing with you. Because it would have been awesome if I'd been able to shake it off and drive away, like that ass weasel who never even stopped after laying into my Z4. If the whole party hadn't cleared out in a panic before the cops could bust them for underage drinking. If Charlotte, or just one of my supposed friends, had stayed behind to ride with me in the ambulance, instead of leaving me there alone, half-delirious from the pain. If my mother hadn't put on all of her best jewelry and gotten lipstick on her teeth before rushing to the emergency room.

It's awful, isn't it, how I remember crap like that? Tiny, insignificant details in the midst of a massive disaster.

I don't really want to get into the rest of it, and I hope you'll forgive me, but going through it once was enough. My poor roadster was totaled, just like everything else in my life. The doctors said my wrist would heal, but the damage to my leg was bad. My knee had been irreparably shattered.

But this story isn't about Toby's twelfth birthday, or the car wreck at Jonas's party—not really.

There is a type of problem in organic chemistry called a retrosynthesis. You are presented with a compound that does not occur in nature, and your job is to work backward, step by step, and ascertain how it came to exist—what sort of conditions led to its eventual creation. When you are finished, if done correctly, the equation can be read normally, making it impossible to distinguish the question from the answer.

I still think that everyone's life, no matter how unremarkable, has a singular tragic encounter after which everything that really matters will happen. That moment is the catalyst—the first step in the equation. But knowing the first step will get you nowhere—it's what comes after that determines the result.

2

SO WHO WAS I in the aftermath of my personal tragedy? At first, I was a lousy sport when it came to the chipper attitudes of the pediatrics nurses. And then I was a stranger in my own home, a temporary occupant of the downstairs guest room. An invalid, if you will, which is probably the most horrific word I've ever heard to describe someone who is supposed to be recuperating. In the context of a mathematical proof, if something is considered "invalid," it has been demonstrated through irrefutable logic not to exist.

Actually, I take it back. The word was fitting for me. I had been Ezra Faulkner, golden boy, but that person no longer existed. And the proof?

I've never told this to anyone, but the last night of summer before senior year, I drove over to Eastwood High. It was late, around eleven, and my parents were already asleep. The landscaped lanes of my gated community were dark and inexplicably lonely, in the way that suburbs sometimes get at night. The strawberry fields on the side of the road looked as though they stretched on for miles, but there wasn't really much left of the old ranch lands—just the small orange grove across from the Chinese strip mall, and the center dividers where last century's sycamore trees grow in captivity.

If you think about it, there's something quite depressing about living in a gated community full of six-bedroom "Spanish-style" homes while, half a mile down the road, illegal migrant workers break their backs in the strawberry fields, and you have to drive past them every morning on the way to school.

Eastwood High is as far north as you can go within the city limits of Eastwood, California, nestled in the foothills like some sort of stucco fortress. I parked in the faculty lot, because screw it, why not? At least, that's what I told myself. Really though, it wasn't a rebellion at all, but a show of weakness—the faculty lot was practically on top of the tennis courts.

A haze of chlorine drifted over the wall of the swim complex, and the custodial staff had already set up the beach umbrellas on the café tables in the upper quad. I could see them in silhouette, tilted at rakish angles.

I fitted my key into the lock on my favorite tennis court and propped the door open with my gear bag. My racquet, which I hadn't handled in months, looked the same as I remembered, with black tape coming loose from the grip. Nearly time for a new one, judging from the dings in the frame, but of course I wouldn't be getting a new one. Not then, and not ever.

I let my cane clatter to the ground and limped toward the back line of the court. My physical therapist didn't even have me on the stationary bike yet, and my other therapist would probably disapprove, but I didn't care. I had to know how bad it was, to see for myself if it was true what the doctors had said—that sports were finished. "Finished." As though the last twelve years of my life amounted to nothing more than third-period phys ed, and the bell had rung for lunch.

I pocketed a ball and prepped my soft serve, that vanilla hit I used so as not to double fault. Barely daring to breathe, I tossed the ball high and felt it connect with the racquet in a way that, while not entirely pleasant, was at least tolerable. It landed neatly in the center of the square without any heat. I'd been aiming for the back right corner, but I'd take it.

I shook out my wrist, grimacing at how constricting the Velcro brace felt, but knowing better than to take it off. And then I gave the second ball a toss and slammed it, angling the racquet to put a slight spin on the serve. I landed on my good leg, but the momentum carried me forward along with my follow-through. I stumbled, accidentally putting too much weight on my knee, and the pain caught me off guard.

By the time it had begun to fade back into the familiar, dull ache that never quite went away, the ball had rolled silently to a stop at my feet, mocking me. My serve had faulted; I hadn't even made it over the net.

I was done. I left the balls on the court, zipped my racquet back into my gear bag, and picked up my cane, wondering why I'd even bothered.

When I locked up the courts, the campus felt spooky all of a sudden, the dark shadows of the foothills looming over the empty buildings. But of course there was nothing to be worried about—nothing besides the first day of school, when I'd finally have to face everyone I'd been avoiding all summer.

Eastwood High used to be mine, the one place where everyone knew who I was and it felt as though I could do no wrong. And the tennis courts—I'd been playing on varsity since the ninth grade. Back when the school was mine, I used to find peace there, between the orderly white lines etched into the forest green rectangles. Tennis was like a video game, one that I'd beat a million times, with the pleasure of winning long gone. A game that I'd kept on playing because people expected me to, and I was good at doing what people expected. But not anymore, because no one seemed to expect anything from me anymore. The funny thing about gold is how quickly it can tarnish.

3

THERE ARE A lot of unexpected public humiliations in high school, but none of them had ever happened to me until 8:10 A.M. on that first day of senior year. Because, at 8:10 A.M., I realized that not only did I have no one to sit with during the welcome back pep rally, but I was also going to have to take the front row, since the bleachers were too cramped for my knee.

The front row was all teachers and this one goth girl in a wheelchair who insisted she was a witch. But there was no way that I was going to hobble feebly up the stairs with the whole school watching. And they *were* watching. I could feel their eyes on me, and not because I'd won a record percentage of the vote in the class council elections or held hands with Charlotte Hyde as we waited in the coffee line in the upper quad. This was different. It made me want to cringe away in silent apology for the dark circles under my eyes and the fact that I had no summer tan to speak of. It made me want to disappear.

A balloon arch and butcher-paper sign decorated each section of the bleachers. I sat directly beneath the *R* in "GO SENIORS!" and watched the leaders of the Student Government Association huddle together in the center of the basketball court. They wore plastic leis and sunglasses. Jill Nakamura, our new class president, was dressed in a bikini top and denim cutoffs. And then the huddle broke apart and I caught sight of Charlotte laughing with her friends in their short Song Squad skirts. Her eyes met mine and she looked away, embarrassed, but that one moment had told me all I needed to know: The tragedy of what had happened at Jonas Beidecker's party was mine and mine alone.

And then a small miracle happened and Toby Ellicott sat down next to me.

"Did you hear about the bees?" he asked cheerfully.

"What?"

"They're disappearing," he said. "Scientists are stumped. I read it in the newspaper this morning."

"Maybe it's a hoax," I said. "I mean, how can you prove something like that?"

"A bee census?" he suggested. "Anyhow, I'm going to buy stock in honey."

Toby and I hadn't really spoken in years. He was on the debate team, and our schedules rarely overlapped. He didn't look much like the pudgy, bespectacled best friend I'd lost somewhere in the first few weeks of seventh grade. His dark hair still flopped all over the place, but he was a lanky six two. He straightened his bow tie, unbuttoned his blazer, and stretched his legs way out in front of him, as though the teacher bleacher was a choice seat.

"You should get a sword cane," he said. "That would be badass. I know a guy, if you're interested."

"You know a sword-cane guy?"

"Don't sound so surprised of my shadowy connections, Faulkner. Technically, he deals in concealed weaponry."

The music started then, a deafening blast of speaker static that gave way to the opening bars of an overplayed Vampire Weekend single. SGA began clapping in that cheesy let's-get-the-party-started way, and Jill squealed into the microphone how super psyched she was for the best school year ever.

Inexplicably, SGA launched into some sort of coordinated hula dance in their sunglasses and leis. I couldn't get over how wrong it was, doing the hula to the African drumbeats of an East Coast prep rock band.

"Please tell me I'm hallucinating," Toby muttered.

"SENIORS, WHERE'S YOUR SCHOOL SPIRIT?" Jill called.

The response was deafening.

"I CAN'T HEAR YOU!" Jill challenged, cocking her hip.

"Kill me now," moaned Toby.

"I would, but I seem to be lacking a sword cane," I told him.

Mrs. Levine, who was sitting next to Toby, glared at us.

"Behave or leave, gentlemen," she snarled.

Toby snorted.

When the song finally ended, Jimmy Fuller took the microphone. He was wearing his tennis warm-ups, and I couldn't help but notice that the team had gotten new uniforms.

"What's up, Eastwood?" he boomed. "It's time to meet your varsity sports teams!"

As if on cue, a side door to the gym opened and the football team poured out in their pads and jerseys. Behind them was the baseball team, then tennis, then water polo, but by that point, I'd stopped paying attention to the teams and their orders. My former life, in its entirety, was standing in the center of the basketball court while I sat on the teacher bleacher, and there was no way in hell that I was going to clap for them. Mostly, I just wanted to get out of that pep rally, and away from all of it.

"Hey, Ezra," Toby whispered loudly. "Got a nicotine patch, buddy?"

"Get out!" Mrs. Levine demanded. "Both of you—now!"

Toby and I looked at each other, shrugged, and shouldered our bags.

It was bright outside, the sky cloudless and impossibly blue. I winced and hung back in the shade of the stucco overhang, fumbling for my sunglasses.

"A *nicotine patch*?" I asked.

"Well, it got us kicked out, didn't it?" Toby said smugly.

"Yeah, I guess it did. Thanks."

"For what? I wanted to get out of there. Mrs. Levine has awful breath."

We wound up passing the time in the Annex, this study room that connected the debate and newspaper classrooms. Everyone else was at the rally, and we could hear muffled screams coming from the gym at regular intervals.

"It sounds like Disneyland or something," Toby offered with a grin.

I was surprised he'd mention it. "Have you been back?" I asked.

"Are you kidding? I'm there every single day. They gave me a free lifetime pass. I'm like the mayor of Adventureland."

"So no, then," I said.

"Have you?"

I shook my head.

"You could get a handicapped pass," Toby pressed. "Skip all of the lines."

"Next time I ask a girl on a date, I'll be sure to mention that."

For some reason, I didn't mind Toby giving me crap about the cane. And I was generally pretty sensitive about it.

You would be too, if you'd spent most of your summer vacation trying to get your well-meaning but overbearing mother to stop hovering outside the bathroom door every time you took a shower. (She was paranoid that I'd slip and die, since I'd refused to let her install those metal handrails. I was paranoid that she'd come inside and catch me, uh, showering.)

"What are you doing for Team Electives?" Toby asked. We had a four-year requirement.

"Speech and debate," I admitted, suddenly realizing that Toby might be in my class.

"Dude, I'm team captain this year! You should compete."

"I'm just taking it for the requirement," I said. "Debate's not really my thing."

Back then, my impression of the debate team was that it was a bunch of guys who put on business suits during the weekend and thought they actually had something meaningful to say about foreign policy because they were enrolled in AP Government.

"Maybe not, but you owe me. I got us out of the pep rally," Toby protested.

"We're even. I told Tug Mason not to piss in your backpack in the eighth-grade locker room."

"You still owe me. He pissed in my Gatorade instead."

"Huh, I'd forgotten about that."

The bell rang then.

"Hey, Faulkner, want to know something depressing?" Toby asked, picking up his bag.

"What?"

"First period hasn't even started yet."

4

THE ONE INTERESTING thing about being signed up for speech and debate was that I'd been given a Humanities Odd schedule. Eastwood High is on block scheduling, and ever since freshman year, my schedule had been Humanities Even, with the other athletes. But not anymore.

I had first period AP Euro, which was unfortunate because 1) Mr. Anthony, the tennis coach, was the AP Euro teacher, and 2) his classroom was on the second floor of the 400 building, which meant that 3) I had to get up a flight of stairs.

Over the summer, stairs had become my nemesis, and I often went out of my way to avoid a public confrontation with them. I was supposed to pick up an elevator key from the front office; it came in a matching set with that little blue parking tag for my car, the one I was never, ever going to display.

By the time I got to AP Euro via a rarely used stairwell

near the staff parking lot, Mr. Anthony had already begun taking roll. He paused briefly to frown at me over the manila folder, and I cringed in silent apology as I slid into a seat in the back.

When he called my name, I mumbled "here," without looking up. I was surprised he'd actually called me. Usually, teachers did this thing when they reached my name on the roll sheet: "Ezra Faulkner is here," they'd say, putting a tick in the box before moving on down the list. It was as though they were pleased to have me, as though my presence meant the class would be better somehow.

But when Coach A paused after calling my name and I had to confirm for him that I was in the room even though he knew damn well that I'd walked in thirty seconds late, I wondered for a moment if I really *was* there. I glanced up, and Coach A was giving me that glare he used whenever we weren't hustling fast enough during practice.

"Consider this your tardiness warning, Mr. Faulkner," he said.

"So noted," I muttered.

Mr. Anthony continued with roll. I wasn't really listening, but when he got to one name that I didn't quite catch, there was a perceptible shift in the room. A new student. She sat way on the other side, near the bookshelves. All I could see was a sleeve of green sweater and a cascade of red hair.

The syllabus was nothing surprising, although Mr. Anthony apparently believed otherwise. He talked about what it meant to be in an Advanced Placement history course, as though we all hadn't taken AP US History with Ms. Welsh as juniors. A lot of the guys on tennis didn't care for Coach Anthony, because they thought he was a hard-ass. I was used to strict coaches, but I was quickly realizing that without any other athletes in the class, Mr. Anthony was just plain strict.

"You should have done the summer reading," Mr. Anthony said, as though it was an accusation, rather than a fact. "*Medieval Europe: From the Fall of Rome to the Renaissance.* If you felt such an assignment was beneath you, then you'll be rearranging your plans for the weekend. You might even consider your weekend plans to be, ah, *history*."

No one laughed.

The Roman Empire: 200 B.C.—474 A.D., he scrawled on the board, and then raised an eyebrow, as though enjoying a private joke. There was this horrible stretch of silence as we tried to figure out why he wasn't saying anything, and then, finally, Xiao Lin raised his hand.

"I am sorry, but I think 476 A.D. is correct?" he mumbled.

"Thank you, Mr.—ah—Lin, for displaying the barest level of competency in reading comprehension," Mr. Anthony snapped, correcting the date on the board. "And now, I wonder if anyone here can tell us why the phrase 'Holy Roman Empire' is a misnomer . . . Mr. Faulkner, perhaps?"

If I didn't know better, I would have thought that was a sneer on Coach A's lip. All right, let's call it a sneer. I got that he was disappointed I couldn't play anymore, but I'd sort of hoped he wouldn't be a jerk about it.

"It only applies after Charlemagne?" I offered, inking over the letters on my syllabus.

"That's a community college answer," Coach announced. "Would you care to rephrase it and try for a UC school?"

I don't know why I said it, except maybe that I didn't want to take crap from Coach A for the rest of the year, but before I could really think it through, I'd leaned back in my chair and replied, "Yeah, okay. Two reasons: One, the 'Holy Roman Empire' was originally called the Frankish Kingdom, until the Pope crowned Charlemagne the 'Emperor of the Romans.' And two, it wasn't holy, or Roman, or even an empire. It was really just, like, this casual alliance of Germanic tribal states."

I'd never really shot my mouth off in class before, and I instantly regretted it. I usually had the right answer when I was called on, and my grades were good enough, but I wasn't what anyone would consider brainy. I'd just done a lot of reading and thinking over the summer, because there hadn't been much else to do.

"Enjoy your weekend, Mr. Faulkner," Coach sneered, and I realized that, instead of getting him off my back, I'd made him want to get back at me.

I'D NEARLY FORGOTTEN we were on Pep Rally Schedule until I was halfway out the classroom door, thinking it was break, and someone tapped me on the shoulder.

It was the new girl. She clutched a crumpled class schedule and stared up at me, as though I'd somehow given her the impression that I was the right person to talk to on her first day. I wasn't expecting her eyes—deep and disquieting and dark blue—the sort of eyes that made you wonder if the skies opened up when she got angry.

"Um, sorry," she said, glancing back down at her schedule. "First period is supposed to end at nine thirty-five, but the bell didn't ring until nine fifty—"

"It's the pep rally," I told her. "Break is canceled and we go straight to third."

"Oh." She pushed her bangs to the side and hesitated a moment before asking, "So, what do you have next?"

"AP American Lit."

"Me too. Can you show me where that is?"

Ordinarily, I could have. On the first day of junior year, I'd even stopped to help a few confused-looking freshmen in the quad, who'd stood gawking at the maps in the backs of their day planners as though they were stuck in some sort of incomprehensible labyrinth.

"Sorry, no," I said, hating myself for it.

"Um, okay."

I watched her walk away, and I thought about how most of the girls at Eastwood, or at least the ones worth noticing, all looked the same: blonde hair, lots of makeup, stupidly expensive handbags. The new girl was nothing like that, and I didn't know what to make of the shabby boys' button-down tucked into her jean shorts, or the worn leather satchel slung over her shoulder, like something out of an old-fashioned movie. She was pretty, though, and I wondered where she'd come from, and why she hadn't bothered trying to fit in. I wanted to follow her and apologize, or at least explain. But I didn't. Instead, I grappled with the stairwell near the faculty lot, crossed the quad toward the 100 building, and opened the door of AP American Lit several minutes in arrears of the bell.

I'D HAD MR. Moreno before, for Honors Brit Lit. He'd supposedly been writing the same novel for the past twenty years, and either he genuinely loved teaching or he'd never outgrown high school, because it was sort of depressing how hard he'd tried to get us psyched about Shakespeare.

Moreno hadn't cared that I was late for class; he hadn't even noticed. The DVD player wasn't working, and he was on his hands and knees with a disc clutched in his teeth, prodding at the cables. Finally Luke Sheppard, the president of Film Club, arrogantly stepped in, and we all sat and watched *The Great Gatsby*—the original, not the remake. I hadn't seen it before, and the film was old-fashioned and sort of bored me. The book had been our summer reading, and the movie wasn't nearly as good.

What I hated, though, was the part with the car accident. I knew it was coming, but that didn't stop it from being any less terrible to watch. I shut my eyes, but I could still hear it, hear the policeman telling the crowd of onlookers how the sonofabitch didn't even stop his car. Even with my eyes closed, I could feel everyone staring at me, and I wished they wouldn't. It was unsettling the way my classmates watched me, as though I fascinated and terrified them. As though I no longer belonged.

When class let out, I briefly considered the quad, with its harsh sunlight and café tables. My old crew sat at the most visible table, the one by the wall that divided the upper and lower quads. I pictured them in their new team uniforms, the first day of senior year, telling stories about summer sports camps and beach vacations, laughing over how young the freshmen looked. And then I pictured sitting down at that table. I pictured no one saying anything, but all of them thinking it: you're not one of us anymore. I wasn't class president, or tennis team captain. I wasn't dating Charlotte, and I didn't drive a shiny Beemer. I wasn't king any longer, so it was only fitting to take my exile. Which is why, instead of gambling my last few chips of dignity, I wound up avoiding the quad entirely and decamping on that shaded stairwell out near the faculty lot with my headphones on, wondering why I hadn't known it would be quite this bad.

THERE WAS ONLY one senior-level Spanish class, which meant another year with Mrs. Martin. She'd urged us to call her Señora Martinez back in Spanish I, but that was completely ridiculous on account of her husband being the pastor of the local Lutheran church. She was one of those cookie-baking, overly mothering types who festooned her sweaters with festive holiday pins and treated us all like second graders.

I was the first to arrive, and Mrs. Martin beamed at me and whispered that her congregation had prayed for me after the accident. I could think of so many more worthwhile things they could have prayed for, but I didn't have the heart to tell her.

"*Gracias, Señora Martinez,*" I muttered, taking my usual seat.

"Yo, Faulkner." Evan nodded in greeting as he and three guys from the tennis team slid into seats around mine as though nothing was the least bit changed. They were carrying Burger King bags and wore matching tennis backpacks, the pro kind we'd been begging Coach to approve for years. I was so distracted by their backpacks that I failed to notice two things: that they'd all gone off campus for lunch and that Evan's uniform sported an extra line of embroidery.

"Aren't you going to congratulate me on making captain?" Evan reached into his bag and unwrapped a massive double burger. The smell of warm onions and clammy meat patties filled the classroom.

"Congratulations," I said, unsurprised. Evan was the most likely choice for it, after all.

"Well, someone had to take over for your gimp ass." Evan's surfer baritone made the insult sound strangely friendly.

Jimmy, who was sitting behind me, held out what had to

be a full-sized bucket of fries. "Want some?"

"Sure you can't finish that yourself?" I deadpanned.

"Nah, I got enough for everyone, in case Señora Martin gets mad."

I couldn't help it, I laughed.

"Dude," Evan said, clapping me on the shoulder. "You in for Chipotle tomorrow? Taco Tuesday, gotta get some tac and guac!"

"No one calls it that." I shook my head, grinning.

It was strange, my crew acting the same as they always had, and for a moment I wondered if it was really that easy. If I could go for Mexican food with a team I no longer belonged to. If I even *wanted* to hang out with them, now that I'd gone from leader to liability.

And then Charlotte waltzed over in an all-too-familiar cloud of fruity perfume and grabbed a handful of fries from Jimmy's bucket. She perched on top of the desk next to Evan's, her Song Squad skirt swishing against her tanned thighs.

"Where are *my* fries?" she demanded, poking Evan with her shoe.

"Well, Jimmy got enough for everyone." Evan's face fell as he realized he'd screwed up.

"But I didn't ask *Jimmy* to get me fries, I asked *you*," she said, pouting.

"Sorry, babe. I'll make it up to you." Evan leaned across the aisle, going in for a kiss, and if I hadn't figured it out before, I knew it then: they were dating.

"Not right now, my hands are greasy," Charlotte said, turning away. "Did you at least get any napkins?"

"Oops. Forgot."

I suppose it should have been painful to see them together, my ex-girlfriend with one of my best friends. That I should have wondered not just how but *when* it had happened, but I felt oddly detached, as though it was too much effort to care. I sighed and took a packet of tissues from my backpack, passing it to Charlotte.

"Thanks." She couldn't even bear to look at me, and I couldn't tell whether it was out of guilt or pity.

Jill Nakamura joined us then, still wearing her sunglasses. She gave Charlotte a hug before taking a seat, like they hadn't just seen each other at lunch.

"Ugh, we have like two classes together this year," Charlotte complained.

I allowed myself to smirk as Jill made up some excuse about Student Government screwing with her schedule. The truth was, Jill and I had been in the same honors courses since tenth grade, but we had an unspoken understanding to keep quiet about that sort of thing.

I watched as Charlotte put the packet of tissues into her handbag—*my* packet of tissues, actually.

"Oh my *God*," Charlotte said, zipping her bag with a flourish. "Look! It's like she robbed the lost-and-found bin."

"The *boys'* lost and found." Jill stifled a laugh.

The new girl stood in the doorway, surveying the mostly filled rows of seats. I could see her trying to be brave about the unwanted attention. Thankfully, Mrs. Martin stepped to the front of the classroom, clapped a short rhythm for silence like we were all in the third grade, and called *"Hola, class!"*

I'd always been fairly ambivalent about Spanish. Usually, I could waste a good five minutes pondering Mrs. Martin's pin-of-the-day, and occasionally we got to sit back and watch Spanish-dubbed Disney movies. But when Mrs. Martin told us that we'd be interviewing a classmate and introducing them to the class *en espanol*, I realized that Spanish had the capacity to be even worse than that morning's pep rally.

I watched as everyone around me, who had been so friendly only minutes before, partnered together. In the past, I'd always had someone to work with. But clearly, things had changed. And then I caught sight of the new girl staring down at a blank page in her notebook.

I claimed the seat next to hers and grinned in the way that girls usually found irresistible. "So what's your name?" I asked.

"Don't we have to speak in Spanish?" she countered, unimpressed.

"Mrs. Martin doesn't care, as long as we do when we give our presentations."

"How challenging." She shook her head, opening to a blank page in her notebook. "Well, *me llamo* Cassidy. *Como te llamas?*"

"*Me llamo* Ezra," I said, writing her name down. Cassidy. I liked the sound of it.

We fell silent for a moment, listening to one of the groups around us struggle on in tortured Spanish. Everyone else was using English because, as I'd said, Mrs. Martin didn't much care.

"Well," Cassidy prompted me.

"Oh, sorry. Uh, *de donde has venido de?*"

She raised an eyebrow. *"Dondo de la Barrows School de San Francisco. Y tu?"*

I hadn't heard of the Barrows School, but I imagined it as some sort of rigid prep school, which only made her appearance at Eastwood High even more odd. I told her that I was from here.

"So, um, *es una escuela donde duerme uno con el otro?*" I asked. My Spanish was rusty, and not that great to begin with.

She burst out laughing, in that unencumbered way you sometimes do at parties or lunch tables, but never in a quiet classroom. Charlotte and Jill whipped around to stare at us.

"Sorry." Cassidy's lips twisted into a smirk, mocking me. "But you seriously want to know if all of the students sleep with each other?"

I winced. "I was trying to ask if it was a boarding school."

"*Si, es un internado.* A boarding school," she replied. "Maybe we should switch to English."

And so we did. I learned that Cassidy had just

completed a high-school summer program at Oxford, studying Shakespeare; that one weekend, she'd nearly gotten stranded in Transylvania; that she'd been teaching herself how to play guitar on the roof of her dormitory because of the acoustics of gothic architecture. I'd never been out of the country—unless driving the three hours to Tijuana with Jimmy, Evan, Charlotte, and Jill last spring break counted. I'd certainly never been to the Globe Theatre, or had my passport stolen by gypsies at Dracula's castle, or climbed out of my bedroom window with a guitar strapped to my back. Everything I had done, everything that defined me, was stuck firmly in the past. But Cassidy was waiting patiently, a fountain pen poised above the pale lines of her notebook.

I sighed and gave her the standard Spanish-class answers: that I was seventeen years old, my favorite sport was tennis, and my favorite subject was history.

"Well," Cassidy said when I had finished, "that was certainly boring."

"I know," I muttered. "Sorry."

"I don't get you," she said, frowning. "Practically everyone goes out of their way to avoid you, but they can't stop staring. And then you sit with *that crowd* in the corner like you're the freaking prom king or whatever it's called and all you can say about yourself is *me gusta el tennis*, which, I'm sorry, but you obviously can't play."

I shrugged, trying not to let it show how much it unnerved me that she'd noticed these things.

"Maybe I *was* the prom king," I finally said.

This infuriated her. I tried not to laugh at how ridiculous it seemed now, that stupid plastic junior prom crown and scepter gathering dust on my bookshelf, when I hadn't even made it to the dance.

We sat there studiously ignoring each other until it was our turn to present.

"*Yo presento Cassidy*," I said, and Charlotte giggled loudly.

Mrs. Martin frowned.

"Butch Cassidy," Charlotte stage-whispered, sending Jill into muffled hysterics.

I knew what Charlotte could be like, and the last thing Cassidy needed was to become the new object of her torture. So I made up a boring story about how Cassidy's favorite subject was English and that she liked to dance ballet and had a younger brother who played soccer. I did her a favor, making her forgettable, rather than giving Charlotte further ammunition. But clearly Cassidy didn't see it that way, because, after I finished, she grinned evilly, pushed up the sleeves of her sweater, and calmly told the class: *This is Ezra. He was the prom king and he's the best tennis player in the whole school.*

5

WHEN I GOT home, I changed into a pair of sport shorts and stretched out on a pool chair in the backyard. The cushion was dusty, and as I listened to the water lap against the landscaped rocks that made up our fake waterfall, I tried to remember the last time anyone had actually used the pool. The sun was hot on my chest, and so bright that I could barely read the instructions in my Spanish exercise book.

"Ezra, what are you doing?" my mom shrilled, startling me.

I rolled over and squinted toward the house, where she hovered behind the screen door, carrying a yoga mat.

"I'm coming in, all right?" I called back.

"What were you thinking?" Mom asked gently as I joined her in the kitchen. She was still in her yoga clothes, which made her look a lot younger than forty-seven.

I shrugged. "I thought I could get a tan. I'm too pale."

"Oh, honey." She took a carton of lemonade out of the fridge and poured us each a glass. "You know you're supposed to stay out of direct sunlight."

I grunted and took a sip of the lemonade, which tasted awful. Everything my mom bought was healthy, which meant that it was helpfully missing at least one key ingredient, such as gluten, sugar, or flavor.

She was right though, about the sunlight thing. I was still on painkillers from my last knee surgery and one of the more delightful side effects was increased sensitivity to sunlight. After twenty minutes in the backyard, I was a bit dizzy, but I wasn't about to admit it.

"How was school?" She frowned at me, the picture of concern.

Quietly humiliating, I thought.

"Fine," I said.

"Did anything interesting happen?" she pressed.

I thought about how I'd gotten kicked out of the pep rally over a hypothetical nicotine patch (incidentally, I'd never even tried a cigarette), and about Coach A's nightmarish AP Euro class. I thought about the new girl, a world away from the disappearing strawberry fields and man-made lake of Eastwood, perched on a gothic rooftop in her funny old clothes, strumming a guitar as she stared out at the bell towers and cobblestones.

"Not really," I said, and then I pretended that I was tired and went upstairs.

OUR HOUSE IS a monstrosity. Six bedrooms and a "bonus room," all painted the same calming shade of free-range eggshell. It looks like one of those models you walk through in the future subdivisions, full of generically bland show-room furniture, the kind of house that you can't imagine anyone actually living in. We moved in when I was eight, an "upgrade" from an older gated community on the other side of the loop. A year later, we inherited Cooper, my mad aunt's massive poodle, when she got remarried and moved into a luxury condo that didn't allow large pets.

Cooper was a standard poodle, the kind that look like furry black giraffes. I used to take him for walks when I was a kid, riding my Razor scooter while he pulled me up and down the streets. I snuck him into my bed when I had nightmares, even though he was supposed to sleep in the downstairs laundry room. He was about eight years old when we got him, and you could tell he considered himself terribly elegant, a regular lord of the manor. All right, I'll admit it: I loved that crazy dog, and the way his fur smelled like popcorn, and how his eyes gave the impression that he understood everything you said.

He was waiting for me in my room, curled up at the foot of my bed with his nose on the copy of *The Great Gatsby* I'd been thumbing through the night before.

How about a walk, old sport? His eyes seemed to ask.

I sat next to him and patted his head. "Sorry," I said.

And I swear he nodded sagely before settling back down on top of Mom's old paperback of *Gatsby*. He just about broke my heart, Cooper. I wanted to grab his leash and take him for our usual jog around the neighborhood, culminating in a full-out race down the steep hiking trail at the end of Crescent Vista. And the thought of how long it had been since we'd done that, and how I'd never be able to take him for a jog again, hit me full force.

I turned on the same Bob Dylan playlist I'd been moping to all summer and lay down on top of the duvet. I wasn't exactly crying, but it hurt like hell to swallow. I stayed like that for a while, listening to that fantastically depressing old music with the blinds closed and trying to convince myself that what I really wanted was my old life back. But I'd felt completely hollow that afternoon, sitting there in Spanish with the old crew talking about nothing, about lunch. It was like the part of me that had enjoyed those friends had evaporated, leaving behind a huge, echoing emptiness, and I was scrabbling on the edge of it, trying not to fall into the hole within myself because I was terrified to find out how far down it went.

I'D MOSTLY GOTTEN it together when Mom called me to dinner through the intercom at precisely six thirty. She'd cooked salmon with quinoa and kale, and not to sound ungrateful or anything, but my father and I would have preferred pizza. But we didn't say anything. You never can, to my mom.

I look a lot like my dad. Same dark curls, although his are gray at the temples. Same blue eyes and slightly cleft chin. He's six one, though, so he has me beat by two inches. He's one of those buddy-buddy corporate lawyers who donates a mint to his old college fraternity. Booming laugh, always smells like Listerine, played tennis once, plays golf now. You know the type.

He kept glancing over his shoulder at dinner, either expecting—or maybe hoping for—the phone to ring. Dad keeps a home office, so he can get work done before and after he comes home from his actual office. He claims it's because New York is three hours ahead and sometimes he has to take a conference call at six in the morning, but really, it's because he wants us to see how important he is, that he can't ever be away from his files and fax machine.

My parents quietly discussed what to do about the neighbor's tree branches that hung over into our backyard, and then the phone in my father's office rang. The call went to voice mail, the familiar notes riffing through his answering machine. Dad dashed for the phone.

"Stop calling, you little bastard," he roared.

Mom pursed her lips and ate another mouthful of quinoa, but I nearly died laughing. When my father had his office line installed, he must've pissed off the telephone company, because they gave him a real gem of a number. Do you remember the first time you figured out that you could play "Mary Had a Little Lamb" by dialing a certain combination of tones on the keypad? That combination just so happens to ring my father's home office.

There's usually a completely clueless kid on the line, punching away at the keypad, unaware he's even made a call. It drives my father nuts, but he's convinced it would be too much of a hassle to have the number changed. Personally, I think it's hilarious. Sometimes, late at night, I'll pick up and try to get a conversation going with whoever's on the other end. A lot of the time they don't speak English, but last December this charming little kid decided I was Santa Claus and made me promise to get him a retainer for Christmas, which just about killed me.

When Dad sat back down at the table, he picked up his fork as though we hadn't just heard him shouting obscenities into the phone.

"So, Ezra," he said, giving me the same schmoozy grin he must use at every UCLA alumni donor reception, "how's the new car running?"

"Yeah, it's awesome," I said, even though it was just your average five-year-old sedan. Not like I'd been expecting our insurance, or my dad, to replace the roadster. But, I mean, it would have been *nice*.

"Well, just remember, kiddo: if you put a dent in that thing, I'll kill ya." Dad started laughing like he'd said something tremendously witty, and I offered up a weak grin in return, hoping I'd missed the joke.

6

IF EVERYTHING REALLY does get better, the way everyone claims, then happiness should be graphable. You draw up an X axis and a Y axis, where a positive slope represents a positive attitude, plot some points, and there you go. But that's crap, because better isn't quantifiable. Anyway, that's what I was thinking about in Calculus the next morning while Mr. Choi reviewed derivatives. Well, that and how much I hate math class.

I got in line for the coffee cart during break, where I had the particular luck to get stuck behind two freshmen girls who wouldn't stop giggling. They kept bumping each other with their shoulders and glancing back at me, as though daring each other to say something. I didn't know what to make of it.

They hung around while I gave my coffee order, and when I grabbed a sugar packet from the little station, the taller girl thrust a stirrer at me.

"Thanks," I said, wondering what this was about. I'd occasionally experienced this sort of thing from love-struck freshmen during junior year, but I was pretty certain that my status as an unattainable upperclassman had been irrevocably withdrawn.

"Hi, Ezra," the girl said, giggling. "Remember me? Toby's sister?"

"Yeah, of course," I said, even though I doubted I would have recognized her in the hallway. She looked like so many other freshmen girls, skinny and brunette, with a pink hoodie and matching braces. And then I realized I'd completely forgotten her name.

I stalled, stirring the sugar into my coffee, and then I felt a tap on my shoulder.

"Good morning," Cassidy said brightly. "What kind of high school has its own coffee cart?"

"Beverage cart," I said. "We had a coffee rebellion last year. Before that, it was just hot chocolate."

I started to introduce Cassidy to Toby's sister, mostly out of politeness, and hesitated, wishing I could remember the girl's name.

"Emily," Toby's sister supplied.

"Right, Emily," I said sheepishly, committing it to memory.

The passing bell rang, and both freshmen looked panicked, as though the world would collapse if they didn't head to class that very second. Ah, to be a ninth grader.

"Shouldn't you two get to class?" I asked, gently teasing them. "Don't want to be late."

They scrambled away as though I'd given orders. I could hear them giggling as they walked, their shoulders pressed together.

"Don't want to be late," Cassidy echoed with a smirk. She'd ditched the oversized boy's shirt in favor of a plaid dress that must've been an antique. It was tight in all of the right places though, and Butch Cassidy she was not.

I threw away my empty sugar packet and headed toward the Speech and Debate classroom.

"It's called a tartle," Cassidy said, following me. "In case you were wondering."

"*What's* called a tartle?"

"That pause in conversation when you're about to introduce someone but you've forgotten their name. There's a word for it. In Scotland, it's called a tartle."

"Fascinating," I said sourly. Actually, it *was* interesting, but I was still upset with her over what had happened in Spanish class.

"Wait," Cassidy persisted. "About what I said yesterday? I didn't know. God, you must hate me. Go ahead, I give you permission to aim an invisible crossbow at my heart."

She stopped walking and stood there a moment, her eyes squeezed shut, as though expecting me to play along. When I didn't, she frowned and caught up with me once more.

"It's not like I was asking around or anything," she

continued. "The whole school's talking about you. And we're going to be late, by the way, if we don't hurry."

"You're the one walking with *me*," I pointed out.

She bit her lip, and I could tell that she'd made a pretty educated guess as to why I hadn't wanted to walk her to English the day before. This strange, silent moment of understanding passed between us.

"What's your fourth period?" I asked, filling the silence.

"Speech and Debate." Her lip curled, as though she'd gotten stuck with the class like I had.

"Me too. Listen, you should go ahead."

"And let you take that invisible crossbow and aim it at my back?" she scoffed. "Don't be ridiculous."

And so we were late together.

"FAULKNER!" TOBY BOOMED. He was sitting on top of the teacher's desk and wearing another shocker of a bow tie. Class hadn't started, and hardly anyone was in their seats. Through the little window built into the door, I could see Ms. Weng in the Annex, in conversation with the journalism teacher.

Toby slid off the desk and practically choked when he saw Cassidy.

"What are you doing here?" he spluttered.

"You two know each other?" I frowned, glancing back and forth between them. Cassidy looked horrified, and I couldn't read Toby's expression at all.

"Cassidy's—well," Toby seemed to change his mind mid-explanation. "She's a fencer."

For some reason, this made Cassidy uncomfortable.

"What, like swords?" I asked.

"He means a picket fencer," Cassidy clarified, grimacing as though the subject was painful. "It's just this term from debate. It's not important."

"Like hell it's not!" Toby retorted. "I can't believe you transferred to Eastwood. You transferred here, right? Because, seriously, this is epic! Everyone's going to freak out."

Cassidy shrugged, clearly not wanting to talk about it. We took a table together in the back, and, after a few minutes, Ms. Weng came in and passed out a course description. She was young, barely out of grad school, the sort of teacher who would constantly lose control of the class and quietly panic until the teacher next door came in and yelled.

She talked about the different types of debate and then made Toby get up and sell us on joining the debate team.

He sauntered to the front of the classroom, buttoned his blazer, and grinned.

"Ladies and gentlemen," he began, "I presume that we all share an interest in booze, mischief, and coed sleepovers."

The color drained from Ms. Weng's face.

"I'm speaking, of course, about getting into college, where one has the option to engage in those sorts of illicit activities after achieving academic excellence, naturally,"

Toby quickly amended. "And joining the debate team makes an excellent résumé stuffer for those college applications."

Toby continued talking about the debate team, the time commitment, and the school's past record ("We're even worse than the golf team!"). He was a decent public speaker, and for a moment I wondered why he'd never gone out for student government. And then I remembered the severed head.

Afterward, Toby sent around a sign-up sheet for the first debate tournament of the year, which no one signed. When the sheet got to Cassidy, her shoulders shook with silent laughter. She slid the piece of paper onto my desk.

Written at the top of the list, in obnoxiously hot pink Sharpie, was this beauty:

EZRA MOTHA-EFFING FAULKNER, YO!
(you owe me for the Gatorade piss)

I couldn't help it—I burst out laughing.

The room went deadly silent, and Toby grinned like he'd just won the Ping-Pong world championship. Ms. Weng frowned at me. I quickly turned my laughter into a fake coughing fit, and Cassidy leaned over and helpfully whacked me on the back. To my deepest shame, this made me actually *start* coughing in earnest.

By the time I got it under control, it had sort of become an event.

"Sorry," Cassidy whispered.

I shrugged like it didn't matter, but when she wasn't looking, I scribbled her name onto the sign-up sheet in payback and then passed it forward. For the remainder of class, we worked in pairs structuring a parliamentary debate. Cassidy and I partnered together.

"What's a picket fencer?" I pressed, when she made no move to start the assignment.

"It's, well, it's when you place first in every round at a tournament." She sighed, fiddling with her still-capped pen. "Your cumulative's a row of ones, like a little picket fence."

I considered this, the idea not just of winning, but doing so without a single defeat, as Toby wandered over and pulled up a chair.

"Yeah, hi," he said. "In case you were wondering, you're not going to have to turn that in."

"You're sure?" I asked.

"I swear it on the grave of my sweet dead hamster Petunia," he said, which wasn't exactly reassuring since, to my knowledge, Toby had never owned a hamster. "Ms. Weng asked me to come up with a random topic during break as an exercise. Technically, I'm not in this class. I'm her student aide."

"So you're her Weng-man?" Cassidy asked.

The three of us laughed, and it struck me that Cassidy and Toby knew each other. That, if anyone was an outsider, it wasn't the new girl, it was me.

When the bell rang, Ms. Weng told us to hold on to our debates, and Toby mouthed, "Told you so."

The classroom began to clear out, and I watched Cassidy fasten the buckles on her satchel. Her hair was half pinned up into this crown of braids, and with the sharp planes of her cheekbones and her pale skin, she looked as though she'd stepped out of a different era, one where people bought war bonds and decamped to the countryside to avoid air raids. I'd never seen anyone like her, and I couldn't help but stare.

"Come on," Toby said, and Cassidy glanced up, nearly catching me staring. "Join me for lunch. You're coming too, Faulkner. I could use a new sidekick."

"Actually, I'm going to Chipotle," I said. "With Evan and Jimmy and them."

But it sounded ridiculous, and even as I said it, I knew I wasn't really going.

"Sure you are." Toby laughed. "I'm not taking no for an answer. Now let's go, for my harem does not eat before I have graced them with my magnificence."

7

THE MOMENT I entered the quad, I realized I'd made a grand miscalculation: Jimmy and Evan hadn't gone to Chipotle after all. All of my old friends had stayed on campus. I could see them there, at the choice table near the wall that divided the upper and lower quads. The water polo and tennis guys were squished around the too-small table, balancing girlfriends on their laps. Charlotte's Song Squad crowd sat on the wall, drinking Diet Cokes and swinging their bare legs. It wasn't quite the same crew as last year, but the composition didn't matter. It was still *that table*, the one where the laughter carried across the quad and everyone who heard it wished they were in on the joke.

"Yo, Captain!" Luke Sheppard called, catching sight of Toby and waving.

I could feel everyone watching as we crossed the quad: Toby in his bow tie, Cassidy in her crown of braids, and me, with the sleeve of my black hoodie pulled low over my wrist brace, trying to look as though I needed my cane less than I actually did.

Toby ushered us over to one of the better-placed tables in the upper quad, an eight-seater with a gray beach umbrella, half full of our year's resident eccentrics. "Meet the rest of our school's illustrious debate team," he said, and for a moment I thought he was joking.

There was Luke Sheppard, the president of the film club, with his hipster glasses and signature smirk. The year before, our whole school had followed this blog called *Auto-Tune the Principal*, and while Luke had never outright claimed credit, everyone knew it was him. Sitting next to Luke was Sam Mayfield, looking like he'd gotten lost on his way home from the country club. Sam smacked of future lawyer, and even though he was a junior, he'd been head of the Campus Republicans for as long as I could remember. Across from Sam, drinking a can of Red Bull and playing some game on his iPad, was Austin Covelli, our school's resident graphic designer. Austin was the guy who whipped up the yearbook cover and designed the school sweatshirts. Back during sophomore year, he'd launched an online T-shirt store.

Mostly, I'd been picturing Toby's friends as a bunch of obscure honor-roll students, the sort who clubbed together out of social necessity and made it through high school largely unnoticed. Not these guys.

"Look who I found," Toby said gleefully.

Luke's jaw dropped. Sam let out an incredulous laugh.

"Well, well, if it isn't Cassidy Thorpe," Austin said, flicking his shaggy blond hair out of his eyes without looking away from his game. "What the heck are you doing here?"

Cassidy smiled hugely. "Waiting to graduate and move on with my life, same as y'all. Now how come none of you ever mentioned that your school has a coffee cart?"

Cassidy slid onto the bench next to Toby, pulled out a packet of peanut butter crackers, and patted the seat next to her. It was the end of the bench, thank God, and I wondered if she'd left it for me on purpose, so I wouldn't have to ask anyone to shift down.

"Oh, right," Toby said a little too theatrically, pretending he'd only just remembered. "You all know Faulkner."

"Hey," I said sheepishly, taking the proffered seat. I guess they'd thought I was just passing by, showing the new student around, but when I sat down, Luke gave Toby a significant look, as though my joining the table needed to be preceded by *his* approval.

I put on my sunglasses and watched everyone pick at their food (lunch starts at 11:30, which is ridiculous, on account of how some nearby food chains are still serving breakfast sandwiches). I hadn't brought anything, and I glanced toward the lunch line in the lower quad, which was an endless stretch of underclassmen.

"Quick, eat these." Phoebe Chang slid a plastic container of grocery store cupcakes onto the table, her nose stud sparkling in the sunlight. There was a pink stripe in her hair that I didn't remember. "I just swiped them from the front office. It's the school nurse's birthday."

She glanced over her shoulder, as though expecting to be apprehended at any moment, and Toby grabbed for one of the vanilla cupcakes.

"Fifty points for irony if we get food poisoning," he said. "By the way, Phoebe, this is Cassidy. And you know Ezra."

Phoebe, who was still basking in the glory of her cupcake heist, glanced at me and nearly dropped her iced tea. "Holy crap. I'm five minutes late and I miss the most historic lunch-table switch in the annals of the upper quad."

"I thought you didn't do annals, Phoebs," Luke said with a wink.

Phoebe picked up a cupcake, smashed the frosting down with her tongue, and offered it to Luke with an evil grin. "I don't know about that. How about some sloppy seconds, Sheppard?"

Luke took the cupcake and bit into it with relish, antagonizing her. I wondered how long they'd been dating. Phoebe, who was not, in fact, a notorious cupcake thief, was actually the editor of the school paper.

"So Ezra," Phoebe said, sliding onto the bench next to Luke. "How's life as a teenage vampire?"

Toby snorted, and Cassidy snickered through a mouthful of cupcake.

"Oh come *on*," Phoebe continued. "You're asking for it. Pale skin, black clothes, no lunch, and that whole brooding thing? It's hilarious. You should get some body glitter and go after an unsuspecting freshman."

"You should!" Cassidy agreed. "Tell her you're a dangerous monster. And mention how good her blood smells."

"Wrong time of the month on that one, and I'm getting slapped," I muttered, and everyone laughed.

"You're funny." Phoebe passed me the last chocolate cupcake. "And I always thought your friends were laughing over their own farts."

"Ninety percent of Eastwood's male population laughs over their own farts," Toby said. "Present company excluded, naturally."

"How many points would I lose if I farted right now?" Luke asked with a chuckle.

"Don't even think about it!" Phoebe warned, preemptively scooting away from him.

I peeled the wrapper off my cupcake and glanced toward my old lunch table, where Charlotte had climbed onto Evan's lap. She was texting, her ponytail spilling over one shoulder. Evan's hand was on her thigh. Suddenly, she looked up and caught me staring. She nudged Evan, who glanced over as well, clearly wondering what I was doing at a different table. But it turned out they didn't really care, because half a moment later, they were sucking face.

"Come on, new girl," Phoebe said, standing up. "Let's go to the bathroom."

Once Phoebe and Cassidy had gone, Luke chuckled and shook his head.

"Can someone please explain why my girlfriend is going to the bathroom with Cassidy Thorpe?"

"I know nothing about the intricacies of female pack behavior," said Sam. "But I do know that we need to expand Friday's guest list."

Luke shot Sam a dark look.

"Sorry," Sam muttered, glancing guiltily in my direction.

"What the heck?" Austin said. "I thought she disappeared, and now she's at Eastwood? It doesn't make sense."

"*What* doesn't make sense?" I asked.

"Any of it." Toby balled up his cupcake wrapper. "But then, Cassidy always liked it that way. You know how I said she was unbeatable at debate? That's not the half of it. She never seemed to try. She'd show up to tournaments in blatant dress code violations, throw a picnic in an elevator, and not even bother to come to the awards ceremony. She competed for this really snotty prep school, which made it even stranger. But she quit after winning the State Quals last year. Gave up her spot at the State championship four days before the tournament, and the rumor was that she'd left school suddenly, just completely disappeared."

"Did you ever find out why?" I asked.

"Like anyone can get a straight answer out of Cassidy." Toby laughed.

"Incoming," Austin muttered, nodding toward Phoebe and Cassidy.

Everyone turned to stare at them guiltily, but I was watching something entirely different—the spectacle of Charlotte and Evan, and their all-too-public face sucking.

When the girls rejoined us, Phoebe glanced at my uneaten cupcake before reaching across the table to pat my hand.

"Don't worry," she teased. "There's some nice O positive in the nurse's office if you're thirsty."

8

I DON'T KNOW if you've ever been in line at the drugstore or somewhere, and the person behind you is chewing gum directly in your ear, and it's so repulsive that you suspect they're doing it on purpose and you're a complete pushover for standing there and taking it. There was something about Evan and Charlotte that made me feel exactly like that. Something so deeply and personally offensive about the two of them all over each other that I just couldn't handle it, even though the initial shock of it had originally fooled me into believing that I didn't care.

So I might as well admit that, deep down, I'd known what I was doing when I decided to eat lunch with Toby instead of sitting with my old crew. Over the course of the week, I went out of my way to avoid my old friends, as I'd done all summer, and they seemed baffled by it, and more than a little bit hurt. I couldn't figure out why they even cared. They couldn't really have thought I'd turn up for that game of paintball or that last-minute rafting trip, or any of the other ridiculous things they'd texted me about. I mean, not one of them had even bothered to visit me in the hospital.

Anyway, Evan and Charlotte were together now, had been together for what seemed suspiciously like a few months at least, and it was plain what that meant. In the grand scheme of seniors worth gawking at, they should have topped the list. But they didn't. Instead, I was the recipient of far too much attention for my liking. And when everyone wasn't whispering and staring at me, they were whispering and staring at Cassidy.

Stories that the debate team had only hinted at spilled out into the schoolwide rumor mill: that Cassidy had turned up at a debate tournament dressed as a boy, complete with an enormous fake mustache, and still won. That Cassidy had organized a flash mob where more than one hundred strangers showed up at a graveyard in San Francisco dressed as zombies and had an enormous pillow fight. That you could purchase T-shirts with a pop art print of Cassidy's face on them from a Spanish fast-fashion retailer. That she'd spent a summer modeling for teen book covers.

In our tiny, nothing-ever-happens town, Cassidy was an oddity, and even though the stories might not have been true, they were more likely to have happened to her than to anyone else.

She never let on that she knew about the rumors, though. And for all I knew, she didn't. Our lunch group had plenty to talk about without resorting to petty gossip, and I was grateful to sit with them, though I could have lived without the unobstructed view of Charlotte and Evan's lunchtime foreplay-dates.

On Thursday night, I had a meeting with Ms. Welsh, my advisor: one of those mandatory things for seniors. Of course I was late, since I'd left my math notebook in the waiting room at my physical therapist's and didn't realize until I was halfway to campus.

Ms. Welsh was nice enough, even about my being late. And so I settled into the world's hardest chair in her office and smiled attentively and listened as she lectured me on the importance of maintaining one's extracurriculars during senior year and reaching out to teachers well in advance for college recommendations. I didn't have the heart to tell her that maintaining my extracurriculars was literally physically impossible, or that I suspected Mrs. Martin might decorate my recommendation letter with grape-scented Fiesta Snoopy stamps.

By the time I finally made my escape after promising to check out some "close to home" colleges I wasn't particularly interested in attending, I was feeling pretty exhausted by the idea of college applications in general. I'd never really thought I'd have to deal with them. It was a given that I'd be recruited to play somewhere, probably one of the nearby state colleges. My father used to tell me stories about his college fraternity, and how future employers would be impressed if

I became president of my frat house. I'd pictured it easily back then, my whole planned-out life: college athlete, fraternity president, getting some suit-and-tie job after school and cruising up to Big Bear or Tahoe on the weekends with my friends. There was more, but you get the idea: the perfectly generic life for the perfectly generic golden boy.

"Ezra?" someone called, derailing my train of thought.

It was Cassidy, coming down the stairwell from the 400 building in this blue sundress that perfectly matched her eyes.

"Oh, hey," I said, attempting a smile. "College advisor meeting?"

"Unfortunately. Mr. Choi doesn't have a sense of humor."

"I've heard he enjoys jokes where the punch lines are mathematical equations," I offered.

"Yeah, he seems like the sort of guy who would get off on a tangent."

I snorted. "That's terrible."

Cassidy shrugged as we fell into step toward the parking lot.

It was getting late. The whole world had darkened while I was in Ms. Welsh's office. The stadium lights were on, bathing the campus in an orange glow and casting the hills into shadow.

"Tomorrow's Friday," Cassidy said, as though I needed reminding. "Wonder what all the cool kids are doing this weekend."

"Jimmy's having a party tomorrow night. I'd give it two hours before someone gets drunk enough to toss the keg into the pool."

"Oh wow, that sounds super fun." Cassidy rolled her eyes.

"Well, what did *you* do on Friday nights before you moved here?"

She shook her head and launched hesitantly into a rambling story about secret parties in the science labs of her boarding school.

"We'd all have to sneak in and out of the dorms through the old steam tunnels. It was like this mark of prestige if you got burned on one of the old pipes. I think one of my brother's friends started it, back in the day. I don't know. It sounds dumb, talking about it."

"No, it doesn't sound dumb."

Jimmy's back-to-school backyard kegger sounded dumb. Only I didn't say anything.

The campus was peaceful at night, surrounded by the gentle slope of the hills, with just the two narrow lanes leading back to town. The hills were covered with hundreds of avocado trees, and every once in a while, a coyote would wander down and terrorize the residents of some nearby gated community.

That was what excited people around here, getting together a mob to shoo the coyote back into the avocado groves, to remove the interloper from our perfect little planned community. No one went looking for adventure; they chased it away.

When we reached the student lot, there was only my Volvo, Justin Wong's souped-up Honda, and a truck with a surfboard strapped on top.

"Um, where's your car?" I asked.

Cassidy laughed. "My *bike* is right here."

Sure enough, a lone red bicycle was locked to the rack. It was a decent bike, a rebuilt Cannondale, but I didn't know much about bikes then.

"Huh," I said, staring at it.

"What?"

"Nothing." I tried not to grin at the image of Cassidy pedaling past the strawberry fields on a bicycle.

"I'll have you know that I care about the environment," Cassidy said hotly. "I'm doing my best to reduce my carbon footprint."

I thought about this for a moment.

"Carpooling reduces your carbon footprint, doesn't it?" I asked.

"Yes."

"So would you like a ride home?"

I don't know where the offer came from, but it suddenly seemed presumptuous.

"There are these coyotes," I said, awkwardly filling the silence. "They come down from the hills sometimes at night and I don't want you to get attacked."

"Coyotes?" Cassidy frowned. "Aren't those, like, *wolves*?"

"Nocturnal wolves," I clarified.

"You're sure you don't mind?"

"I offered, didn't I?"

"All right," Cassidy relented.

I had an unfortunate fit of chivalry and told Cassidy to get into the car while I dealt with her bike. It damn near killed me too, getting that thing into the trunk.

"Thank you," she said when I climbed into the driver's seat.

"No problem." I reached for my seat belt. "So where do you live?"

"Um, Terrace Bluffs?"

"That's no trouble. I live in Rosewood, I'm right next to you on the loop."

She buckled her seat belt, and I threw the car into reverse, realizing how intimate it was with just the two of us, and the empty rows of parking spaces.

"Rosewood's the section across the park, isn't it?" she asked.

"Yeah. My bedroom looks out over it."

"So does mine." Cassidy grinned. "Maybe we can see into each other's bedrooms."

"I'll remember to close the blinds next week when I commit a double homicide," I promised, flashing my brights on the blind curve out of the foothills.

"I like you like this," Cassidy said.

"Like what?" I asked as I merged onto Eastwood Boulevard.

"Talking. You hold back if there are too many people around."

I put on my turn signal, in case a coyote was curious which way I wanted to turn at the deserted intersection, and thought about this. The way I figured it, keeping quiet was safe. Words could betray you if you chose the wrong ones, or mean less if you used too many. Jokes could be grandly miscalculated, or stories deemed boring, and I'd learned early on that my sense of humor and ideas about what sorts of things were fascinating didn't exactly overlap with my friends'.

"I don't hold back," I protested. "I just don't have anything interesting to say."

Cassidy looked skeptical. "Yeah, sorry, not buying it. You have this maddening little smile sometimes, like you've just thought of something incredibly witty but are afraid to say it in case no one gets the joke."

I shrugged and turned left onto Crescent Vista, catching the traffic light that made two minutes last even longer than they did in Coach Anthony's class.

"Actually, I don't know which is worse," Cassidy mused, "when people laugh at things that aren't funny, or when they don't laugh at things that are."

"The first one," I said darkly. "Just ask Toby."

"What, you mean the severed-head thing?"

She said it exactly like that, as though we might have been talking about irregular verbs or the Pledge of Allegiance.

"He told you?"

"Last year at some debate tournament. We were sitting out on the balcony under a tent we'd made from bedsheets and I'd mentioned how I'd never been to Disneyland. I think it's hilarious. I called him 'the catcher on the ride' for ages."

I shook my head over her terrible pun and turned on the radio, trying not to think about Cassidy and Toby keeping each other company late at night in hotel rooms, probably in their pajamas. The Shins drifted through the speakers, and I waited for Cassidy to say something as we sat at that endless light, but she didn't. Instead, she picked up a straw wrapper I'd stuffed into the cup holder and began to fold it into a little origami star.

"Make a wish," she said, cupping the little star in the palm of her hand.

The glow of the streetlight washed over her, and it struck me almost as an afterthought that she was beautiful. I don't know how I'd missed it those first few days, but I knew it then. Her hair was thrown back into a ponytail, with these copper-colored pieces framing her face. Her eyes shone with amusement, and her sweater slipped off one shoulder, revealing a purple bra strap. She was achingly effortless, and she would never, in a million years, choose me. But, for the next few minutes, I contented myself with the magnificent possibility that she might.

The gate guard outside Cassidy's subdivision gave me the third degree, which, incidentally, is the sort of burn that can kill. When he was finally satisfied that we weren't about to wreak havoc on the unsuspecting suburban streets, he opened the gate, and I drove through into Terrace Bluffs.

It wasn't that different from my subdivision; the houses were all set back from the street, with circular driveways and balconies that weren't really supposed to be used. There were only four models, like a computer animation that kept repeating. Some little kids had been drawing in the street with chalk, and I felt terrible as I drove over it, as though I was wrecking a second grader's sand castle.

"How do I get to your house?" I asked.

"Do you ever just not want to go home?" Her face was pale in the lamplight, and I could see it in her eyes that she was serious.

"Yeah, absolutely," I admitted, even though it was pretty personal. I thought about my mom sitting in the family room, watching the news and worrying over everything. About my father in his home office, a mug of tea going cold at his elbow as he typed out another brief. About my bedroom, which felt as though it wasn't mine anymore after I'd spent three months sleeping in the downstairs guest room.

"I have an idea," Cassidy said. "How about we go somewhere, right now?"

"It's Eastwood," I said. "There's nowhere to go."

"Let's go to the park," Cassidy pleaded. "You can point out your bedroom window, and I can point out mine."

"All right," I said, reversing over the chalk drawings.

The gate guard gave me a dirty look when I pulled through, and Cassidy laughed and flipped him the bird when we were too far away for him to see.

"I freaking hate that guy," she said. "Do you read Foucault? What am I talking about? Of course you don't read Foucault."

"Mostly, I just don't read," I deadpanned, making Cassidy laugh.

"Well, Mr. Illiterate Jock, let me enlighten you. There was this philosopher-slash-historian called Foucault, who wrote about how society is like this legendary prison called the panopticon. In the panopticon, you might be under constant observation, except you can never be sure whether someone is watching or not, so you wind up following the rules anyway."

"But how do you know who's a watcher and who's a prisoner?" I asked, pulling into the empty parking lot.

"That's the point. Even the watchers are prisoners. Come on, let's go on the swings." She was already out of the car before I could even put on the handbrake.

"Wait," I called.

Cassidy turned around, her dress rippling in the warm Santa Ana winds. I locked the car and stood there, awash in embarrassment.

"I don't think I can go on the swings," I admitted.

"Then you can push me."

She took off toward the small playground and the bright plastic play set as though we were running a race. I stepped cautiously into the sandbox, feeling my cane sink into the sand like a beach umbrella. Cassidy kicked off her sandals and tied her sweater around her waist. Sitting there on the swing set, in her bare feet and blue dress, her hair slipping out of its ponytail, she was so gorgeous that it hurt.

"Go on," she said, twisting on the swing so that the chains made an X. "Push."

I laid my palms against her back, touching bare skin. I gulped and gave her a push, nearly losing my balance before I figured out how to manage it.

"Keep going!" she called.

I kept going. She rose higher and higher on the swing, and to be honest, I was rising a bit myself.

After a while, she didn't need me anymore. She was just up there, impossibly high, the chains slapping against the top bar.

She tilted her head back, grinning at me. "We'll escape the panopticon together," she promised.

And then she jumped.

The swing buckled as she flew forward, laughing and shouting. She landed unsteadily on her feet, at the edge of the sandbox.

"Did we escape?" I called.

"Not even close."

I sat down on the swing, hoping that would disguise my problem. Cassidy took the other swing, making a complicated design in the sand with her toes.

"Do you see that house just to the right of the tallest tree?" I asked, breaking the silence.

"With the two chimneys?"

"Yeah."

"My bedroom's the one with the fake balcony. It's right above our pool with the fake waterfall," I added, earning one of Cassidy's rare smiles.

"I'll send you secret messages," she promised. "In Morse code. With my Hello Kitty flashlight."

"You better."

Suddenly, Cassidy's phone buzzed. She slipped it out of her pocket and I glimpsed a list of missed calls.

"I should get back," she said, standing up. "Pop your trunk so I can get my bike?"

"I don't mind driving you."

Cassidy shook her head. "I'd rather bike. It's like, my mom's already pissed? I'm not used to living at home, and I forgot to check in."

"Well, if you're sure."

"I'll see you at school," she said, and then grinned evilly. "Unless I'm attacked by nocturnal wolves, in which case you'll just have to live with the guilt."

She scooped up her shoes, and I watched her silhouette as she ran across the grass, and I thought about how it usually wasn't like this when it came to me and girls.

9

I SUPPOSE I'D better explain about Charlotte Hyde and how we'd started dating. I asked her to be my girlfriend in October of our junior year, during a scorcher of a weekend when we'd all driven out to Laguna Beach for the day. It was the usual crew piled into the usual cars, about fifteen of us.

Jimmy had packed a cooler of beers, bought with his older brother's ID. In typical Jimmy fashion, he'd forgotten to bring anything that might disguise the open containers, so the guys kept sneaking them into the public toilets. The cops parked out on Beach Boulevard must've thought they all had the shits.

The girls wanted to sunbathe, as usual. They rarely did anything besides recline in beach chairs and flick through magazines, and it baffled me how anyone could go to the beach to willingly engage in the same pass-the-time activities that passengers suffered through on airplanes.

The seniors in our crowd put Evan and me to work

grilling hot dogs on a public barbecue near the lifeguard stand. Evan complained about being a grunt, but I honestly didn't mind. It was peaceful standing there, the heat from the coals drying my bathing suit, the sun slanting off the water. It was the beginning of junior year, and we had everything to look forward to.

After we ate the hot dogs on hamburger buns ("No one fuckin' told me what *kind* of buns," Evan had protested) and the girls pretended to be upset over it, Brett Masters, the captain of the water polo team, challenged the tennis guys to five-on-five volleyball.

They destroyed us because, unlike tennis, water polo plays all on the same court and knows how to pass the damn ball. I'd managed a pretty spectacular spike out of sheer luck, but Jimmy and Evan were drunk enough that it was actually entertaining to watch them fumble and curse at their own ineptitude.

The sun had begun to set during the game, the ocean breeze turning cold. The girls put back on their sundresses. Charlotte unhooked her bathing suit top and removed it from beneath her dress as if by magic. She caught me looking and grinned, sensing that I was under her spell.

"Ezra, come over here," she demanded, pouting cutely.

Dutifully, I went.

"Jill and I found this quiz in *Pop Teen* magazine about how to tell if a guy likes you," she said, and before I knew it, the girls had trapped me on their matching hot pink towels and were making me take the quiz from their magazine. The questions were ridiculous, and when we finally reached the last one, Charlotte insisted on looking up my horoscope.

"Love is in the cards for all of you stubborn Tauruses!" she told me, and then frowned. "Well, what do you think?"

"I think I just learned the plural form of *Taurus*," I joked, and Charlotte pretended to be upset that I wasn't taking the horoscope seriously.

Ever since the end of sophomore year, I'd suspected that Charlotte liked me, but that day at the beach was the first time I sensed that she wasn't just flirting for the fun of it— that she had something specific in mind.

"You're so sweet," she murmured, leaning into my shoulder as we sat side by side on her towel. "It's a shame you're not over Staci."

Staci Guffin and I had broken up a month earlier, for reasons I didn't fully understand and didn't particularly care to. She'd traumatized me with a *Sex and the City* DVD marathon when I thought I was going over to her house for, uh, something more orgasmic than shoes. Maybe she'd just wanted to break up so she could have an ex-boyfriend to complain about to her friends. I honestly didn't know.

"Trust me," I said, glancing down at the long blonde hair piled on top of her head, and her endless, tanned legs, dusted with a fine layer of sand. "I'm definitely over Staci."

I didn't know much about Charlotte back then, just that she was gorgeous and sexy and always had gum in her purse that she'd offer me with a smile, like she'd brought it just for me. I didn't know that she listened to her iPod in the kitchen while she made elaborate cookies and cupcakes from gourmet baking blogs, or that she thought it was bad luck to eat the batter. I didn't know that she'd danced since she was three, that she did yoga with her mom before school, or that she collected everything to do with ladybugs. I didn't know that we'd be together for more than eight months, the longest relationship I'd have in high school.

We wound up taking a walk to the other end of the beach, where the rocks jutted into the surf, forming little tide pools. She wore my Eastwood Tennis sweatshirt, because she'd gotten cold. I was secretly glad, since it made her seem more real somehow, the way she kept pushing up the sleeves of my hoodie as we walked through the tidal foam.

We scrambled onto the rocks, the barnacles stabbing into the soles of our feet. In the distance, I could see our friends beginning to pack up, and it filled me with a strange sense of urgency. I watched Evan heft the cooler, dumping its contents over Jimmy's head, and I judged that we had maybe five minutes for whatever it was that had brought us apart from everyone else.

"I'm glad you're not a complete jerk," Charlotte said. She had slipped her phone out of the pocket of my sweatshirt and was texting.

"Thanks, I guess?"

"I didn't mean it like that." Charlotte looked up from

her phone with a guilty smile. Her hair streamed behind her in the breeze, and the bridge of her nose had turned pink from the sun. "Sorry. Jill wanted to know where I'd put her sunscreen. Anyway, I just meant how we're, like, *destined* to date each other. The most popular girl in the junior class and the most popular guy."

"I'm not the most popular guy in our year," I protested, dropping my gaze to the tide pools.

"Um, duh. Of course you are. Why else would I have brought you here?"

"*You* brought me here?" I raised an eyebrow, teasing her.

"Yes, I did. Now shut up and kiss me."

I shut up and kissed her. She tasted like strawberry lip-gloss and diet soda, and she smelled like suntan lotion and my mom's favorite detergent, and we were sixteen and not fully dressed, even as far as the beach is concerned.

"So?" Charlotte asked with a sly smile when we pulled apart.

"You should keep my sweatshirt," I said. "It looks nice on you."

"*Ezra*," Charlotte chastised. She put her hand on her hip, waiting.

"Um, would you like to go out with me?"

"Of course." She grinned triumphantly and kissed me again, her hands warm and soft on my back. "Mmm, you're so *cute*. We should take you shopping. I bet you'd look super hot in some new jeans."

So there it is. The day it happened: a romantic tale filled with beers consumed in a public urinal, getting creamed at volleyball by varsity water polo, kissing a girl in the tide pools, and not knowing what I was getting myself into.

Back in ninth-grade science, we had a unit on ecology, and I'd read Steinbeck's *Sea of Cortez* for extra credit after failing to impress Mr. Ghesh with my tenuous understanding of the water cycle. Steinbeck wrote about tide pools and how profoundly they illustrate the interconnectedness of all things, folded together in an ever-expanding universe that's bound by the elastic string of time. He said that one should look from the tide pool to the stars, and then back again in wonder. And maybe things would have been different if I'd heeded his advice that day on the beach with Charlotte, but I didn't. Instead, I linked my hand in hers and failed to appreciate the bigger picture, and the only stars I saw were wearing varsity jackets.

10

YOU CAN ALWAYS tell when it's Friday. There's an excitement specific to Fridays, coupled with relief that another week has passed. Even Toby's friends, who I didn't think ever did much over the weekend, were in a good mood that first Friday.

Luke, Austin, and Phoebe were already there when I got to the table during break. Luke had his arm around Phoebe, who was eating a Pop-Tart, and Austin was engrossed in some mobile gaming device.

"No, no, bad portal," he scolded, totally oblivious to the world. "Stop—evil—eurgh! Suck my flagellated balls, douchenozzle!"

Phoebe sighed. "Help, help, Austin! Your flagellated balls are on fire!"

Austin didn't even look up.

"Told you he was in the gaming zone," Phoebe said.

"What'd I miss?" I asked, sliding onto a bench.

"Well, I heard Jimmy's having a sick kegger tonight," Luke said, in this sarcastic way that let me know he still wasn't all that thrilled to have me around. "It's a Tier One party, of course."

"Yeah, I heard that too," I said, not liking the way Luke had casually thrown around the term my old friends used to express the exclusivity of their little events. "It's like *Animal Farm*."

"You mean *Animal House*," Luke corrected. "The movie about college frat parties."

I shook my head. "No, I mean *Animal Farm*. You know: 'Some animals are more equal than other animals.'"

Phoebe laughed and squirmed out from under Luke's arm to throw away her Pop-Tart wrapper.

"Ezra, you're taking me to Jimmy's party, right?" she asked, fake-pouting.

"Definitely," I said, playing along. "Should we bring a bottle of wine or an assortment of cheeses as a host gift?"

Luke broke off a piece of Phoebe's Pop-Tart and she squealed in protest, ignoring my question.

"What up, minions?" Toby slid a preposterously large coffee thermos onto the table. "Ooh, is that Mortal Portal Three?"

Austin still didn't look up.

"He's in the zone," Phoebe said. "Honestly, what *is* it with boys and video games? No wonder print is dead."

"*I* read," Toby protested as Sam and Cassidy joined us,

eating fresh cookies from the bakery line. "For instance, last night I read that you can levitate a frog with magnets."

Phoebe rolled her eyes, unimpressed.

"Hypothetically, or scientifically proven?" Cassidy wanted to know.

"Scientifically proven," Toby said triumphantly. "These Nobel Prize–winning scientists did it."

"How many beers do y'all think it takes before one internationally respected scientist turns to another and says, 'Dude, bet you twenty bucks I can levitate a frog with a magnet?'" Sam drawled.

"Well, which magnetic charge?" Cassidy asked. "I mean, it has to be either positive or negative, doesn't it?"

"You think you're so clever, don't you?" Toby teased.

"Just a tadpole," Cassidy replied.

Everyone groaned.

And then the bell rang.

Cassidy and I had English together—with Luke, actually, but he usually walked Phoebe to class.

"So," I said as Cassidy and I headed toward Mr. Moreno's room, "I didn't see any secret messages last night."

"I didn't want to be predictable," Cassidy retorted. "But at least now I know you're paying attention."

GOOD OLD MORENO and his pop quizzes. I'd nearly forgotten about those. He slammed a tough one on us—themes and metaphors from the first one hundred pages of *Gatsby*.

I was slogging my way through the questions on the Smart Board when it hit me how the billboard that Wilson thought was watching him—the one with the eyes of Dr. T. J. Eckleburg—wasn't so different from the idea behind the panopticon. I scribbled my revelation down as my final long-answer question and finished just before Mr. Moreno called time.

He made us trade papers with the person sitting behind us, which, lucky me, was Luke. Luke grinned as I tore my page out of my notebook and handed it over.

"Hope you studied, Faulkner," he said, uncapping his pen.

I got Anamica Patel's paper. At the top of it, she'd written her name, the date, our teacher's name, our class period, and "Gatsby Quiz #1" in the neatest handwriting I'd ever seen.

Mr. Moreno went over the short-answer questions and the true-false. Anamica missed one of the true-false.

"All right, hand them back and then pass them forward. I'll grade the long-answer questions myself," Mr. Moreno said.

I passed Anamica's quiz forward and she scowled at me, as though it was my fault she hadn't gotten a score as perfect as her handwriting.

"Hey, uh, Luke?" I asked. "Can I have my quiz back?"

"Nice essay, Faulkner," he said, leaning back in his chair, still holding my paper. "Which version of CliffsNotes did you use?"

"I didn't know there were different versions," I said. "Which one do *you* recommend?"

Luke muttered something under his breath and passed back my quiz. There was a piece of computer paper beneath it, folded in thirds.

I was about to mention it, but Luke shook his head slightly in warning, so I slipped the piece of paper into my bag and passed my quiz to the front.

"MS. WENG WANTS to see both of you," said Toby, when Cassidy and I arrived at the lunch table with our mini-pizzas. "By the way, that means now."

I crammed a slice of minipizza into my mouth and indicated that I was good to go.

"Great, now when he *does* eat, it's disgusting," Phoebe noted.

Cassidy sighed and sat down. "I'm going to pretend I didn't get that message until the very end of lunch. How about you, Ezra?"

I swallowed thickly. "What message?"

"Good boy." Cassidy put on her sunglasses and nibbled her way through half of her pizza before getting up.

"Are you seriously not finishing that?" I asked.

"Why?" Cassidy grinned, dangling the pizza half over a trash can. "Do you *want* it?"

"*I* want it," Austin said, finally glancing up from his game console. "I'm broke. I spent all my money on MP Three."

"I knew that's what you were playing!" Toby said. "Dude, what level are you? Is it true the Eyes regenerate twice as fast if you Infinity Drop them?"

"Let's go," Cassidy said with a sigh, and I followed her to Ms. Weng's classroom.

Ms. Weng was eating last night's leftover spaghetti out of a plastic container at her desk and reading a celebrity gossip magazine. I'm not going to lie; it was pretty sad.

"You wanted to see us?" I asked.

She startled and guiltily slid an attendance folder over the magazine. I pretended not to notice.

"Yes, our two new recruits! I'm so happy to have both of you on the team."

Suddenly, I remembered that sign-up sheet the first day of class and how I'd put Cassidy's name down. I was screwed. I glanced at Cassidy, and her expression was a mixture of shock and horror.

"Um, about that?" I began. "I don't think—"

But Ms. Weng wasn't listening. She rambled on about how wonderful it was to have a seasoned pro like Cassidy, and how she was sure Cassidy or Toby could answer any questions I might have about competing.

Cassidy's face had gone gray. "Ms. Weng," she finally said. "I think there's a mistake. I didn't sign up."

"Oh, I've already registered both of you for the San Diego open tournament in two weeks," Ms. Weng said, misunderstanding. "And I've reserved the school van to drive everyone down for the weekend, unless either of you have any, er, *special needs* you'd like to discuss privately?"

"Nope," I said through clenched teeth. "No 'special needs.'"

I made the phrase sound good and dirty, and Cassidy shot me a look of sympathy.

"I'm so glad," Ms. Weng said, handing us each a thick packet. "Now you'll need to have these permission forms signed by a parent or guardian."

"My parents are out of town," Cassidy said. "Yeah, they're in Switzerland at this medical symposium for the rest of the month."

I was pretty sure Cassidy's parents were at no such thing, but Ms. Weng just smiled and assured Cassidy that her old coach could fax over last year's form for the time being. There was such a finality to her tone that we didn't dare to question it.

Cassidy and I slunk from Ms. Weng's room in defeat. The moment the door closed, Cassidy turned toward me, eyes blazing.

"What the *hell*?" she demanded. "She cornered us back there. And I *never* signed up to compete—it's like she was planning this all along. I knew there was a reason I got put in debate class! 'Oh, there aren't any other team electives open,' my advisor said. 'It's this or phys ed.' Yeah, freaking right. I'm not some champion pony they can parade around whenever they feel like it. I don't compete anymore, and they have no right to force me into it like this."

"Um," I said.

"And *you* didn't sign up for it, either!" Cassidy jabbed a finger at my chest. "You should have seen your face when Ms. Weng asked if you had any special needs. I wish you'd punched her."

"Yeah, that would've been productive."

Cassidy sighed. "God, Ezra, you really don't get it. Our names are already *entered*. We compete or forfeit on the tournament listing."

Crap. I wasn't familiar with the rules of debate competitions, and I hadn't realized the only way out was to forfeit publicly.

"Um, Cassidy?" I had to tell her. "Remember that day in class with the sign-up sheet and how you were laughing at me?"

"Yeah?"

"I sort of signed you up as a joke," I admitted.

"You WHAT?"

"I didn't know!" I quickly amended. "You'd pulled that stupid stunt on me in Spanish and then Toby had signed *me* up so I just figured—"

"You just figured what, exactly?" Cassidy said coldly. "That it would be *funny*?"

"Um, I guess? I didn't know you felt like that about debate. I didn't know that you'd stopped competing."

I hung my head, waiting for Cassidy to laugh and say

that it was okay. But she didn't.

"That's right," Cassidy said fiercely. "I stopped competing. Just like how *you* stopped competing in tennis. But you know what? I *get* that you don't want to talk about it. Just because I don't limp around with a freaking cane doesn't mean I have to explain myself to people I've known for five seconds for quitting. So screw you for signing me up for this because you thought it would be *funny*."

Her eyes burned with revulsion as she stomped past me. And I didn't blame her. I felt awful. Like I should go back into Ms. Weng's office and explain everything. But then the bell rang, and I realized I was going to be late for Spanish.

11

BY THAT EVENING, my weekend was shaping up to be pretty lousy. I'd come straight home from school and spent the day alternating between doing the key terms for Coach Anthony's class and playing Zombie Guitar God on mute to keep my mind off how badly I'd screwed things up with Cassidy. But it wasn't working.

Worse, I could tell that my mom kept coming to check on me, hovering just outside my bedroom door and listening. Cooper, who was curled on a bathrobe at the foot of my bed, would glance at the door and then sigh, settling back into his nest.

Well, it is *Friday night, old sport,* his eyes seemed to say. *And there's a whole world out there.*

Cooper was right; maybe I *should* go to Jimmy's backyard kegger. I briefly considered it before remembering what happened the last time I went to a house party. So yeah, that was definitely out. And then the little Skype icon on my computer screen dinged. It was Toby, and did I want to come over?

I changed out of my pajamas, grabbed my keys, and practically opened my bedroom door into my mom's face.

"Oh, you're up," she said.

"Well yeah, it's nine o'clock. I'm going out."

"Where are you going?" she called after me. "I need to know where you're going!"

"Why?" I asked, mildly curious as to when this had become a new house rule.

She spluttered over that one for a good ten seconds.

"Look, I'm going to Toby's," I said, which was pretty charitable. "I have my phone, and we're not going to huff rat poison or anything."

"Ezra!" She sounded shocked. "Don't be rude. I have every right to worry."

"I know," I said in exasperation. "You *keep reminding me.*"

As I pulled out of the driveway, I wondered what everyone from school was doing. I could pretty much guess the crowd that was headed to Jimmy's party to drink a few beers in their bathing suits. And everyone else was probably headed to the Prism Center, this outdoor mall with an IMAX cinema and lots of dramatically lit palm trees. The Prism was really the only place to go in Eastwood besides the Chinese strip mall, and even there, the cops would hassle you to start heading home when it was still early because of the town curfew. I privately thought of them as the Prism Wardens, which was funny for about two seconds, and then became infinitely depressing—and not just because the name now reminded me of Cassidy and her panopticon.

It was strange, driving over to Toby's. I'd only ever biked there, on the trails that connect the different subdivisions. Toby lived in Walnut Ranch, one of the older developments south of the loop. I'd practically lived at his house during elementary school, and as I drove, I remembered flashes of what we'd been like as kids: how we'd taped notes to the undersides of each other's mailboxes, written in a code that only we could decipher. The year we dressed as Batman and Robin for Halloween and then switched costumes, just to see how long it would take my dad to notice, the answer being a disturbingly long time. The Cub Scout camping trip when the scout leader's obnoxious son put a worm in my pudding cup, so Toby and I caught a frog and zipped it inside his sleeping bag. Writing swear words in the air with our sparklers on the Fourth of July. Begging my mom to take us to Barnes and Noble at midnight to get the latest Harry Potter book and promising we wouldn't stay up all night reading but doing it anyway.

I'd completely forgotten what Toby had been like, back then. How he'd always been the one to devise our elaborate schemes, how he'd constantly gotten me into trouble, and then out of it with an aw-shucks routine and apology. He'd grown up into exactly the unabashedly nerdy, quick-witted guy you'd expect from a kid who went door-to-door selling homemade comics to raise the start-up capital for our summer lemonade stand when we were ten. And I'd grown up into a massive douche—with a cane.

TOBY'S HOUSE LOOKED the same as I remembered, complete with an unwashed burgundy minivan parked in the driveway. I rang the bell and a tiny dog started yapping.

Toby's sister opened the door. She was wearing a bright pink bathrobe and carrying an angry little terrier that looked like an ankle biter.

"Hey, Emily," I said.

"Omigod." She seemed shocked that I'd turned up at her house, as though she'd forgotten I used to know her garage door code.

Toby's house was pretty compact, and the front door opened directly into the living room, where three of Emily's friends were watching one of those terrible vampire romance things in their pajamas, sleeping bags already laid out.

"Hiiii, Ezra," one of the girls said, giggling.

"Um, hi?" I said. Poor Toby. No wonder he'd wanted me to come over. Thankfully, he came dashing around the corner, fastening a pair of cuff links.

"Welcome to purgatory," he said. "Come on in."

Toby's room hadn't changed much; there was a new shelf

displaying some action figures I didn't recognize, a police box, and some random dude dressed like Toby in a blazer and bow tie, plus a couple of samurai swords. And then I caught sight of the top shelf of his bookcase and stopped dead.

"You kept them?" I asked.

"I finished them." Toby pulled out the thick stack of homemade comics and tossed them onto his bed.

I reached for *Superhero Academy, volume I*. It was laughingly amateur, done in colored pencil on computer paper, with the byline in alternating blue and red bubble letters: *created by Toby Ellicott & Ezra Faulkner*.

We'd worked on *Superhero Academy* every day after school in the fifth grade. I think we'd gotten four volumes in before suffering from artistic differences. But there were at least eight volumes scattered across the bed. A few of them were computer-illustrated and almost professional-looking. I picked up *Justice University: The Final Battle* and flipped to the end.

"Okay, there's no way Invisible Boy could defeat the Arch Alchemist with a *samurai sword*," I argued.

"You're just bitter because I made your character evil," Toby snapped.

"Not at all, I just don't get how the Arch Alchemist became mortal all of a sudden."

"Because he split his soul into seven pieces and hid them all over Justice City," Toby retorted.

"You turned our comic book into a *Harry Potter rip-off?*" I spluttered.

"Are we seriously having this discussion?"

I felt my cheeks heat up, and I tossed the graphic novel back onto the bed with a shrug. Toby sorted them into the right order and returned them to his shelf.

"So are we going or not?" he asked.

"Where? Jimmy's party?" I sincerely hoped he wasn't going to annoy me into showing up at that.

"I could kill Luke," Toby said. "He *really* didn't invite you?"

"Invite me to what?"

"The Floating Movie Theater? You know, that piece of paper with some random words on it and a URL?"

Suddenly, I remembered the sheet of paper Luke had passed me in Moreno's class that afternoon. I'd thought it was some stupid flyer for Film Club.

"Crap," I said. "He gave me something, but I never opened it. I was sort of distracted."

Toby snorted. "Yeah, I'll *bet* you were distracted."

"What's that supposed to mean?"

"Cassidy, dude. I know you're into her, but trust me, it's better to just forget it. She'll get into your head and mess you up."

"Believe me," I said with a sigh, "staying away from Cassidy won't be a problem."

And then I explained how I'd accidentally forced her

into joining the debate team.

"You are so dead," Toby said.

"I didn't realize it was such a big deal," I admitted. "*You* put *my* name down."

"And I figured you'd cross it off." Toby shrugged. "But Cassidy's different. A FORFEIT next to her name on the tournament lists would cause gossip. She's the defending champion, you know? Everyone thought she'd rank nationally, but she withdrew from the state tournament two days before the primaries, just totally disappeared. To have her name posted as a forfeit from *Eastwood*, the most pathetic debate team out there? Anyway, are we going to Luke's screening or not? Because we need to pick up coffee filters on the way."

TWENTY MINUTES LATER, we were in Toby's spectacularly dinged, hand-me-down burgundy minivan (known fondly as the "Fail Whale"), trying to coax the broken antenna to pick up an FM frequency as we cruised up Eastwood Boulevard.

"Tonight's going to be fun," Toby promised. "You'll see."

And I guess it might have been, if I wasn't still lugging around the memory of my earlier douche-baggage. Because the more that I thought about Cassidy on the swing set in her bare feet, smiling at me as she promised that we'd escape the panopticon together, the more I wished I hadn't wrecked everything.

"Yeah, fun," I muttered, watching a tumbleweed blow through the crosswalk and latch itself to a yield sign in the center divider.

According to Toby, the floating movie theater was something of a closely guarded legend in nerd circles, and my being invited was a pretty big deal. The history went back to our Cub Scout days, when an enterprising Eastwood High senior named Max Sheppard had stolen the janitor's key ring and quietly made himself a copy. He used the keys to play a series of nasty pranks on the administration, successfully evading capture. On his sixteenth birthday, Luke Sheppard inherited the keys to the kingdom from his older brother, but chose to use them for good. And so began the Floating Movie Theater, a series of secret film screenings never held in the same place twice.

The campus was pretty deserted, and Toby double-parked his van, straddling the principal's and vice principal's spots.

"Grab the filters," he told me.

"Remind me why I just spent five bucks on coffee filters?"

"Because you have five bucks and I don't?" Toby grinned. "Naw, it's just part of what we do. I mean, we don't want to be caught—we want to be *noticed*. So we watched *Dead Poets Society* in Mr. Moreno's room and left behind a ton of whiteboard markers. We watched the *Princess Bride* in the library and donated a box of books. And tonight, we're screening *Rushmore* in the teachers' lounge. Hence the coffee filters."

Toby stopped walking, waiting for the sheer awesomeness of the Floating Movie Theater to wash over me.

Instead, this is what I said: "We're breaking into the teachers' lounge?"

"More like 'letting ourselves in,'" Toby assured me. "Come on."

I planted my feet firmly at the edge of the parking lot.

"You better be damned sure we won't get caught," I warned. "Because I can't exactly run if the cops show up."

Toby started laughing. "Funny story," he said. "Max Sheppard? Why, just the other week, he let me off on a warning for my busted taillight. Now let's go."

THE MOVIE HAD just started. Toby and I grabbed seats on the side, and I tried to follow along, but mostly, what I wound up following was Cassidy's expression.

I suppose she didn't think anyone was looking and had let her guard down, the way you do in an empty room. The way I did when I closed the blinds and stared up at the ceiling fan above my bed, equally fascinated and horrified by the thoughts racing through my brain.

She seemed so sad, even though the movie was a comedy and everyone else was laughing, as though she wasn't paying attention to the film at all, but was haunted by images of something else. I'd never seen her like that, and it made me wonder about what Toby had said, how she'd disappeared without warning, and how no one had known what to make of it.

A couple of people stood up when the movie ended, but Luke insisted that we had to watch the credits. Surprisingly, they sat back down, looking thoroughly chastised; I hadn't realized Luke carried that sort of power, but it made an odd sort of sense. I'd heard him referred to as the "king of the nerds," and I had never understood why, but I could see it easily then.

"So what did you think?" Toby asked as we deposited our coffee filters on a table with everyone else's loot.

"About the movie?"

"Obviously the movie is a classic and *Napoleon Dynamite* is a pale imitation of this far superior film," Toby said wryly, "but no. About this: secret screenings, coded invitations, positive vandalism."

"It's awesome," I said. And I meant it. I hadn't known that people did things like this, especially in Eastwood. It was strange, realizing that these sorts of clandestine activities happened at a school I used to think I ran, that there were other things going on besides my old friends' parties. "Why don't more people know about it?"

"Because Evan McMillan would turn this into some obnoxious drinking game," Luke said, joining us.

"Yeah, probably," I admitted. "Beer funneling through coffee filters."

We stood there in silence for a bit, Luke with this knowing look on his face, as though he was glad I'd finally seen what he could do.

"So Luke," I said, breaking the silence, "how about screening *One Flew Over the Cuckoo's Nest* in the nurse's office? I know it'd be a tight fit, but it would be sort of perfect."

"Dude," Toby said. "That would be epic."

"I didn't ask for your ideas, Faulkner," Luke said coldly, drifting over to play host to a nearby group of juniors.

"He really doesn't like me," I noted.

"Nah, 'course he does," Toby said unconvincingly. "You're pals."

I gave him a look.

"His girlfriend used to have the world's biggest crush on you," Toby admitted. "Probably still does."

"Phoebe?"

"'Oh Ezra, you're like some sexy vampire,'" Toby mocked.

I winced, but I had to admit, he had a point.

"Hey there, sexy vampire," someone said, tapping me on the shoulder.

Cassidy tucked her hair behind her ears and smiled as though that afternoon—and the past few hours—had never happened.

"Hi?" I said cautiously.

"How much do you love Bill Murray?" she asked, rambling about the movie we'd just sat through. "*I* adore him. If he popped the question, I'd Bill Murray him in a second."

"Um," I said, confused. Had I missed something? Last time I'd checked, Cassidy hated my guts, and I'd gotten the impression that we weren't speaking to each other any time in the foreseeable future.

"Listen," Cassidy said. "I could use a protégé, so tag, you're it. I'm going to teach you everything I know about debate, and you're going to win first place at the San Diego tournament."

"I am?"

"Yes! And the heavenly cherubs will play tiny ukuleles of joy and you will lay incense and coniferous fruits at my altar."

"Sounds like a plan," I said dryly. "Coniferous fruits and goddess worship. Check."

"That's more like it!" Cassidy grinned.

"Oh, look over there," Toby deadpanned, shooting me a sly glance. "It's someone I suddenly feel the need to go bother."

"I thought you were mad," I said after Toby left.

"Like Hamlet, my madness is fleeting," Cassidy informed me.

"No, I thought you were mad at *me*," I clarified.

"Ezra, you're being ridiculous. I'm over it. That's what girls do; they get angry, and then they get over it. Haven't you ever been friends with a girl before?"

Of course I hadn't; I'd dated my fair share of them, but

I'd never wanted to be friends with any of the girls in my old crowd. What would have been the point?

Maybe Cassidy was right—maybe it was only *girlfriends* who stayed mad at you. Still, there was something in her smile that I didn't quite believe. But I accepted my good fortune, knowing better than to question it.

12

ONCE EACH SEPTEMBER, the teachers had a training day, and we got the day off. Junior year, Evan and Jimmy and I went down to Balboa, ate cheeseburgers on the boardwalk, and watched some terrible 3-D movie. But that year, I had totally forgotten about Teacher Development Day until the day before.

Unsurprisingly, Toby and the debate crew had a grand adventure planned; they'd purchased tickets to a show in LA called *Spring Awakening*, and Toby was trying without success to convince everyone to dress up as turn-of-the-century schoolboys.

"Really, you guys should come with us," Phoebe said, when everyone sheepishly realized that Cassidy and I hadn't been included in the original plan. "We bought our tickets over the summer, but you could still come even if you got seats in a different section."

"That's all right," Cassidy said casually. "Ezra and I

already have plans."

This was news to me. Toby gave me a significant look, and I shrugged, having no idea what Cassidy was talking about.

"Yeah? You two going gleaning?" Sam asked, which made everyone except Cassidy crack up.

I should explain—"gleaning" is when you pick rotting and bruised crops, the stuff migrant workers leave behind in the fields because it's not good enough to sell as produce. It's actually a required field trip for eighth graders. They bus us over to the old ranch lands for the day, complete with a yearbook photographer, and it's just as terrible as it sounds.

Toby quickly filled Cassidy in on what we were laughing about.

"You're not serious," Cassidy said. "Y'all had a field trip to pick rotting tomatoes? What about going to museums?"

"Yeah," Toby said dryly. "Not so much. Welcome to Eastwood."

On the way to third period, I asked Cassidy what she meant about our having plans. She was wearing a white lace dress with straps that wouldn't stay put, and I couldn't help but imagine running my hands over her shoulders, slipping the straps down.

"Oh that." Cassidy shrugged. "I figure it's the perfect time to start your training. You're going to be my protégé, remember?"

"How could I forget?" I teased.

"Good." Cassidy grinned. "Pick me up outside Terrace Bluffs at eight thirty tomorrow morning. And bring a backpack full of school supplies."

SOMEHOW, EIGHT THIRTY on Wednesday morning felt horrendously early, as though my brain was convinced it should have the opportunity to sleep in on a day off. I yawned my way through a cup of coffee and joined the line of cars waiting to exit the Rosewood gates on their way to work.

When I pulled onto the shoulder outside Terrace Bluffs, Cassidy was sitting on the curb, fiddling with a pair of Ray-Bans. She wore jeans and a plaid button-down shirt, a navy blue backpack by her feet.

I'd been expecting another of Cassidy's antique clothing concoctions, and this seemed out of character somehow. But even dressed normally, Cassidy was still someone you'd look at twice without quite knowing why. It was as though she was disguised as an ordinary girl and found the deception tremendously funny.

"I saw a coyote this morning," she announced, climbing into the front seat. "It was in our backyard obsessing over the koi pond."

"Maybe it just wanted a friend."

"Or it was looking for a koi mistress," Cassidy observed wryly.

It was a reference to a poem, I guessed, but I couldn't place it. I shrugged.

"*Had we but world enough and time,*'" Cassidy quoted. "Andrew Marvell?"

"Right." It sounded vaguely familiar, like something Moreno had put on an identification quiz back in Honors Brit Lit, but I wasn't exactly a big poetry fan. "So where are we going?"

"Where we have no business being, other than the business of mischief and deception," she said. "Just drive over to the University Town Center."

So I did. And while I drove, Cassidy told me her theory about winning at debate tournaments. The most successful debaters ("I'd call them master debaters, but clearly you aren't mature enough to handle that, Mister Smirkyface," she teased) knew to reference literature and philosophy and history.

"And the more sophisticated your references are, the better," Cassidy said, toying with the air vent. "You don't want to quote Robert *Frost*, for God's sake. Quote John Rawls, or John Stuart Mill."

I hadn't heard of either of those last two guys, but I didn't say anything. Actually, I was trying to figure out if we were on a date, albeit one that had started at eight thirty in the morning.

"We could still go gleaning," I said, nodding out the window as we passed one of the remaining orange groves.

"I don't know why you think that's funny."

"Haven't you heard? It's my hillbilly way of taking you to a museum."

Cassidy shook her head, but I could see that she was smiling.

The University Town Center was an odd place to be at 8:45 in the morning. I hardly ever went there, since it was a fifteen-minute drive in the direction of Back Bay, this snotty WASP beach town. Actually, the Town Center straddled the border between Eastwood and Back Bay, said border consisting mostly of a Metrolink station, a medical complex with which I was intimately familiar, and a golf club where my father was a member.

"Ironic, isn't it?" I said, pulling into the lot, "how the Town Center is on the border of two towns but in the center of neither?"

Cassidy snorted appreciatively.

"Well, come on," she said, putting on her sunglasses. "We're going to be late for class."

"Ha ha," I said, but Cassidy didn't seem like she was joking. "What are we really doing here?"

The Town Center was the unofficial hangout for the University of California Eastwood, whose campus was just across the street.

"I already told you," Cassidy said impatiently, climbing out of the car and shouldering her backpack. "Mischief and deception. We're crashing some classes at the university, getting you good and educated in the liberal arts so you make a stunning debut at the San Diego tournament. Voilà, here's our class schedule."

I looked down at the purple Post-it she'd handed me.

"History of the British Empire?" I read aloud. "Seventeenth-Century Literature? Introduction to Philosophy?"

"Exactly," Cassidy said smugly. "Now hurry up. We're taking the road *beyond* the road less traveled, and being on time will make all the difference."

"WON'T THE TEACHER notice?" I asked, struggling to keep up with Cassidy's fast pace as we took the elevated pathway from the Town Center to the main campus. "We're not exactly enrolled here."

"First of all, it's *professor*, and no, they won't notice. I used to spend spring break staying with my brother when he was at Yale, and I'd randomly sneak into classes when I got bored. They never caught me. Besides, I picked survey courses, the ones with like a hundred students. We're just going to appreciate the lectures, take notes on whatever we can use in debate, and then go on our merry way."

Which is basically what happened—in History of the British Empire, at least. We joined a hundred other students in an echoing, tiered lecture hall and sat through a mildly interesting but mostly dull fifty minutes on imperialism, capitalism, and war economy. I dutifully scribbled down some notes, which was more than I could say for the bearded guy two rows down who spent the entire class playing Angry Wings on his phone.

"So?" Cassidy asked, once the class had let out and she'd dragged me into the line for the nearest coffee cart. "What did you think?"

"Interesting," I said, because I knew that was what she wanted me to say.

"'Though this be madness, yet there is method in't.'" Cassidy grinned and poured some sugar into her coffee. "*Hamlet*. And speaking of which, time for some seventeenth-century literature."

WHEN WE GOT to the lecture hall, something seemed wrong. It wasn't until I noticed the textbooks that I realized why.

"I think we're in the wrong room." I whispered. "Should we go?"

And then a professor in a funny, flat-bottomed tie strode to the front of the room and it was too late to do anything but sit there and listen.

Somehow, we'd wound up in Organic Chemistry. I'd done honors chem as a junior, which had been one of the least pleasant experiences of my high-school career, and I assumed that organic chemistry would be an equally painful continuation of the same.

The professor, this tiny Eastern European guy with a penchant for stroking his little blond chin beard, rolled up his sleeves. He drew two hydrocarbon chains on the board— that much at least I could recognize. One was shaped like an M, the other like a W.

"Who can tell me the difference?" he asked, surveying the lecture hall.

No one was brave enough to hazard a guess.

"There *is* no difference," the professor finally said. "The molecules are identical, if you consider them in three-D space."

He held up two plastic models and rotated one of them. They *were* identical.

"Now, if you please," he continued, drawing two new molecules on the board. "What is the difference here?"

It was mind-blowing, the way I could suddenly see exactly what he was asking, now that I knew to look past the scribbles on the board and to imagine the molecules as they actually were.

"Come on, doesn't anyone play Tetris?" the professor asked, earning a few laughs.

"They're opposites," someone called.

"They're opposites," the professor repeated, picking up two new models and rotating them, "in the same sense that your left hand is the opposite of your right hand. They are mirror images of each other, which we shall call *enantiomers*."

He went on, talking about how opposites could actually be the same thing, and how they occurred together in nature, not actually opposites at all, but simply destined to take part in different reactions. It was nothing like the grueling equations we'd been forced to crunch in honors chem, numbers with exponents so high that I sometimes felt bad for my calculator. There wasn't any math to it at all, just theories and explanations for why reactions proceeded the way they did, and why molecules bonded in three dimensions. I didn't understand all of it, but the stuff I did get was pretty interesting.

When the class ended, Cassidy turned toward me, a little furrow between her eyebrows.

"I'm really sorry I mixed up the classrooms," she said.

"What are you talking about? That was awesome."

I'd never before walked out of a classroom with my mind racing because of what I'd learned, and I wanted to savor the feeling as long as possible. It was as though my brain was suddenly capable of considering the world with far more complexity, as though there was so much more to see and do and learn. For the first time, I was thinking that college might not be like high school, that the classes might actually be *worth* something, and then Cassidy started laughing.

"What?" I asked, a bit annoyed that she'd interrupted my private Zen moment.

"No one likes organic chemistry. It's, like, the worst requirement there is for pre-med."

"Well, maybe I liked it because I'm *not* going to be pre-med."

"No, you're planning to be a field hand." Cassidy rolled her eyes.

"Obviously. I'll operate on a seasonal schedule. I'll call it Spring Gleaning."

Cassidy whacked me with her notebook.

After an unexciting philosophy lecture on something called consequentialism, we walked back to the Town Center. It was around noon, and the weather had turned scorching. The sky, which was a brilliant blue directly overhead, lightened to white gray as it stretched over the mountains.

I took off my button-down, which I'd worn over a T-shirt in case it was a date.

Cassidy glanced over as I stuffed the collared shirt into my backpack.

"What happened to your wrist?" she asked.

"Nothing, it's just a brace," I said, not wanting to get into it.

"So it's some kind of jock fashion statement?" Cassidy teased. She pushed her sunglasses up into her hair, suddenly becoming serious. "Is that why you always wear long sleeves?"

"No," I said, mocking her. "I always wear long sleeves because it's some kind of jock fashion statement."

She stuck out her tongue, which made her look like a little kid.

"Very mature," I said. "I thought we were pretending to be college students."

"Not anymore. Class is dismissed. Now it's lunchtime."

We got sandwiches at Lee's, one of those chains you

grow up thinking must be everywhere, but in reality exists only in California.

At Cassidy's insistence, we took our sandwiches across the street to this little slope of rocks and grass that ran alongside the man-made creek and had our picnic in the shade of an oak tree. On the trail above us, bicyclists whizzed by on their narrow path, and across the water, I could see another couple spreading out their picnic. Not that Cassidy and I were a couple.

I turned up the speakers on my phone and put on an old Crystal Castles album while Cassidy rooted through the grass, picking tiny white flowers and knotting them together into a crown.

"Here," she said, leaning in to place the circlet on my head.

Her face was inches from mine. I could see the freckles that dusted her nose and the gold flecks in the disquieting blue of her eyes.

When she pulled away to study what I looked like with the crown of flowers in my hair, I had the brief impression that she knew how much she confused me and was enjoying it.

"When can I take this off?" I asked.

"When you tell me where you're applying to college," she said mischievously.

I shrugged. That question was easy.

"Probably here, maybe some other state schools."

I could tell instantly that I'd said the wrong thing.

"So that's it?" Cassidy asked. "You're fine with spending your whole life in the same twenty square miles?"

Wordlessly, I took off the crown and examined it.

"Well, it isn't as though I'm going to be *recruited* anywhere."

"Oh." Cassidy's cheeks reddened, and she fiddled with her napkin for a moment. "Sorry. I hadn't realized."

"No, it's fine. One state school's as good as the next. I wasn't exactly aiming for the Ivy League."

"Why not?" Cassidy asked curiously. "Everyone from Barrows is."

It wasn't the sort of question I was used to encountering: why not Harvard or Yale? The answer was obvious: because no one expected me to attend schools like those. I'd never shown a serious interest in academics, and I'd played tennis hoping our team would make All State, not training for the Olympics. The vast majority of my classmates, myself included, had never even seen it snow.

"I don't really think I'd fit in," I finally said.

"No, of course not." Cassidy's tone dripped scorn. "You'd prefer to fit in with the brainless jocks who win high-school popularity contests and the vapid girls who worship them."

"In case you hadn't noticed, I don't exactly fit in with them, either."

Cassidy started laughing.

"Ezra," she said slowly, "*everyone* has noticed."

I leaned over and placed the crown of flowers onto her head, letting my hands linger in her hair just a moment more than was necessary.

And I suppose I should have tilted her face up toward mine and kissed her then, but I didn't. I couldn't tell if she was just trying to see if I would, or if she really wanted me to, and I didn't want to find out.

Instead, I told her about how it had been for me ever since the accident. I told her how I'd spent nearly two weeks in the hospital while the rest of my classmates finished junior year without me; how I'd missed prom and the student government elections and the Junior-Senior Luau; how the first surgery hadn't worked and my mom had cried when she found out I had to have another; how my tennis coach had come by the hospital and I'd heard him fighting with my dad out in the hallway, blaming me; how my so-called friends had sent a cheesy card they'd all signed, rather than visiting; how the doctors made such a big production of telling me that I'd never play sports again that I thought they were going to say I'd be in a wheelchair for the rest of my life; how the worst part was having to go back to school with kids I'd known since kindergarten, and the only thing that had changed was me, because I didn't know who I was anymore, or who I wanted to be.

When I finished, Cassidy didn't say anything for a long time. And then she closed the short distance between us and brushed her lips against my cheek.

They were cold from her diet soda, and it was over in an instant. But she didn't move away. Instead, she sat down with her jeans touching mine and leaned her head on my shoulder. I could feel the flutter of her eyelashes against my neck with every blink, and we sat there for a while, breathing quietly together, listening to the thrum of traffic on University Drive and the gurgle of the creek.

"There's this poem," Cassidy finally said, "by Mary Oliver. And I used to write a line from it in all of my school notebooks to remind myself that I didn't have to be embarrassed of the past and afraid of the future. And it helped. So I'm giving it to you. The line is, 'Tell me, what is it you plan to do/With your one wild and precious life?'"

We stared out at the creek, watching the couple across from us gather their things and head back to the path.

"Well," I said. "What are my options?"

"Let me consult the oracle," Cassidy mused, leaning forward to pull up a blade of grass. She examined it in her palm as though she was reading my fortune. "You can sound your barbaric yawp over the rooftops . . . or suffer the slings and arrows of outrageous fortune . . . or seize the day . . . or sail away from the safe harbor . . . or seek a newer world . . . or rage against the dying of the light, although that one doesn't start with *s*, so it sort of ruins the poetry of it all, don't you think?"

"And here I thought you were going to say doctor,

lawyer, or business executive." I laughed.

"Honestly, Ezra." Cassidy stood up, brushing the grass off her jeans. "You'll never escape the panopticon thinking like that."

13

THAT NIGHT, I took Cooper out to the end of our cul-de-sac and tossed a ball for him. It wasn't the same as taking him for our run down the hiking trails, but he seemed to enjoy it all the same. He even found a wild rabbit to chase, although I don't think the rabbit particularly appreciated the game, or being hunted as game.

When I brought Cooper back to the house, my mom was at the kitchen table with a mug of tea at her elbow, flipping through the *TV Guide* even though we have On Demand and streaming.

"Where'd you go?" she asked.

"End of the block," I said, pouring fresh water into Cooper's bowl. "Tossed around a ball."

"Off the leash?" She looked horrified. "Ezra, it's dark outside! He could've been hit by a car!"

"It's a cul-de-sac, so I highly doubt it."

"*Tone*, young man."

"Sorry." I took a pack of cookies out of the pantry and opened them. "Want one?"

"Not this late," she said. "Bring those to the table and tell me about school."

I suddenly regretted my foray into the pantry.

"School's fine," I said through a mouthful of cookie. "Although these are terrible. I thought they were chocolate chip."

"Carob chip. It's healthier. How are your classes?"

"Good. I need you to sign a permission form for debate. There's an overnight tournament in San Diego next weekend."

"An *overnight* field trip?" She shook her head. "Honey, I don't know. Don't you have physical therapy on Saturdays?"

"I can call Dr. Levine and reschedule," I said impatiently. "And it's not a field trip, it's a tournament. I joined the debate team."

Cooper whined for a cookie, and I shot him a look that said *Trust me, you don't want to try these.*

"Is that what your friends from student government are doing this year?" Mom asked cheerily. "The debate team?"

"Not exactly." I tried not to grin at the thought of Jimmy Fuller, our sports team liaison, or Tiffany Wells, our social events chair, hanging out with my new lunch crowd. "Toby Ellicott asked me to join. He's captain this year."

"Oh, Toby! I haven't seen that boy in ages." Mom closed the *TV Guide* and leaned across the table, dropping her voice to a whisper. "Tell me, did he turn out to be gay?"

I choked on the carob cookie.

"Mom!"

"What? I'm just curious, honey."

I stared at her, appalled. It was one of those questions you don't go around asking about people.

"Are you going to sign the permission form or should I ask Dad?" I pressed.

"Leave it on the counter for me in the morning. I can take you to Nordstrom after school."

I'd just gotten up from the table, and when she mentioned shopping, I froze.

"Well, you're going to need a suit for debate, aren't you?" Mom went on, warming to the idea. "And we can get you some new clothes as well. Your jeans are a bit baggy now, and I don't want you tripping over the hems."

She was smiling as though the men's department of Nordstrom was a perfect opportunity for us to spend some quality time together. And then I came up with an idea.

"Actually," I said, "I'll go with Toby. He'll know what I'll need for the tournament."

"That's a great idea." Mom beamed. "Just use your father's credit card. Gay boys have such wonderful taste in clothes!"

"YOU CAN'T JUST buy a suit *off the rack*." Cassidy gawked at me, horrified.

That same Vampire Weekend song from the Back to

School Pep Rally seeped through invisible speakers, permeating the men's department of Nordstrom. I sighed, overwhelmed by the endless stretch of clothing racks.

"Toby," Cassidy whined. "Tell him."

"Seeing how all of *my* suits came from the fine atelier of Messrs.' Salvation and Army, I wouldn't know." Toby grinned, enjoying my discomfort. "But he definitely needs a pink button-down."

"Like hell I do. You guys suck."

"Do we need some help over here?" A smiling saleslady who could have been one of our classmates' mothers asked.

"We do, actually," Cassidy said brightly. "Do y'all do complimentary tailoring on suit jackets?"

An hour later, I had a trunk full of shopping bags and a tailoring slip for a new suit, which I could pick up in a week.

"It could've been worse," Cassidy said, patting me on the shoulder as we climbed back into my car. "You could have spent two hours trying on different types of trouser pleating with your mom."

"You haven't met his mom." Toby laughed. "It would have been three hours. And a surprise haircut."

"When did you two join forces?" I grumbled.

"Not soon enough, apparently." Cassidy grinned. "Now who wants to study for Mr. Anthony's quiz?"

Toby's schedule was a flip of ours; he had English first and then history.

"How about you just give me the answers at break

tomorrow?" Toby suggested.

"How about I glue your bow tie around your neck?" Cassidy retorted.

"I'd like to see you try." Toby laughed and turned on the radio. "Now let's get the hell out of the Prism Center now that we've got what we came for."

"Are we studying somewhere, or am I dropping you back at the Fail Whale?" I asked.

"We're studying." Toby sighed.

We drove over to this giant sprawl of superstores near school called the Legacy. It was nice spreading out our stuff in the Barnes and Noble café, drinking coffee and studying with other people like it was some sort of social activity. I'd never done it before.

Well, I mean, I *had,* when Charlotte insisted we do our homework together in Starbucks back when we'd first started dating, but that was mostly her rubbing my pant leg under the table until we had to give up on studying and go back to her house, since her parents were never home. So I suppose I'd never studied *effectively* with other people. Sure, Cassidy teased me, pretending she'd messed with my drink when I came back from the bathroom (she hadn't; she just wanted to make me suspicious), but we actually got work done.

By the time we were reasonably prepared for the quiz, it was getting late.

"So Faulkner," Toby said. "I might be wrong, but I think

you want to buy me dinner because I was so much help picking out a tie."

"Fine," I said. It had always been like this, even when we were kids. My five-dollar-per-week elementary school allowance had financed the bulk of his Sour Patch Kids and Pokémon Cards addiction. "Let me tell my mom I won't be home for dinner."

I took out my phone, stepped into the magazine section, and quickly assured my mom that no, we weren't having fast food, and yes, I'd bought everything I needed.

The conversation wasn't ending anytime soon, so I sat down on the bench and flicked through a copy of *Rolling Stone* someone had left, wishing she'd just learn how to text.

"Yeah, I got, like, loafers or something . . . with rubber bottoms, I remembered that part . . . I don't know, sort of red brown."

I sighed, wishing she'd lose interest.

"*Mom*," I said forcefully. "Everyone's waiting, I have to go . . . Yeah, I'll be home before nine. Okay . . . okay, bye."

"Oh, shut up," I said when I got back to our table in the café.

"I didn't say anything." Toby grinned broadly.

"Your silence is judging me."

"That's probably true," Toby admitted.

We walked across the parking lot to In-N-Out Burger, which doesn't technically count as fast food, since you have to wait for it.

"Do you know about their secret menu?" Toby asked Cassidy. "Because you can order all sorts of things. Root beer floats, animal-style fries . . ."

"Obviously." Cassidy rolled her eyes. "I *have* lived in California before."

"No! Really?" Toby mocked.

"Well, do you know about the palm trees?" I asked.

Both of them stared at me. I grinned.

"There are two palm trees planted in an X outside of all the In-N-Outs," I said. "It's from some old movie the owner liked, because in the film a treasure was buried there."

"That's terrible," Cassidy said. "Pretending a fast-food place is a buried treasure."

"I don't know," I said. "I think it's cool. Most people don't know about it, but when you do, you look for the X every time you drive past an In-N-Out."

"Like IHOP," Toby said. "My cousins call it 'dohi,' since that's IHOP upside down. It gets in your head. You'll just see an upside-down dohi sign next time you pass one, trust me."

Immediately, I thought of the hydrocarbon chains in organic chemistry; the same thing upside down, and how knowing to look for it changes your whole perspective. I almost mentioned it, since Cassidy would know what I was talking about, but I didn't. Not because they'd think I was weird, or nerdy, but because the moment was so perfect that it just didn't need anything else.

◄◄--►►

"DUDE," TOBY WHISPERED as we took our order receipt. "Did you know that Justin Wong worked here?"

I shrugged. "Must pay well."

Justin was in my math class. He was a pretty forgettable guy, except for his car—this ridiculously souped-up Honda, the kind kids at school referred to as a rice rocket.

We were filling our drinks from the soda machine when I first heard it: a familiar peal of laughter. My shoulders stiffened.

"Oh, kill me." Toby leaned against the soda machine, staring at them.

Sure enough: Charlotte, Evan, and Jimmy were in the good corner booth, the big one by the windows, where we always used to sit when we came here.

"Do you think we should just get it to go?" Toby muttered.

"Go where?" I asked. "There can never be burgers in my car, because then my car will *smell like burgers*, and trust me, that's a risk I'm not willing to take."

"We could put them in the trunk," Toby suggested desperately.

"I'm not eating a burger that's been in anyone's trunk," Cassidy said.

"We could eat them in the parking lot," Toby said.

"Because that isn't obvious." I rolled my eyes. "They're sitting right by the window."

We clustered around the ketchup pump, eyeing the

table. They'd just gotten their food and clearly weren't planning to leave anytime soon.

One of the In-N-Out employees, some kid from a different school, dropped off three more burgers and fries at their table.

"Hey, Ezra?" Justin Wong called. "I had Angelo bring your food over to your table."

I stared at Justin, not comprehending. And then I realized: those burgers were *ours*.

"Awesome," I said hollowly. "Thanks."

"Shit stickers," Toby swore softly.

"Well, come on." I said it as though we were standing outside of the funeral service and might as well go in.

"Oh good, you mean I get to hang out with your old friends?" Cassidy grinned hugely.

"Be nice," I warned.

"You'd think I brushed my teeth and sharpened my tongue every morning, the way he goes on," Cassidy complained.

"More like brushed your teeth and dulled your wit," said Toby.

IT WAS EVAN who spotted us first. His surfer's baritone carried across the restaurant as he raised his soft drink in the air like some sort of toast and called, "Yo, Faulkner! Get your gimp ass over here!"

"Hey," I said sheepishly as we shuffled toward the table.

"What's going on?"

"Just chillin'," Evan said.

Jimmy nodded enthusiastically. He was eating a 4 x 4 Animal Style, a gooey, thick stack of meat patties oozing sauce. There was another identical burger on his tray, because apparently one wasn't enough. He took a bite, and it reminded me of this video I'd seen on YouTube of a mountain lion devouring a gazelle.

"So, funny story," I said, "but Justin sent our food over to your table."

"Who?" Charlotte asked blankly.

"Justin," I repeated. "The guy behind the counter? He's in our year at school."

I couldn't figure why she didn't know who I meant. And then I realized that Charlotte had always done this— pretended not to know which classmate you were taking about, as though she was above remembering certain people.

"Oh." Charlotte frowned, disinterested. "Well, whatever. You're here now, so join us."

"Yeah, dude, plenty of room. Pop a squat," Evan said.

We hadn't discussed it, but I knew the plan was to get our food and calculate the physics of which table was the farthest from this booth, that table being the optimal place to enjoy our dinner. But I couldn't exactly refuse. Not after the way I'd blown everyone off without explanation ever since school started.

"Sounds good," I said with a shrug, sliding into the booth.

I could feel Cassidy's hand on my sleeve, as though she wanted me to know that she'd slide in first so I could take the end, but I gritted my teeth and scooted along the pleather seat, not wanting my old friends to see how useless I was.

"Where's Jill?" I asked, unwrapping my food. I dumped half of the fries onto my tray and wordlessly passed Cassidy the little paper container, since we were sharing.

Charlotte watched me split the container of fries as though it meant something significant.

"She's stuck doing some Student Government crap, I don't even know. But it'll give us a chance to know your new friend." Charlotte's smile dripped venom as she stirred the straw in her milk shake.

We all bit into our burgers. Three tables away, a kid too big for his high chair screamed for dessert while his parents calmly ate their food, ignoring him.

"Faulkner, you didn't come to my party!" Jimmy accused.

"Yeah, sorry. How was it?"

"Connor MacLeary showed up wasted and tossed the keg into the pool." Jimmy shrugged philosophically. "And my bitch-ass neighbor called the cops. We had to pretend it was a church barbecue."

"That actually worked?" Toby asked, floored.

"No." Jimmy took another bite of his burger.

"So, *Cassie*," Charlotte said brightly, "Where did you

move here from, again? Chino? Compton?"

Cassidy smiled at the insult, as though she found Charlotte extremely funny.

"San Francisco," Cassidy said. "But I've lived all over the world, really. London, Zurich, even down in Louisiana for a couple of years."

"Oh," Charlotte's face fell as she considered this. "I've always wanted to visit Europe."

"Well, where does your class trip go?" Cassidy wanted to know.

We all looked at her blankly.

"You don't have those?" Cassidy asked, disbelieving. "Seniors don't go to Spain or somewhere to traipse through museums and churches for a week?"

I started laughing. "We go to Six Flags."

"Good thing it's not *Disneyland*," Charlotte said sweetly, with a glance in Toby's direction.

At this, Evan burst out laughing.

"Babe," he spluttered, trying to get it under control, "you're pure evil."

"Whatever, you love it," Charlotte retorted, touching her index finger to the tip of his nose. It was so adorable that I almost threw up all over my adorable pile of fries.

"So, has everyone studied for Mr. Anthony's quiz?" I asked, hurriedly changing the subject without thinking.

"What quiz?" Jimmy asked nervously.

"AP Euro," Cassidy said.

"Dude, none of us are in AP." Evan chuckled, cramming a fistful of fries into his mouth.

"It's senior year," said Jimmy. "I've only got five classes, counting tennis."

"Counting tennis, that takes balls," Toby muttered.

Cassidy snorted, and I tried not to.

Evan reached over and snagged a handful of fries off Charlotte's plate. She fake-pouted and slapped at his hand as he crammed them into his mouth, laughing.

"I'm hungry," Evan said by way of apology. "Rocked it hard at practice this afternoon."

"Hell yeah!" Jimmy affirmed. They bumped greasy fists over the napkin dispenser. Toby winced.

"So Ezra," Charlotte said, "how come you're not sitting with us at lunch anymore?"

All eyes were on me. I shrugged and took a pull of my drink, stalling. The family with the screaming kid left their trays and trash at the table as they got up.

"It's, well . . ." I trailed off, unsure of how to answer.

Did she honestly want me to say it out loud? That it felt wrong for me to go back, like they only wanted me around out of some sense of residual pity? That they'd been lousy friends when I was in the hospital? That she'd cheated on me the night of the accident, and that, just a little bit, I blamed her for what had happened? That, if it came to it, I'd rather eat lunch on a cot in the nurse's office than bear daily witness to Charlotte sitting on Evan's lap?

Thankfully, Toby came to my rescue.

"Faulkner's on the debate team now."

They all burst out laughing, as though Toby had claimed I'd joined forces with the kids who brought their laptops and headsets to school to play *World of Warcraft* during lunch.

"Dude, for real?" Evan asked.

"Sure," I said. "Why not?"

"Can we talk?" Charlotte batted her eyelashes, her smile curving dangerously.

Unasked, Cassidy and Toby got up so I could extract myself from the booth. In thick, awkward silence, I followed Charlotte over to the condiment bar.

We hadn't talked. Not since Jonas Beidecker's pre-prom party, when she'd run after me insisting I better not back out of prom. And there was so much to say, and to avoid saying, that I didn't know where to begin. But Charlotte clearly did.

"What is *up* with you?" she demanded. "You're hanging out with *Toby Ellicott* and joining the debate team?"

Charlotte was still in her song squad skirt, ribbons tied around her ponytail, a little blue paw print painted on her cheek. But her expression was far from cheerful.

"Well?" she asked, waiting for an explanation.

But the thing was, by my reckoning, I didn't owe her one. Not for something as trivial as whom I chose to eat lunch with.

"So you and Evan," I countered. "Awesome. You'll have my vote for Homecoming Court."

"Oh, please," Charlotte protested, a little too vehemently. "That's *not* why we're together."

"Of course not." I held back a smile, noting how my comment had infuriated her.

"This is ridiculous," Charlotte said. "You should come back to our lunch table. It's not your place to sit with those losers. Bring your snotty prep-school girlfriend, even. I don't care."

"They're *not* losers. And Cassidy and I are just friends."

"Yeah." Charlotte laughed. "Because *so many* girls see you and think, 'Now *that's* a guy I'd like to be *just friends* with.'"

"What are you talking about?"

I was fairly certain that most girls saw me and thought, *That's the kid who almost died at Jonas's party. Used to be a star athlete, but he's, like, crippled now. Isn't it so sad?*

I raised an eyebrow, waiting for Charlotte to voice the truth of what everyone wasn't saying. Instead, she sighed and swished her skirt as though I exasperated her. It was a move I recognized from the halcyon days of junior year, when we'd just started dating.

"Ohmigod, Ezra! Get a clue. You're all brooding and depressed now, and don't *even* ask me why, but dark, deep, and twisty *totally* works for you. You could have anyone you want, so ditch the social outcasts and stop sulking over your sprained knee."

My sprained knee—right. I didn't even know what to

say to that, so I did what I always did around Charlotte—around all of my old friends, really. I shrugged and said nothing.

"Listen," she said, stepping closer and pouting cutely. "I'm having a party next Friday. You're coming, right?"

Now I was *sure* she was flirting. But the thing was, I wanted no part of it.

"Actually, I'm not. I'm busy."

"Doing what?"

"Debate tournament," I said, enjoying myself. "All weekend, unfortunately. Out of town."

"You're not serious."

I leaned in, closing the distance between us and knowing that I would get away with whatever I said next.

"I'm as serious as a car crash."

I gave her my most winning smile before heading back to the table.

AS WE WALKED back to my car, I turned around only once. The sun was setting, and the lights strung between the palm trees in the parking lot had just come on. But even in the purpling night, with the glow of hundreds of tiny lights reflected against the In-N-Out window, I could see them sitting there in the large corner booth, the one they'd taken for just the three of them. Their food was finished, but they hoarded the best table in the place as though it was theirs as long as they wanted it.

Not so long ago, I would have been there with them, inhaling a Double-Double after tennis practice, dipping my fries into my milk shake just to make Charlotte squeal in disgust. I would have laughed at Evan and Jimmy's antics, because we all knew they were only doing it to see how long until I made them stop.

"We're going to get kicked out," I'd warn, shaking my head. "They'll take a mug shot of us in those stupid paper hats and hang it on the wall to shame us."

And eventually, when Justin Wong came over to pointedly clear our trays, I would have shot him an apologetic look when the others weren't watching, knowing that we'd been wrong but had gotten away with it anyway.

"Well," Cassidy said, climbing into the front seat, "that was exquisitely unpleasant."

"Welcome to the OC, bitch?" Toby offered.

"Let's just go." I put on some music, not wanting to talk about it. Arcade Fire was on the local college station, crooning about growing up in the suburbs. I concentrated on the lyrics until I turned back onto Princeton Boulevard.

"Tumbleweed," Toby noted. "Fifty points if you hit it."

"In Soviet Russia," I said, doing a terrible accent, "tumbleweeds hit you."

"There *are* no tumbleweeds in Soviet Russia," Cassidy put in. "But speaking of the KGB, what was up with your ex-girlfriend?"

I laughed hollowly.

"She informed me that I'm upsetting the status quo. And also that she's having a party next Friday."

"So are we," Toby said. "And I can guarantee you, ours is going to be far better, and far more exclusive."

"It will," Cassidy assured me. "You've yet to experience the undiluted awesome that is a hotel-room party."

"My single regret in life," I replied.

"I don't know," Toby mused, "that mullet you had in sixth grade was pretty bad."

Cassidy laughed.

"He's lying," I said. "It's physically impossible for my hair to mullet."

"Since when is *mullet* a verb?" Toby grinned.

"Since you started lying about my having one," I said, turning into the school lot. It was just starting to fill up with cars for that night's football game.

"I'll drive Cassidy home," Toby said, digging for his keys.

"I'm *fine*," Cassidy protested. "I don't know why you're all so afraid of coyotes."

"I'm not," Toby said. "I'm afraid Faulkner's gonna offer to put your bike in his trunk again, and we all know he'll kill himself lifting it."

"You're an asshole," I informed him.

"At least I didn't have a mullet in the sixth grade!"

14

CASSIDY AND I never told anyone where we'd gone during Teacher Development Day. We hadn't sworn to keep it a secret or anything, but it felt strangely private, tangled in the things I'd confessed and in the brief moment when she'd pressed her lips against my cheek. Somehow, though, Toby could sense that something had passed between us, and he was less than thrilled about it.

"That's why I drove her home," he explained in the lunch line on Friday. "It's . . . she's not what you think. She's unpredictable."

"Then stop trying to *predict* that she'll wreck me," I replied, paying the lunch lady for my sandwich. "What's this about, anyway? How well do you even know each other?"

"Biblically, Faulkner. We know each other biblically."

"Yeah, I'm sure."

"Well, our teams hung out sometimes. We invited each other when we had room parties," Toby said. "And there are these little flirtations that happen—debate-cest or whatever you want to call it. She'd act like she couldn't get enough of someone for about a day, and then she'd lose interest completely. She leaves a trail of broken hearts, and she either doesn't realize or doesn't care."

I took my change from the lunch lady.

"That's the problem? Remind me never to tell you what goes on at tennis camp," I said, grabbing some napkins.

"I'd make a dropping-the-soap joke, but I sense that the lunch ladies won't appreciate it." Toby picked up a Styrofoam container of "General Chicken" and gave it a dubious sniff before handing over some crumpled dollar bills. "There's something different about Cassidy this year, and I don't know what's changed, but I have a bad feeling about it. Now what do you think? Is this chicken in general, or some specific type of chicken they've neglected to identify?"

"It looks disgusting."

"Obviously. But does its disgustingness remind you of anything?" Toby pressed hopefully. "General Tso's chicken, perhaps?"

I glanced at it again.

"It's generally disgusting chicken," I informed him.

"Hmmm," Toby regarded it sadly. "I think you're right."

I SPENT THE weekend digging myself out from beneath a pile of work. Moreno wanted a "practice essay" on *Gatsby*, which apparently differed from a real essay, most likely in a way that didn't exist. Coach Anthony wanted fifty key terms by Tuesday, handwritten, to prevent us from using copy-paste. And I had a take-home quiz in Calculus. The only bright point was Sunday night, when Cassidy finally flashed Morse code at me from her bedroom window.

HI, she said, flashing it twice. HI HI.

I still remembered Morse code from my Cub Scout days, and I reached for the switch on my desk lamp and flashed HI back at her, wondering and half hoping that she'd ask me to slip out and meet her in the park.

But her window stayed dark after I replied, even though she knew I was there, watching. So I went to sleep thinking of her, of the curve of her back in a light cotton dress, of her hair twisted up into its crown of braids, of her, leaping from the zenith of the plastic swing set and clearing the sandbox, turning a neat lap around the whole of Eastwood, California, while I stood there, trapped in the dreariness of it all, numbly watching.

TOBY CALLED TWO practice sessions for the debate team after school that week. We matched up for mock debates on Tuesday, and I got paired with Phoebe. Cassidy played judge, sitting cross-legged on Ms. Weng's desk and toying with the fringed ends of her scarf.

Toby had just taught me how to flow, or take notes, the day before, and I was still using one of those photocopied grids with the arrows drawn in. It made me feel remedial.

The only good thing was that Phoebe, whom I'd suspected would crush me, wound up being surprisingly terrible at debate, and had only competed at one tournament so far. After our closing statements, we handed Cassidy our notes and went over to examine the trophy case in the back of the classroom.

The most impressive ones were a few years old at least; the legacy of students long graduated. What had once been a championship team had become a nerdy hangout destination, with its participants seeking fun rather than glory. I couldn't imagine such a thing ever happening to our school's tennis team—or any sports team, really. *You'll have fun if you're winning,* my dad used to say, as though it was possible to control such things.

"Any of these recent?" I asked Phoebe, nodding toward the case.

"A couple. The hilariously little one is Toby's. And the plaque is Sam and Luke's, they're actually decent team debaters when Sam doesn't get carried away with his Republican agenda." She laughed slightly. "You're surprisingly good at public speaking, you know."

"Yeah, well, you may have a decent delivery, but your flow's a mess," Cassidy said, climbing down from Ms. Weng's desk and passing back our notes. Mine looked like her pen had hemorrhaged all over it, while Phoebe's only had a few marks.

"And you're the opposite," Cassidy continued, frowning

at Phoebe. "The outline's solid, but your delivery is unconvincing. Come on, let's see how you two do with a different topic."

We practiced until four thirty, when Austin had SAT prep and I had to get out of there for PT, only I said it was the dentist. I know physical therapy's nothing to be embarrassed about, but it still sounded bad: "therapy," as though I needed professional help to function.

At least it was just PT, not one of those trauma counseling sessions the hospital had insisted upon after the accident. Those I couldn't stand, but thankfully I was down to like once a month with Dr. Cohen, the world's biggest douchenoodle of a clinical psychologist. Seriously, his teeth were so white that they probably glowed in the dark.

So I sheepishly drove over to the medical center, where I spent an hour on the stationary bike and treadmill, listening to the sample debates Toby had given me on audio file and trying not to wonder about Cassidy. She acted as though she'd never gotten upset over my signing her up for the debate team, and I couldn't understand if she'd just overreacted, or was hiding her anger.

Maybe it was like Toby had said, and she was just unpredictable. But I doubted it. Because, every night around eleven, from the other side of Meadowbridge Park, Cassidy's bedroom window would darken, and her flashlight would blink the same greeting at me in Morse code. Always HI. HI HI. Nothing more. A beginning of an unfinished conversation that I didn't have the guts to take control of.

I went to sleep every night that week waiting for whatever it was between the two of us to start traveling at the speed of flashlights, but it never did. As always, she left me wanting more, and dreaming of what it would be like if I ever got it.

15

THE TOURNAMENT WAS being held at SDAPA, the San Diego Academy for the Performing Arts. It was one of those Mission-style campuses, all white adobe arches with mosaic tiles. I half expected to be able to hear the crash of the surf from the parking lot.

We were running late, on account of the traffic, and barely had time to change. Cassidy, Phoebe, and I had to grab our garment bags and change in the bathrooms while the rest of the team, who had worn their suits to school, rushed to make check-in.

All around us, the campus had become a frantic hub of students in business suits and private-school uniforms. We passed two guys wheeling file boxes stacked three high and bungee-corded together, and a girl who was reciting a monologue at a brick wall. The whole place had a desperate, last-minute air of preparation that reminded me of the morning I'd sat the SATs.

I changed into my suit, which, I had to admit, *did* fit a lot better than the ones I'd rented for formal dances. The girls took longer, and I spent a few minutes standing awkwardly outside the bathroom like some sort of bodyguard, waiting for them.

"Awww," Phoebe said when they finally emerged, "someone looks adorable in his suit."

"Lies. I look like a senator," I complained, tugging at my collar.

"A liberal senator," Cassidy assured me. "The kind who has a sex scandal with a high-class prostitute."

And that was when I saw what Cassidy had done to herself: the gold and red ribbing on her sweater-vest, the matching stripes on her tie, the gray uniform skirt, and the navy blazer draped over her arm . . .

"Is that a *Gryffindor* tie?" I asked.

"And an official Harry Potter Merchandise sweater-vest," she confirmed smugly.

"Ms. Weng'll make you change," Phoebe said.

"She can't." Cassidy grinned. "I'm not out of dress code. Technically. Now come along Cedric, Cho."

We headed toward the indoor cafeteria where all of the teams were making camp, and I realized that I was nervous. Deeply, horribly nervous. Not about doing well at the tournament, because I knew I was pretty hopeless in that regard. I was nervous that I'd fail to see what was so wonderful about putting on a suit and talking about government. Nervous that I didn't really belong with this group of friends after all. That I was destined to forever be someone whose defining characteristic was lost forever at seventeen, rather than found.

The cafeteria was crowded, and Cassidy reached over and grabbed my hand as we walked in. I glanced over at her; she seemed so different from the girl who had placed a crown of flowers in my hair by the creek and told me to make a wish on a paper star. For the first time, Cassidy seemed on edge.

Toby spotted us, waving us over to our team's table, where Ms. Weng quickly filled us in on the schedule: We'd have two preliminary rounds that evening, then two more prelims the next morning, to be followed by two final rounds and an award ceremony.

"Cassidy, what are you wearing?" Ms. Weng asked.

"My Oxford tie?" Cassidy frowned, a perfect picture of confusion. "It's from my summer study."

I don't know how we all managed to keep from laughing as she got away with it, but we did. And then a flurry of commotion went up on the other side of the cafeteria: The first round had been posted. The room erupted into utter chaos as three hundred teenagers surged forward to get a look.

Cassidy insisted I stay behind, so I stood around awkwardly with Ms. Weng for a moment, until Cassidy returned wielding a purple Post-it with my room number scribbled down.

I stared at the Post-it, my nerves doubling.

"You'll be fine," Toby said, clapping me on the back. "We suck, remember? Go lose one for the team."

I laughed, feeling slightly better. I could do this. It was just a speech, something I'd done all the time at SGA meetings and pep rallies. A speech in a room where hardly anyone was listening. A speech that hadn't even been written yet, so I wouldn't even have to worry about forgetting my lines.

I glanced over at Cassidy, to see how she was holding up, since she'd been acting weird all day. She was so pale that she looked as if she might faint, and her expression seemed haunted.

"You okay?" I asked.

"I'm fine," Cassidy said, attempting a smile. "Now don't worry about me, little protégé. Go on, fly away."

"Well, good luck," I said.

"Break a leg!" Cassidy called teasingly after me as I headed toward the A building.

I took a route that avoided the main stairs and wound up massively turned around. I arrived at the East corridor by mistake, and was pretty disgusted with myself as I doubled back along a third-floor hallway. And then I saw Cassidy.

Her back was turned, and she was standing next to a

decrepit water fountain, talking to this old lady coach I didn't recognize. The coach had her hand on Cassidy's shoulder, and her expression was so grave that I didn't dare to interrupt.

"—but it's wonderful to see you back here, competing again," the coach said.

"Thanks," Cassidy muttered.

I hesitated, sensing this wasn't something I was supposed to see, and then Cassidy turned around.

"Hey," she said, embarrassed. "What are you doing here?"

"Attempting to locate the west corridor?" I admitted.

"It's this way," Cassidy said. "I'll show you."

She hustled me around the corner, and sure enough, the little letters next to the room numbers changed from "East" to "North."

"What was that about?" I asked.

"I have no idea." Cassidy shrugged. "Actually, I'm glad you showed up. This coach I've never seen before randomly pulled me aside. She kept calling me Elizabeth and acting like my mom had cancer."

"Weird," I said.

"There must be some school that actually has Gryffindor uniforms." Cassidy grinned, pulling at her sweater-vest. "Well, 'West' should be just around the corner. I have to head back."

"See you later, Elizabeth!" I called after her.

"Hate you," she yelled back.

WHEN I GOT back to the table after my round, Toby, Austin, and Phoebe were already there. Phoebe had unearthed a box of Fruit Gushers, and she offered me a pack.

"Thanks," I said, tearing it open. "Haven't had these since I was a kid."

"That's the point," Phoebe said, grinning. "They taste like childhood."

"So how'd it go?" Toby asked.

"Fine," I said. "I guess. It's weird; I can't tell if I won or lost."

"That happens sometimes." Austin looked up from his game console. "Although I *definitely* lost. I matched with one of those assholes from Rancho—they wear National Forensics League pins in their lapels—anyway, it was a disaster."

"Sucks," I offered.

Austin shrugged and ate a handful of Fruit Gushers.

"It's okay," he said, waving his game console. "I got like three street passes from walking there, plus a new unlock code, so Rancho can suck it."

Phoebe rolled her eyes.

"Austin believes that winning or losing in binary is meaningless when there's a high score to beat."

"True that," Austin said, saluting her with his stylus.

"So Austin," Toby asked, "do you beat your own high score every day?"

It sounded so dirty that we all cracked up.

"Are you asking if I'm a master debater, Ellicott?" Austin returned.

By that point we were all nearly in hysterics. That was how Cassidy found us—cracking up so hard that it was actually taking an effort not to choke on our food.

Luke and Sam drifted back from their round ten minutes later, since team debates always take slightly longer. By the time they reached the table, we were clustered around Austin's iPad watching ridiculous YouTube videos and taking turns showing our favorites.

The second round posted, and once again, Cassidy darted off to retrieve my room number. I guessed that she was trying to be helpful, but it was a little much. I didn't have the heart to tell her, though. So I dutifully accepted my Post-it and trotted off to debate one of the Rancho guys, this scrawny freshman with a Blackberry clipped to his belt, as though he was already running a company. *The enemy,* I thought, realizing that I was starting to develop a sense of team loyalty.

We wound up debating the merits of free market economics, which definitely wasn't my strong suit, and I argued pro again. I thought I'd managed to present the argument okay, but the moment that freshman adjusted his belt, straightened his tie, and shot me a look like he expected me to suck it, I knew I was done for. He filleted me.

It was so frustrating, knowing that, if we were on a

tennis court, I could've killed him with my backhand, slicing it to land short and watching him run like hell. But this was debate, and my superpowers were nonexistent. I almost wished he'd debated Cassidy in her ridiculous Harry Potter costume, so she could've wiped the smirk off his muggle face.

16

"BEFORE I GIVE you kids the room keys, here are the rules," Ms. Weng said, hell-bent on humiliating us in the bustling hotel lobby. "Rooms are single sex. If I find out otherwise, you're off the team. You can eat dinner in the hotel restaurant or the shopping center across the street. If you go to the shopping center, you're back here by eight. No leaving the hotel at night, and no smoking, I don't care if you're old enough to buy cigarettes. We'll meet back here at seven forty-five tomorrow morning to check out. Any room charges are your responsibility. Everyone got it?"

We muttered that we did, and she made us all take her phone number before she handed Toby the envelopes with our keys.

"I'm in Room Two thirty-nine," she called as we all headed toward the elevator. "If there's an emergency."

Cassidy laughed, clapping a hand over her mouth.

"Sorry," she said, "but one of those jerks from Rancho

invited me to get shit faced in their room tonight. They said to come by Room Two thirty-seven."

The hilarity of what was going to happen hit us all full force.

"Poor Ms. Weng," Toby said sadly. "However will she read her salacious romance novel in the bathtub in peace with those hooligans playing Beer Pong in the next room?"

"Dude," I said, wincing. "Mental picture."

"Naw, seriously, that's what she does," Austin told me. "It's why she agreed to coach debate. Weng lives with her parents, man. She'd advise the wrestling team if it came with a free hotel room once a month."

"She always asks at the front desk if the room has a tub," Toby said. "The first one of us to laugh loses fifty points."

"What are the points for?" I finally asked.

I thought it was a valid question, but apparently not, since everyone stared at me, horrified.

"Oh, Ezra," Cassidy said sadly, "now you've gone and lost all of yours."

"Is it possible to have negative points?" I asked as the elevator doors opened, depositing us on the fourth floor.

"I'm not permitted to explain the rules of the game," Toby said. "Nor to acknowledge whether or not we're playing one. Come on, team. Move out!"

We had two rooms next to each other. The guys trooped into one, and the girls headed into the other.

"Um," I said, surveying the two double beds and trying

not to point out the obvious, that there were five of us.

And then Luke opened a door that I'd initially taken for a closet, but which actually opened into the girls' room.

"Hi," Phoebe said as she and Cassidy trooped through and joined us.

That was when I realized: No one intended to keep single-sex sleeping arrangements.

"Everyone ready to get dinner?" Toby asked.

"We're not going to change?" I looked down at my suit.

"Nope," Phoebe said, grinning. "Rite of passage. Team dinner in our team uniforms. And it's your problem if you spill."

"She says that," Luke confided, "but really, she'll iron everyone's shirts in the morning if we ask nicely."

"I will not!" Phoebe picked up a pillow and threw it at him.

The shopping center across from the Hyatt wasn't bad, although I felt self-conscious about the seven of us in our suits. Well, six of us in suits, and one in a Hogwarts uniform. We wound up at the Cheesecake Factory, which I thought was an odd choice, when there was a Denny's and a Burger King. It wasn't something we talked about, but I knew Toby never had much cash.

"Who wants appetizers?" Toby asked cheerfully, cracking open the giant menu. He caught my expression and started laughing. "Dinner's on Faulkner."

"That's not funny," I said. "Even tennis doesn't pull that

on the new guys."

"Relax." Toby flashed a credit card. "It's coming out of our team budget. Which, technically, *you* approved last April. Rather generously, I might add."

"Oh, right," I said sheepishly. I *had* approved the next year's Team Activities budgets. "Appetizers for everyone, then. You can thank me later."

"Actually, the new guy buys the booze," Luke told me.

Phoebe shook her head. "He's kidding."

We ordered a couple of appetizer platters, and everyone filled me in on the rivalry with Rancho.

"Basically, they hate us," Austin said. "They think we don't take debate seriously."

"We *don't* take debate seriously," Sam drawled.

"Yeah, but we *used* to," Austin said. "We were like, sister teams, or whatever it's called, during freshman year. Before your time."

Sam and Phoebe were both juniors, but I kept forgetting.

"Debate sucked back then," Luke said. "Coach Kaplan would surprise us and search the hotel rooms."

"It sucked," Toby agreed. "Poor Kenneth Yang."

"What happened to Kenneth Yang?" Cassidy asked, taking a sip of her drink.

Everyone sighed, and I got the impression that this was a story they'd all heard a million times. But Toby was determined to tell it again. He grinned.

"So Coach Kaplan comes by at two in the morning

to make sure we're all in bed and not still awake, because Kenneth Yang made this huge show of bringing a *Monopoly* board with him. So Coach is all, 'Open up! I can hear you little shits playing Monopoly in there,' and no one opens the door, because there's liquor *everywhere*. So he wakes up everyone sleeping in the *adjoining room* and bursts through, and there's Kenneth Yang with three neckties around his head, doing sake bombs while ironing his pants."

We all crack up.

"And Coach Kaplan is all, 'What the fuck, Yang?' Because Kenneth Yang was team captain back then, and one of the best policy debaters around. And Kenneth Yang looks at Coach with the three neckties still around his head, in his goddamn underpants, and says, 'It's not what you think. I got a chance card in Monopoly, Coach.'"

Even Phoebe was choking on her soda at this point.

"What happened?" I asked.

"A week's suspension," Toby said. "And he got banned from overnight competition for the rest of the year. Carly Tate took over as captain. And she'd hooked up with the Rancho captain the year before, so that was awkward."

"And that, Dragon Army," Austin said, "is why Rancho is the enemy."

"And also why the enemy's gate is down," Luke added, earning a few eye rolls for reasons I didn't understand.

We ordered an entire chocolate cheesecake for dessert. It arrived at the table along with half of the Cheesecake

Factory staff, who were clapping and singing some permutation of "Happy Birthday."

The cheesecake went down in front of Cassidy, a single candle poked into the blob of whipped cream in the center. She turned red when she realized what was happening, but took the joke well, blowing out the candle and claiming that she was going to keep it as a souvenir of our immaturity.

IT TURNED OUT everyone's suspiciously oversized duffel bags were full of party supplies. Specifically, gin and whiskey and wine—the fancy stuff my parents drank, not the cheap beer that went into Solo cups at high-school parties. There were speakers too, sleek expensive ones that plugged into Austin's iPod, and tonic water with lime, and little wedges of gourmet cheese, and a baguette, which I found particularly hilarious as Phoebe pulled it out of her mini-suitcase. I didn't know any sixteen-year-olds who bought baguettes as party supplies.

Before I knew it, I was standing in the midst of a party. A bunch of people from some school called Wentworth showed up with a bottle of prosecco, which Cassidy whispered to me was poor man's champagne. They went to a tiny K–12 school in Los Angeles and gave the impression of being older and jaded, even though some of them were just sophomores.

Sam played bartender, rolling up his sleeves and filling plastic champagne flutes and glass cups from the bathroom. He seemed to know what he was doing, rattling off the names of cocktails and bemoaning the fact that we didn't have a bottle of St. Germain, and that Luke had bought the wrong kind of vermouth. The Wentworth team—there were six of them—drifted onto the balcony, smoking and drinking near-champagne.

Austin set up the speakers and docked his iPod. "Requests?" he called.

"Make us feel young and tragic," Cassidy said, sitting cross-legged on one of the beds. She was sipping something that looked like Sprite but probably wasn't.

The opening bars of some Beyonce disaster drifted through Austin's speakers, and everyone groaned.

"I'm joking!" he assured us, switching it to Bon Iver.

Toby passed me a whiskey on the rocks, and I tasted it cautiously. I wasn't much of a drinker, but there was good music playing, and a baguette on the ironing board, and Cassidy sitting cross-legged on the duvet in a schoolgirl outfit, so I tossed it back, because I was sick of being cautious.

Sam refilled it instantly and I downed the second glass as an afterthought, not realizing what I had done until my head began to spin from the combination of pain medicine and liquor, a combination the little prescription labels had warned against. I sat down next to Cassidy, who was talking with a cute blonde girl from Wentworth.

"But you're here." The girl frowned, and I got the impression that they were talking about Cassidy's old school.

"Haven't you heard?" Cassidy smiled tightly. "I go to Eastwood now."

The girl laughed, skeptical.

"I'm serious," Cassidy insisted. "We have pep rallies and everything. It's adorable."

"Yeah, adorable." The girl glanced at me for a second, her lips twisting into a knowing smile.

"Have you met my baby brother Cassius?" Cassidy asked, slinging her arm around my shoulder like we were actually related. "Hard to believe he's only fourteen."

For a second the girl believed her.

"I thought—" the girl began, frowning.

"I was kidding," Cassidy interrupted coldly. "God."

"I'm Ezra," I said, offering a handshake since it seemed to go with the suit.

"Blair," the girl said with a toss of her hair. She glanced up at me through her eyelashes, and I realized that she was the kind of girl who enjoyed competing for a boy's attention. "God, you're charming. Come on, charming, let's dance."

I couldn't dance. Not before, and certainly not then, with two tumblers of whiskey warming my veins and a decided lack of balance.

"Honestly, I can't," I protested as she pulled me up.

And then the lights went off, plunging us into darkness.

"Hey, I'm uncorkin' a bottle of wine here," Sam complained, his accent even thicker after a few drinks, like a parody of itself.

"Shh!" someone said.

The door to the adjoining room opened, and Toby stood there holding a candle.

"All rise for the team captains," someone said.

Austin cut the music, and everyone stood.

The candlelight flickered as Toby and the other team captain, this preppy-looking guy in his grandfather's old Rolex who'd introduced himself as Peter, made their way to the two chairs in the corner. Peter was carrying a gavel (of course he had a gavel), which he banged against the padded armrest, I suppose for the ceremony of it.

"A toast," he cried, raising his drink. "To the virgins, to make much of time!"

Everyone laughed and drank, whether or not the term applied to us personally, although I rather thought it applied to the vast majority, considering we were in a room filled with high-school debaters. I could feel Cassidy standing at my side, and when I glanced at her, a bit unsteady on my feet from the liquor, I sensed an unsteadiness inside of her, a different kind.

Luke turned the lights back on, leaving them dimmed, and Sam shut the door to the balcony. And thus began the meeting.

It was the most bizarre meeting I'd ever been to, like some sort of sarcastic secret society. Toby and Peter took turns choosing different members of their teams to debate each other on ridiculous subjects, like whether the president of the United States should be chosen by lottery ticket, or if the Pope could defeat a bear in a fistfight. We all voted on who had won each debate, and the loser had to take a shot of gin.

Essentially, the whole thing was one elaborate drinking game.

To my surprise, I won my debate, on whether Truth or Dare was an effective alternative to a criminal trial. But my victory was short-lived, since they made me drink anyway, because I was new.

Cassidy's debate was after mine, and when she flounced to the front of the room to face off against Blair, everyone got quiet. For a moment, I thought Cassidy was going to refuse, or be terrible on purpose, but she didn't do either of those things.

Instead, she stood there calmly sipping her drink while Blair argued that vampires shouldn't have voting rights and then she straightened her tie, grinning.

"My admirable opponent argues that vampires do not deserve suffrage, as many great yet misinformed politicians have done before her while calling for the continued marginalization of women, or other minorities," Cassidy began. "Yet vampires were, at some point, human. At what point can a man's voting rights be revoked, if he is proven to be of rational mind? And who here would agree to such an egregious breach of liberty? No, the real threat to our electoral system is the werewolf! Can the werewolf cast a vote in wolf form, or only when he appears to be a man? And can we ensure that he is not merely casting the vote of his pack's alpha wolf, rather than his own?"

It was both hilarious and intelligent. And it was completely Cassidy. I wouldn't want to follow that, and apparently neither did Blair, because, when it was time for her rebuttal, she shook her head and drank from the gin bottle, conceding defeat.

Cassidy took a shot as well. She wobbled over to the bed and sat back down next to me, putting her head on my shoulder.

"Werewolf suffrage?" I asked.

"I'm tired," Cassidy mumbled. "I don't even remember what I was talking about."

Toby and Peter shook hands, calling the debate to an end, and Austin turned the music back up.

Someone pulled the blankets off one of the beds and turned the balcony into a fort. Couples ducked in and out for snatches of privacy, and I wondered if Cassidy would suggest we go inside, but she didn't.

Austin broke the baguette in half and dueled Toby, sloppy drunk and laughing, until Phoebe crawled out of the blanket fort and yelled at them.

"Do you have any idea," she fumed, "how difficult it is to keep a baguette from going stale in a suitcase *overnight*?"

This set everyone into hysterics.

I was decently buzzed by that point, the room spinning

gently as I sat on one of the beds with Cassidy curled against my shoulder like a cat. We were playing Fruit Assassin on Austin's iPad, trying to sabotage each other with renegade swipes. The music was still on, quieter stuff now.

"Hey," Cassidy said, putting down the iPad. "Hi."

"Hi back," I said. Yep, definitely drunk.

"I think Blair likes you," Cassidy said, biting her lip to keep from giggling. "I've talked with her approximately twice ever, so I am an expert in this and trust me, she is probably even in love with you."

"Well, of course she is," I teased. "I'm irresistibly charming."

"Oh, you are?" Cassidy grinned. Her face was inches from mine. Her braid had come undone, and her hair tumbled over her shoulders, smelling of mint shampoo.

And then Toby bellowed, "Fine! You guys can all be *beautiful snowflakes*! I'm gonna go over here and be an *awkward snowflake*!"

Cassidy glanced at me and started to laugh while Toby spluttered indignantly at Sam and Austin, not truly angry. And I felt the almostness of our moment drift away, over the railing of the hotel balcony, and into the shopping center where we'd all pretended to celebrate Cassidy's birthday dinner. And maybe it was just as well, after all, since I wanted our first kiss to be more than some drunken thing at a debate tournament.

The party ended around two, everyone making a

halfhearted attempt to clean up the evidence before the Wentworth team went back to their own hotel rooms to catch a couple hours' sleep. Cassidy brewed coffee for everyone in the little coffeemaker, and we drank it out of plastic champagne flutes.

"Okay, time to figure this out," Toby said, swaggering out of the bathroom in a hotel robe, his hair wet and his contacts swapped for glasses. "Who's bunking with whom?"

Phoebe appeared in the doorway to the other room wearing a towel and flip-flops long enough to announce that she and Luke were sharing a bed in there.

Sam and Austin looked at each other and shrugged.

"I don't mind if you don't snore," Sam said.

"Yeah, same." Austin shuffled past Toby and disappeared into the bathroom.

"Either of you want a bed to yourself?" Toby asked Cassidy and me.

Cassidy glanced at me, but I knew better than to say anything.

"We'll just share this one," she said, patting the duvet. "Captain's privileges, Ellicott. You get your own bed."

And that was how I wound up sharing a bed with Cassidy Thorpe.

Before I knew what was happening, Cassidy had changed into a tank top and pajama shorts and crawled under the covers. I came out of the bathroom in my boxers and T-shirt, feeling horribly self-conscious. Austin and Sam were already asleep, scooted toward opposite edges of their bed, both of them snoring.

Cassidy put a finger to her lips and nodded at Austin, whose mouth was wide open.

I grinned.

"Hey," I whispered, "I didn't bring pajamas. Do you mind if, er, is it okay?"

I was trying to be a gentleman about climbing into bed with her in my boxers since I'd stupidly underpacked, but Cassidy shook her head and peeled back the covers.

"Just get in," she said.

I sat down, plugging in my phone on the nightstand, an action that felt incredibly grown up when there was a girl on the other side of the bed. And then I felt Cassidy's hand on my leg.

"Does it still hurt?" she asked, sliding her fingers over my knee.

"No," I lied quietly.

Cassidy's fingers traced over my scars, and I could tell she didn't believe me.

"You don't have to worry," I said. "About kicking me in your sleep or anything."

"But I wouldn't want to." She propped herself on one elbow, staring at me. "You'll have to hold me tight, to make sure I don't."

And with that, she rolled over and turned off the light.

I crawled under the covers, waiting for my eyes to adjust

and having the strange idea that Cassidy could see me just fine in complete blackness. The blinds were drawn, and the room was thick with an expectant sort of darkness filled with sleeping bodies and girls wearing tiny blue pajama shorts.

If I stretched, our arms would touch. The possibility of it, of our skin meeting under the covers, thrilled me. I wondered if she was thinking about it too. And then she sighed.

"What?" I whispered.

"Shhh," Cassidy whispered back, scooting toward me until her head was on my shoulder. "Don't ruin it."

Even though it was late and I was tired, I must have lain there for an hour, frustrated and hard and unable to do anything about it as Cassidy slept with her cheek against my shoulder.

17

I WOKE UP the next morning to the chorus of everyone's coordinated cell phone alarms, feeling like death. My arms were wrapped around Cassidy, and somehow my head was on her shoulder, though I was certain it had been the other way around when we'd fallen asleep.

"Hey," I said gently. "Wake up."

"Mmmmm," Cassidy murmured sleepily. Her hair spilled off the pillow in a fierce tangle, and it was so incredibly intimate, waking up with her there, in my arms, that I could hardly stand it.

From the next bed, Sam groaned.

"Dude, I thought you were gonna stay on your side!" he complained.

"That's so sweet," I called. "Who was the big spoon?"

"Shut up, Faulkner," Austin grumbled.

Cassidy snuggled against my arm, curling into a ball.

"Five more minutes," she whispered.

"Come on," I said, nudging her, "you have to get up and iron my shirt."

That got her.

Cassidy's eyes flew open, and her mouth twisted into a smirk.

"Good morning to you too," she said.

I DON'T KNOW how we managed to get dressed, gather our stuff, and get down to the lobby on time, but we did. I thought Ms. Weng was going to suspect us for sure, the state we were in, but she hardly noticed. There were circles under her eyes and she kept yawning. The jerks from Rancho had probably kept her up half the night with their Beer Pong.

"Can we stop somewhere for coffee?" Toby asked, and Ms. Weng actually agreed, so by the time we arrived at SDAPA, we were all handling the morning a lot better.

Ms. Weng drifted off toward the coaches' lounge, and we headed toward our table in the cafeteria to drop our stuff and wait for the next round to post. The girls left to apply makeup in the bathroom and Toby wandered off toward a quiet corner of the cafeteria, motioning for me to follow.

"*So*," he said pointedly, grinning as though he was accusing me of "nailing it," "are you two together now?"

Reflexively, I glanced toward our table, even though the girls still hadn't returned.

"I don't know," I said truthfully. "Maybe."

"You're certainly acting like it."

He was right; we were acting like it. I'd spent the whole night with a girl cuddled against my shoulder like we'd just had sex—a girl I was in love with, and whom I'd never even kissed. And I had no idea what to do about it.

"Would it bother you if we were?" I asked.

"Well, I'm not going to fly into a jealous rage or anything, if that's what you're worried about." Toby smirked, but saw that I was serious. "Honestly? I've sort of known it was going to happen. She's into you."

"You're sure?" I asked.

"No, I want you to make a fool of yourself and actually be rejected for the first time in your life. I'm like the proverbial ostrich that kicks sand in your face, my friend."

"Actually, they bury their beaks in the sand," I said.

"Just testing."

The third round posted then, before I could say anything, and everyone crushed toward the far wall to get a look. Toby and I pushed our way to the front, finding our last names and school name printed on the tournament roster. We memorized our room numbers, muttering them under our breaths.

We were walking back to the table when Cassidy grabbed my arm. Her expression was serious, and I noticed that she wasn't wearing the Gryffindor tie anymore, just a plain school uniform.

"Hey," she said.

"Third round is posted." I nodded toward the wall. "I'll

wait for you so we can walk together."

"Ezra," Cassidy said. "We have to talk. Now."

And I knew that whatever it was she needed to say, it wasn't going to be good. I followed her out of the cafeteria and into the courtyard. She stopped by this mosaic wall featuring a perfect day at the beach; it was sort of cruel, if you thought about it, putting something like that up in a school. Cassidy looked nervous, which didn't bode well. And she still wasn't saying anything. I was suddenly overcome with a heavy sense of dread.

"You can tell me," I said. "Whatever it is."

Cassidy tucked her hair behind her ears. She was wearing it down, in loose waves, and it made her look younger, somehow, and more vulnerable.

"You can't go to your third round," she said. "You have to go to mine. I switched us."

Whatever I'd been expecting her to say, this wasn't it. This wasn't even close. I frowned, not really understanding.

"You've been competing as me," she explained. "The judges don't see our names, just, like, a string of numbers, so I sent you to my rounds yesterday, not yours."

"Wait," I said, as the full impact of what Cassidy was saying sunk in. "All this time, we've been *cheating*?"

"No!" Cassidy said fiercely. "I just . . . I'm done competing, Ezra. I left this, and you brought me back. So I figured you'd be my way out of having to really do this. Like I wasn't really here after all, if you were me."

"Yeah," I said slowly, "but if I'm competing as you, then you're competing as me. Which is cheating."

Cassidy shook her head.

"I threw the first match," she promised. "Neither of us is going to make the finals."

"It's still wrong," I said. "Even if neither of us wins. So, what, I'm supposed to keep competing as you all day?"

"Basically," Cassidy said, her chin jutting stubbornly. And then, as if in slow motion, I watched her bravado crumple. Her shoulders sagged, and her eyes welled with tears.

"I'm sorry," she whispered. "I didn't mean for you to find out like this. I don't want to be here, to be a part of this. I thought you'd understand."

"Maybe I'd understand better if you told me what this is actually about." But even as I said it, I knew she wouldn't tell me. Not there, with last night's alcohol seeping through our pores, by that ridiculous beach mosaic, as hundreds of teenagers floated past in their blazers and button-downs.

"Ezra," she said, "please."

I sighed, looking at her. Cassidy's eyes were liquid, her face pale.

"I'm sorry," she whispered. "But neither of us can take back what we did. You signed me up. I switched us. Go along with this and we're even."

"I don't care about being even," I said. "Something's going on with you."

"Nothing's going on," Cassidy snapped. "You remember the first week of school, how everyone stared at you and you walked around like you wanted to disappear? That's what being here feels like for me. That's what I'm acting like. I thought you'd get it. I thought we were alike."

"We are," I said, wondering how she'd done that, made me go from being upset to comforting her. "You're right, and I'm sorry. Just . . . give me a minute to think."

I didn't use CliffsNotes, or copy my friends' assignments, or buy term papers off the internet. I was hopelessly moral about those sorts of things. Cassidy had been wrong to switch us, but it was randomized which debaters matched against each other in the preliminary rounds. If neither of us made it to the finals, it didn't really matter. We weren't taking anyone's spot, or using an unfair advantage to get ahead. We were simply switched. So I supposed, if it came to it, it *was* a moral sort of cheating. And if she'd forced me to cheat, I was the reason she felt like she had to.

"We have to see it through," I said. "If we switch back and match against someone we've already debated, it would be a disaster."

"I knew you'd do this for me, Ezra. I knew you'd understand." Cassidy pulled me into a hug, burying her face in my chest, and I believed then that she'd eventually decide to tell me what all of this was about, and that, whatever it was, I was probably imagining something far worse.

◄◄→►

I DIDN'T SAY anything to Toby about the cheating. Cassidy and I went off to each other's rounds that morning and acted like nothing at all was the matter, like the biggest thing between us was that we'd shared a bed.

Final rounds were posted that afternoon; none of us had made it. Everyone looked at Cassidy in shock, asking who had beaten the unbeatable Cassidy Thorpe, but she just grinned and refused to say anything, as though the joke was so good that she couldn't bear to share it.

Except she had shared it—with me. It was my joke too, and I didn't find it at all funny.

Cassidy had said we were alike, and I almost believed it. She'd made me feel like I was rescuing her, but the more I thought about it, the more I wondered why she hadn't simply won the tournament, a final demonstration of why she was this unbeatable champion. And then I wondered if it really mattered. Because every time I closed my eyes, I pictured her nestled against me in that hotel bed, her legs soft and warm against mine, and out of all the things I wanted but knew I couldn't have, part of me hoped that Cassidy would be the one exception.

18

THAT NIGHT I sat at my desk going over Moreno's corrections on my *Gatsby* practice essay. The lampposts in Meadowbridge Park had been on for hours, illuminating the honeysuckle bushes. I thought about Cassidy's flashlight, about how I stood at my window waiting for her room to go dark, and how F. Scott Fitzgerald would have loved that.

Cooper whined for attention. He'd draped himself across my feet and was chewing on a rawhide bone, holding it vertically between his paws like he was smoking a pipe. I leaned down to pet him, and he sighed.

"You're right," I said. "I know. I'm hopeless."

I reached for the switch on my desk lamp and flashed HELLO.

The lights switched off in Cassidy's bedroom, and her flashlight flicked on.

SORRY.

"She's sorry," I told Cooper, because he didn't understand Morse code.

He lifted his head as if to say *But you already knew that, old sport.*

Her flashlight flickered again.

FORGIVE ME.

This time, I didn't hesitate.

ALWAYS, I replied.

MY MOM WOKE me up way too early the next morning.

"Ezraaaaa," she trilled, poking her head into my room. "You have company."

"Ughhh, what time is it?" I managed.

"Nine o'clock," she said. "Really, honey, you've been so tired lately. Do I need to call Dr. Cohen?"

Blearily, I realized that I needed to stop using "I'm tired," as an excuse to spend time alone in my room.

"I was up late finishing an essay."

"Well, there's a very nice girl downstairs who wants you to go have breakfast with all of your friends from the debate team."

I sat up.

"*Cassidy's* here?"

"I had her wait in the kitchen with your father. She's very pretty, honey. And her parents are both doctors."

I had this horrifying realization that my nightmares were true: While I was sleeping, my parents had been downstairs grilling the girl I liked on what her parents did for a living.

When I dashed into the kitchen five minutes later, still buttoning my shirt, I found Cassidy sitting cross-legged on the tile, scratching Cooper behind the ears.

"Hi!" she said brightly. "You forgot about team breakfast, didn't you?"

"Oops," I said sheepishly, mostly for my parents' benefit, since I was fairly certain there *was* no team breakfast.

"Can we bring Cooper?" Cassidy asked.

Cooper lifted his head, halfway interested.

"To a restaurant?" Mom asked, dismayed.

"Of course not, Mrs. Faulkner," Cassidy said. "Everyone's coming over to my house for pancakes. Our housekeeper won't mind. It's just across the park."

"Well, I suppose," my mom said doubtfully.

The moment we were out the front door, Cassidy holding Cooper's leash, I raised an eyebrow. "What's *really* going on?" I asked.

"You mean you didn't believe me?" Cassidy made her eyes go wide and innocent. "Honestly, Ezra, I'm hurt."

I followed her toward the pedestrian gate that led out into the park. Cooper bounded ahead, prancing importantly. He had part of his leash dangling from his mouth, and he looked very pleased with himself.

"There's sunscreen in my purse, by the way. If you want to borrow some," Cassidy said, holding open the gate.

"Why would I want to borrow sunscreen?"

"We're going on a treasure hunt. Didn't I mention?"

"No, you told me we were eating pancakes with the debate team. At *your* house," I said.

"Clearly that was code for 'We're going on a treasure hunt.' Which is why we need Cooper here. So he can be our truffle sniffer."

She turned right on the path, which led toward Eastwood's hiking trails.

"All right," I conceded. "Give me the sunscreen."

She dug it out of her purse, and I slathered it on while she played with Cooper. He gave me a look as if to say *So this is the girl, old sport.*

"You're in charge of the GPS," Cassidy told me, handing me her phone. "Don't close the app or we'll have to start over."

Cassidy led me into the trails, explaining as we went that we were searching for a *geocache*, or tiny capsule. They were hidden all over the United States, and you had to solve puzzles to find them.

"Sometimes they have nothing inside, and sometimes they're filled with little treasures," she said. "But if you take something, you're supposed to leave something in its place."

"The law of conservation of geocaches," I said.

"Why yes, Mr. Illiterate Jock, exactly like that." Cassidy smiled at me, her hair fiercely red in the sunlight. There was a little smear of sunscreen below her ear.

"Wait," I said, reaching to wipe it away. "You had

sunscreen on your cheek."

"Did you get it?" Cassidy asked.

"No, I smeared it bigger."

"Whatever," she said. "At least I don't have sunscreen in my *hair*."

"It's not sunscreen. You're turning my hair white."

I navigated us through the hiking trails, telling Cassidy stories about the invisible world Toby and I had concocted there when we were kids. We found the geocache behind a loose brick on this wall down by the back of the Catholic Church. It was filled with junk—cheap fast-food toys, mostly. But it didn't matter what was inside, just that the hiking trails really *were* filled with buried treasure.

And I understood then that Cassidy was making it up to me. That this adventure was her apology for what had happened at the debate tournament, because simply saying sorry was too normal for a girl like Cassidy Thorpe.

"Don't you want to sign the log?" I asked, motioning toward Cassidy's phone, which had finished playing this little congratulatory fanfare and was displaying a list of names.

"Why?" Cassidy asked.

"So the next people who find this know we were here?" it sounded lame even as I said it. But Cassidy's eyes lit up.

"Hmm," she said, grabbing the phone and typing quickly.

"My turn," I said, taking it back. But then I frowned at what she'd written. "Who's Owen?"

"My brother," Cassidy said sheepishly. "We used to do this, to mess with the universe."

"So you signed each other up for weird newsletters and stuff?" I asked.

"Everyone does that. *We'd* switch library cards, put each other's names on blog comments, screw with the grand cosmic record of who did what."

"Why?" I asked, confused.

"The world tends toward chaos, you know," Cassidy said. "I'm just helping it along. You could too. Just write down a made-up name, or even a fictional character. And to the next person who finds this geocache, it's as though things really happened that way. You have to at least allow for the possibility of it."

"Fictional people?" I teased. "Only you would think of that."

But I know now that isn't true; history is filled with fictional people. And even the epigraph Fitzgerald placed at the beginning of *The Great Gatsby* is by a writer who doesn't exist. We have all been fooled into believing in people who are entirely imaginary—made-up prisoners in a hypothetical panopticon. But the point isn't whether or not you believe in imaginary people; it's whether or not you want to.

"I think I'll stick with reality," I said, handing Cassidy back her phone.

She stared at it, and then me, disappointed. "I'd think you of all people would want to escape."

"Imaginary prisoners are still prisoners," I said, which was apparently the right thing, because Cassidy slipped her hand into mine and told me more about Foucault as we walked back toward the park.

THAT NIGHT, WHEN Cassidy clicked on her flashlight to say hello, I did the unthinkable: I replied by text message.

Actually, I was stunned that it worked. But after a relatively short back and forth, she'd given me her address and agreed to wait outside while I drove over. When I pulled up, Cassidy was leaning against a streetlamp, bathed in its soft orange glow. She carried the green sweater she always wore, one sleeve trailing.

"Hi," she said. "Where are we going?"

"You forgot about team dinner," I joked, throwing the car into reverse.

Cassidy laughed, buckling her seat belt. Her hair was wet, and its wetness had left an abstract pattern across the shoulders of her blue blouse. I told her that I wanted to show her something, and that it was a surprise. I reached for her hand, and we drove like that, in the reassuring quiet of Sunday night in Eastwood, all the way to the freeway, listening to the Buzzcocks.

The moment I merged onto the 5 North, the quiet was replaced with the emptiness of the freeway at night, and we rolled down the windows, shedding music like ballast. After a couple of miles, I began to hear it in the distance—the dull thud of what we'd come to see.

"What's that noise?" Cassidy asked suspiciously.

"Just wait." I grinned, enjoying the suspense.

And then a firework burst over the Harbor Boulevard overpass. It hung there, shimmering in the night sky before blinking into a cloud of smoke.

"A firework!" Cassidy turned toward me, delighted.

Three more fireworks shot up over the freeway, contorting into purple stars as they burst against the dissipating smoke. The sky was stained the color of charcoal, and the fireworks kept coming, louder now, and enormous.

"Disneyland fireworks," I said, exiting the freeway. "I thought we could park and watch."

There was a diner right off the freeway, open more out of optimism than demand. I pulled into the empty lot and Cassidy reached up to open the sunroof. Her smile was luminous, even brighter than the fireworks, as she shimmied out the sunroof, her legs dangling. One of the laces on her Converse had come untied, and it swished gently against the hand brake.

"Climb up!" she insisted, and I did, because she was waiting for me beneath the fireworks shaped like planets and stars.

We sat there, side by side, holding hands in that childhood way with our fingers zipped together, our faces turned toward the sky. The fireworks sparkled overhead, pounding like drums.

"Hey," Cassidy said, nudging me with her shoulder.

"Hi."

"This is nice."

"Very nice," I agreed. "The nicest parking lot I've ever seen."

Cassidy shook her head at my terrible attempt at humor. Three fireworks burst in tandem: purple-green-gold.

"There's a word for it," she told me, "in French, for when you have a lingering impression of something having passed by. *Sillage*. I always think of it when a firework explodes and lights up the smoke from the ones before it."

"That's a terrible word," I teased. "It's like an excuse for holding onto the past."

"Well, I think it's beautiful. A word for remembering small moments destined to be lost."

And I thought she was beautiful, except the words caught in my throat, like words used to, back when I sat at a different lunch table.

We turned our attention to the fireworks display, although I was having trouble concentrating, because my fingers were laced with her smaller ones, and the leg of my jeans was pressed against the pale cotton of her skirt, and the breeze carried just a hint of her shampoo.

"Wouldn't it be incredible," I said, "if you could send secret messages with fireworks? Like Morse code."

"Why?" Cassidy asked, her face inches from mine. "What would you say?"

I closed the distance between us, pressing my lips against hers. We kissed like we weren't in a parking lot in a not-so-nice part of Anaheim, sitting on the roof of my car on a school night. We kissed like there was a bed waiting for us to share at a debate tournament, and it didn't matter if I'd remembered to pack pajamas. And then we kissed again, for good measure.

She tasted like buried treasure and swing sets and coffee. She tasted the way fireworks felt, like something you could get close to but never really have just for yourself.

"Wait," Cassidy whispered, pulling away.

Sillage, I thought. *The lingering impression of a kiss having ended.*

She dropped through the sunroof, crawling into the backseat with a mischievous smile and motioning for me to follow. I learned three things that night: 1) sharing a bed isn't nearly as intimate as making out in a too-small backseat, 2) inexplicably, some bras unhook in the front, and 3) Cassidy hadn't known I was Jewish.

19

I DROVE CASSIDY to school every day that week, pulling up outside her house with two travel mugs of coffee and waiting for her to slip out the front door, swinging her leather satchel as she hurried down the front walk.

Her house was enormous, one of those Spanish-tiled villas with a four-car garage, the kind you're almost certain is two houses attached, because of the oversized symmetry. I remembered when they'd built this subdivision, two years after mine, and how I'd woken up every morning in the fifth grade to the sound of the workmen, not even bothering to set an alarm after a while. I remembered the eerily quiet Monday morning when the hammering finally stopped, and how my mom had yelled at me for oversleeping.

How could I have known, back then, that the white house across the park would belong to Cassidy Thorpe? That out of a row of nearly identical McMansions, there'd be one window in particular I searched out every night before bed, looking for secret messages?

It took about five minutes for everyone at school to figure out we were together. I suppose we were lousy at keeping it a secret, or maybe we weren't even trying. I'd dated Charlotte for such a long time that I'd forgotten how these things went, how everyone would stare as we climbed out of my car in the Senior Lot in our sunglasses, carrying identical mugs of coffee.

Word had definitely gotten around by break; it felt as though the entire quad was watching as we sat down at our table with the rest of the debate team.

"Honestly," Phoebe said, giving me a stern look, "I wore *sweatpants* today. You could have *warned* me this was going to happen."

I assumed Phoebe meant the, uh, camera phones aimed in our table's general direction. It was unsettling, being newsworthy at this particular lunch table, being entirely certain that you were the reason everyone was staring, and being unsure whether it was envy or disapproval.

The stream of attention slowed to a trickle over the course of the week as everyone realized that Cassidy and I weren't going to climb onto each other's laps and mash faces at the table. That's not to say we were totally innocent of any public displays of affection; there was some hand-holding and the occasional hurried good-bye kiss on even days, when we had different sixth periods.

During break on Wednesday, I went into the main office

and asked Mrs. Beams, the school secretary, for an elevator key.

"Ezra," she said, leveling me with a stern glare over the top of her rhinestone reading glasses, "you were supposed to pick this up on the *first day of school*."

"I forgot?" I tried sheepishly, although a more accurate answer would have been that I'd made it my top priority to avoid doing so.

"It's almost October, young man," she chastised.

"You're right, I know."

She handed over the key, and I put it into the pocket of my jeans, trying to look extra pathetic on my way out of the office, in case she had second thoughts. I didn't use the key until that afternoon, when the bell rang for fifth period. Cassidy started to walk toward Mrs. Martin's classroom our usual way, via the staircase by the faculty lot, but I stopped her.

"Actually," I said, "let's go around the other side."

Cassidy raised an eyebrow, but went along with it. I took out the key and twisted it into the call slot for the handicapped elevator, trying not to look too pleased with myself.

"Ladies first," I said grandly.

"What's going on?" Cassidy asked suspiciously, stepping inside the dented metal elevator.

I shrugged and waited for the doors to close before sliding my arm around her waist.

"Ever wanted to make out in an elevator?" I asked, grinning.

WHILE THE REST of the school quickly became obsessed with watching Cassidy and me, our lunch table was obsessing over news of a silent rave in Los Angeles that Friday. Toby volunteered to drive, and Phoebe promised she'd try to get out of babysitting, and by the time I got up enough nerve to ask what exactly a silent rave was, everyone stared at me like I was crazy.

"It's a type of flash mob," Cassidy explained. "Hundreds of strangers gather in a public place, put in their headphones at exactly the same moment, and start dancing."

I tried and failed to picture it, but I had to admit that it sounded more interesting than a three-hour historical musical about depressed German teenagers, which had been the last thing they'd all gone to LA for.

"So there's one tomorrow?" I asked.

"Yep. And we're going to be in the middle of it," Toby informed me.

Luke and Sam already had plans to go paintballing with some guys from their church, and Phoebe couldn't get out of babysitting after all, so it wound up being Toby, Austin, Cassidy, and me who piled into the Fail Whale after school on Friday.

Toby made us stop at a gas station for snacks so it felt like a real road trip, even though the drive was two hours at most. Cassidy got a pack of licorice, and Austin dumped an energy shot into a cherry slushie, which we all made fun of.

"It's *good*," Austin protested. "Honestly, haven't you ever had a Red Bull slushie?"

"I don't see the point in caffeine without coffee. Or coffee without caffeine, for that matter," I informed him.

"Whatever." Austin put up his hood as he took his change from the cashier. "One day the world will recognize Red Bull as a legitimate food group, and who will be laughing then?"

"Everyone," Cassidy said dryly. "They'll be too jacked on caffeine shots to do anything else."

We piled back into the Fail Whale, which featured—get this—a tape deck. Toby had a bunch of mix tapes he'd picked up at swap meets and thrift stores, so we listened to "Happy Bday Heather!!!" as we merged onto 5 North. It was like playing Russian roulette with terrible eighties music in five out of six chambers.

"Ugh." Cassidy made a face. "Switch it. Ace of Base overload."

Toby ejected the tape, and Austin, who was riding shotgun, put in a different one and hit rewind.

"There's nineties nostalgia," Austin observed while we waited for the tape to rewind, "and then there's antiquated technology. Unfortunately, this is the latter."

Toby didn't take well to anyone insulting his car. As he put it, the Fail Whale was "a magnificent relic of the enduring crisis of solidly middle-class suburbia."

"Austin, you drive a *Jetta*."

"It was my sister's!" Austin protested. I could see his face turn red in the rearview mirror.

I didn't say anything, since I'd, uh, earned a Beemer by turning sixteen. Cassidy offered me one of her Red Vines, and I accepted it absently, biting off each end before I realized what I was doing.

"Toby," I called. "Remember making straws out of licorice at Cub Scouts?"

"I thought I was the only one who did that," Austin said.

"Well, did any of you squish those little paper cups they have next to water dispensers into pots?" Cassidy asked.

I had no idea what she was talking about, but Toby did.

"Yeah. You had to blow into them and smash the bottoms at the same time to get it to work."

And then we spent the rest of the ride reminiscing over old Nickelodeon programs, and Furbys and I-Zone cameras and Tamagotchis, and how weird it was that everyone did video calling and watched television on their computers.

"Dude," Austin said as we exited the freeway, "in fifty years, all of the old folks' homes are going to be filled with seniors listening to Justin Bieber on the oldies station and talking about how movies used to be in two-D."

"All of our longings are universal longings," Cassidy said. "I'm paraphrasing, but it's Fitzgerald."

"I don't think he was talking about *Neopets*." Toby's

voice dripped scorn as he edged into the center of the intersection, waiting to turn.

"Well, he was talking about the human condition," Cassidy retorted. "And if, for our generation, that happens to be a collective longing for a world before smart phones, then so be it. There's no sense in speculating on the enduring impact of the recently past; if popular culture was that predictive, everything would be obsolete the moment it came into existence."

For a moment, no one said anything. And then Austin laughed. "Jesus, what are they *teaching* kids in prep schools these days?"

"Conformity," Cassidy answered, as though Austin had been serious.

THERE WAS THIS hectic undercurrent to the shopping center. Everyone was staring at everyone else, wondering who was there to participate in the flash mob, and who was on an innocent shopping expedition.

We were slightly early, so we went into the Barnes and Noble. Toby and Austin headed for the graphic novels, and Cassidy and I wound up on our own in the art section, where we looked at a book on Banksy, this subversive graffiti artist I hadn't heard of.

"What I love about him," Cassidy said, her eyes bright and excited, "is how he printed up all of this fake money and threw it into a crowd. People thought it was real and tried to spend it in shops, and they were so angry when they found out it was fake. But now, those bills sell for a fortune on eBay. It's simultaneously real and not real, you know? Worthless as currency, but not as art . . . my brother asked for one of those bills for Christmas a few years ago, and my mom assumed he wanted it framed, and he said he'd just stick it in his wallet because it was one of the few works of art you could carry in your pocket."

Cassidy trailed off, closing the book.

"We should find Toby and Austin," she said.

"They can wait," I insisted, tilting Cassidy's face up toward mine and stealing a kiss.

"Oh, really?" Cassidy murmured, her lips against mine.

When we came up for air, Toby was standing there, making a face. Cassidy and I shuffled toward the escalator, mildly humiliated at having been caught.

"Hey," I said, reaching into my back pocket. "I brought you something."

I handed Cassidy the iPod I'd borrowed off my dad, and she stared down at it, completely baffled.

"It's a loan," I explained. "I put on some songs."

Cassidy's lips curved into a smile.

"You made me a flash-mob playlist?" she asked.

"Sort of. You just hit play. I synched it to mine, so we can dance to the same songs."

I'd had the inspiration around midnight the night before, and had stayed up until two deciding on the perfect tracks to use. I'd pictured it quite romantically, the two of us in the middle of a crowd of strangers, dancing to the same music. But Cassidy's smile disappeared, and I had the impression that I'd disappointed her somehow.

"What?" I asked.

"Ezra," she said. "It's a *flash mob*. The point is that everyone dances to their own music, and it's so beautifully random that it works. Hundreds of strangers, all choosing a different song to encapsulate their own experience. It's a dance floor where every genre of music is playing at once, and no one's supposed to know what anyone else is listening to."

"Sorry," I muttered, embarrassed.

She handed the iPod back to me with a reassuring smile.

"Don't worry about it," she said. "You didn't know."

"You could put it on shuffle," I suggested. "That way it wouldn't be the same music as mine."

"That's okay," Cassidy said, her smile widening until it was genuine. "I'd rather dance to my own songs and watch you try and guess what they are."

Toby and Austin had walked down the escalator, and were waiting at the door of the bookstore. Austin had bought a book and was zipping the plastic bag into his omnipresent backpack.

"Come on," Toby said impatiently. "Two minutes!"

We all crowded into the central courtyard, where tons of high-school and college students were milling around, trying to look nonchalant. Everyone had their phones out, waiting for it to hit five o'clock exactly. A group of hipster-looking guys nodded at us, informing Toby that his bow tie was "quality."

"See?" Toby said, grinning. "Bow ties are cool."

We staked out a place near the fountain that Toby judged would be right in the middle of everything. The Grove was packed, which was unsurprising for five o'clock on a Friday. Families with strollers and tourists with fancy cameras wandered along the pedestrian paths, going about their business of shopping and sightseeing. For another agonizing minute, we waited in the palpable collective anticipation of hundreds of strangers trying to pretend they weren't up to anything out of the ordinary, until Toby whispered, "Now."

On an invisible cue, everyone put on their headphones and hit play. Teenagers began pouring out of shop fronts, running toward the central courtyard, joining the dance party.

It was fantastic, strangers smiling at one another, break dancing or rocking out or swaying to some mysterious beat that only they could hear. I turned up the volume on my headphones, dancing awkwardly to the Clash.

Cassidy was wearing a pair of expensive DJ headphones, gold-plated and glinting in the sunlight. She pressed them tightly around her ears, closing her eyes and dancing like no one was watching. The hem of her turquoise dress rose dangerously high, and the old pocket-watch necklace she wore bounced up and down over her chest, and she was so beautiful that I could hardly stand it.

Toby was dancing ironically, doing "the sprinkler" and "the shopping cart," having the time of his life as he cracked himself up. And Austin was performing some complicated hand contortions to what I guessed was techno.

All around us, strangers paired up and danced together, laughing. I was overwhelmed by the number of people recording video of the event, unable to be present in the moment. There was an older guy in a banana costume doing pelvic thrusts, desperate for attention. I wondered what he did for a living, if it was some respectable bank job or something totally demeaning.

But the flash mob wasn't about the banana-suit guy, or the people standing awkwardly with video cameras, or the gawking crowds that had come out of the stores to see what was happening. It was about being able to dance like Cassidy did, as though no one was watching, as though the moment was infinite enough without needing to document its existence. And so I closed my eyes and tried.

When I opened them, Cassidy was standing there, her headphones around her neck. She motioned for me to do the same, and when I did, the quiet of what was happening shocked me. I'd been so sure that my private soundtrack was a part of everything that I hadn't realized what we looked like, hundreds of strangers dancing in absolute silence.

We'd danced for maybe half an hour, until it became

more of a spectacle than a flash mob. No one wanted to head back quite yet, so we drove over to Santa Monica and had dinner at some old-fashioned burger place. We walked around the promenade afterward, making up hilarious and tragic life stories for the guy who'd worn the banana costume. Los Angeles seemed to change into a different city at night, a more vibrant and mysterious one. I was quiet, because we'd done a lot of walking, and I wasn't sure how much more I could handle. It was getting pretty bad when Cassidy squeezed my hand and said, "Hey, let's go sit on a bench and people-watch."

"Sounds good," I said, relieved.

Toby and Austin ducked into a bookstore to track down some graphic novel the other store hadn't carried, and Cassidy and I sat down to wait for them. I thought I'd done a pretty good job of pretending I was okay, but something must have given me away, because Cassidy sighed and shot me a stern look.

"You could have *said* something," she scolded.

"I'm fine," I lied.

"No, you want everyone to *think* you're fine. There's a difference."

I shrugged and didn't say anything. Cassidy shivered, and I pulled her closer against me.

"Do you think they're together?" she mumbled, her cheek pressing warmly on my neck.

"Who?"

"Toby and Austin."

I was fairly stunned by the question, because things like that just didn't occur to me.

"Why would you think that?"

"I don't know." Cassidy shrugged. "Just an impression I had. But I could be wrong. Austin doesn't quite seem the type."

"And Toby does?" I didn't realize it was a rhetorical question until I'd asked it.

It was strange, thinking that Toby might be gay. It made an odd kind of sense, but it didn't bother me, or anything like that. He was still Toby, our fearless captain.

It wasn't long before Toby and Austin came out of the bookshop.

"We should head back," I said, in case they were up for walking another mile or two.

Cassidy kept giving me these glances out of the corner of her eye as we walked back to the Fail Whale, as though she thought I should say something, but no way in hell was I going to ask Toby to bring the car around.

"Backseat!" Austin called, scrambling for it. He stretched out, folding his arms across his chest. "Don't wake me."

Toby rolled his eyes. "I'm not driving back with all of you jerks sleeping. Faulkner, get up front."

I'd already reclaimed my seat from the drive up, and a nap sounded awesome, like maybe I could sleep through the ache in my knee.

"Actually, I'll keep you company," Cassidy said, climbing into the passenger seat.

Our eyes met in the rearview mirror, and I shot her a look of gratitude before tossing my hoodie over my lap like a blanket and drifting asleep on the crowded lanes of the 10 East.

20

CASSIDY TOOK ME shopping over the weekend at a sec-
ondhand clothing store. It was in this group of vinyl shops
and vegetarian restaurants a couple of blocks from the big
luxury mall, a place I'd driven past dozens of times but
never thought to stop and explore.

There were weird sculptures everywhere, which Cassidy
called "art installations."

One art installation in particular was made of rusted
barrels, and I suggested that maybe they should uninstall
it, which made Cassidy laugh. Her hair was down, the way I
liked it best, falling over her shoulders in loose waves. She'd
put on a pair of boots with big heels, and the extra height
made holding hands feel different, as though she was closer,
and easier to reach.

She dragged me into a narrow store bursting with sec-
ondhand clothing. I halfheartedly flicked through a rack of
T-shirts, more people-watching than shopping. There was

a blonde girl with dreadlocks and a nose ring behind the counter, and an Asian guy with tattoo sleeves and stretched earlobes standing outside the dressing room.

"Oh my God, perfect!" Cassidy exclaimed, holding up some sort of blue feathered monstrosity that might have been either a coat or a bathrobe.

"No," I told her.

"You're trying it on!" she insisted, laughing as she put it back.

After a while, it became clear that Cassidy was teasing me with the worst things she could find.

"That is a black T-shirt," she informed me, looking at what I was holding. "Come on, Ezra, I'm not going to do it for you. You need to express yourself. You're not an Abercrombie button-down and baggy jeans."

I stared down at the black T-shirt, realizing that Cassidy hadn't dragged me to a shop so she could make me buy some new jeans. She was determined to help me figure out who I wanted to be, now that I sat with the debate team and participated in flash mobs and snuck into college lecture halls. And I could see her point. If I didn't want to hang out with my old friends, I probably shouldn't keep dressing like I did, especially since I'd dropped enough weight over the summer that nothing in my closet fit anymore.

"Got any suggestions?" I asked, because that seemed safe.

"Hmmm." She sized me up as though enjoying a private

joke. "How about a leather jacket?"

When I dumped my pile of clothes onto the counter to pay, the girl with the dreadlocks smiled at me.

"Awesome jacket," she said, ringing it up. "You should wear it with the black jeans."

"Yeah, okay," I said, taking out a credit card.

"Just not with that shirt." She laughed as she rang up my purchases and stuffed everything into a bag.

"You're sure you didn't want the feathered bathrobe too?" Cassidy teased as we climbed back into my car.

"Nah, it would just make Toby jealous."

"So jealous," Cassidy agreed.

A car was waiting for my parking spot, riding my ass so I could barely pull out.

"Seriously," I muttered. "Why is the world filled with douche-bag drivers?"

"Well, you are under a tree. Maybe he's just a *schattenparker*," Cassidy said, turning on the radio. She hit my presets, getting three stations of commercials in a row before giving up.

"What's a *schattenparker*?"

"It's German." Cassidy grinned. "And it translates roughly as 'someone who always parks their car in the shade so their interior doesn't get hot.' German's full of really good insults."

"Like what?" I asked.

"Um." Cassidy considered for a moment. "*Vomdoucher*.

That means someone who can't stand to take cold showers. And I like *backpfeifengesicht* a lot. That one translates to 'a face that cries out for a fist in it.' It's very Shakespearean."

I shook my head. "Where do you learn this stuff?"

"Don't you ever get bored?" Cassidy asked.

"Yeah, but I don't Google 'German insults.'"

"Why not? It's fascinating."

I shrugged, merging onto the freeway. "I guess it just never occurred to me."

"Do you know what just occurred to *me*?" Cassidy asked playfully.

"What?"

"I've never seen your bedroom."

THANKFULLY, MY PARENTS were out shopping for new lighting fixtures or lamps or something. I hadn't really been paying attention when my mom had explained it that morning, but the point was, they weren't home, and wouldn't be back for a while.

"Should I be afraid?" Cassidy asked warily as I led her up to my room. "Is this going to be one of those messy boy bedrooms that smells like old cheese?"

"Definitely. I've got posters of girls in bikinis, too. And like, a whole bedside drawer of lube."

"I would be disappointed if you didn't." Cassidy laughed.

My room wasn't all that exciting, except for the fact that it contained a large bed. Mostly, it was just really clean. If it wasn't, my mom straightened up before the maid came on Tuesdays, which meant that she went through all of my stuff.

I wasn't allowed to put posters up or anything like that, so there were a couple of framed prints: McEnroe and Fleming at Wimbledon, plus some sailing stuff my dad had liked, even though we never went sailing. I had a big bookshelf that held photographs from school dances, a couple of game consoles, and the empty space where my tennis trophies used to sit before I put them in a box in the closet.

I opened the door, and Cooper pushed past us and jumped onto the bed, laying his head down on my Wii controller.

"Cooper, get out!" I said, laughing.

"Awww, poor dog." Cassidy sat down on my bed and scratched him behind the ears.

"That's not helping," I said.

"Why do you have a framed picture of a sailboat?" she asked.

I shrugged and sat down next to her.

"Let me guess," Cassidy said, "because someone else picked it out and put it up in a room meant to encapsulate who *you* are, even though you have no interest in boats."

"If I say yes, do I get to kiss you?"

"Not in front of the dog!" She pretended to be shocked.

"Cooper, get out!" I said, prodding him.

Cooper sat up, considered it, and then promptly lay back down.

Cassidy finally coaxed him off the bed and shooed him out the door.

"There," she said. "We have successfully sexiled your poodle."

"Achievement unlocked." It was a phrase I'd picked up from our lunch table, and it made Cassidy smile.

She bent down to take off her boots, and then padded barefoot around my room, examining it.

"Where are your books?" she asked.

"Under the bed," I admitted sheepishly.

Cassidy got down on her hands and knees and peered under the bed.

"It's the lost library of Alexandria," she said dryly.

"I don't get it, but okay."

"You should put them on your shelves. Unless you're afraid the football team might come over and discover that you're a *giant nerd*."

"I haven't read many of them," I said, in case she thought that I had. "They were my mom's in college."

"You're never going to read them if they're under your bed."

"I'll put on my new leather jacket and go read one in a coffee shop tomorrow," I promised, grinning.

"You're so full of it," Cassidy teased, scooting onto the bed. Her arms were goose bumped from the air-conditioning, and her tank top was askew, revealing a lacy bra strap.

"Mmm, come here," I said, pulling her on top of me.

I'd forgotten to put on music to set the mood, but it didn't matter. For once, we had a huge bed all to ourselves, and a lock on the door, and an echoing, empty house beyond that lock.

I kissed her neck, slipping the straps of her tank top over her shoulders, and then kissed those too. I pushed her tank top down around her waist, hoping she'd get the hint that I wanted her to take it off.

"Very subtle," she said, sitting up and wriggling out of her top. Stripes of late-afternoon sunlight seeped though the blinds, creating golden bands across her skin.

"It's purple," I said stupidly, mesmerized by the appearance of her lacy bra and the soft curves of her waist.

And then Cooper let out a pitiful whine and scratched his paw against the door. Cassidy glanced over, and Cooper whined again, louder this time.

"Hush, Cooper!" she called, but if anything, the mention of his name seemed to encourage him.

"Just ignore it," I told her.

And we tried to, for a while. But it's pretty hard to pretend your dog isn't sobbing his eyes out on the other side of the door.

"It's getting worse," Cassidy said, trying not to laugh. "Can't you do anything?"

"He's never like this," I grumbled, getting up.

I stuck my head out the door. Cooper stared back at me, his brown eyes quivering. He let out an experimental whine.

"No!" I told him. "Hush, Cooper! Go away!"

Not going to happen, old sport, his eyes seemed to say. He lay down, settling his head on top of his paws, and whined softly.

"Better," I said, shutting the door with a sigh.

Cassidy was sitting up on the bed in her bra and jeans, her hair tumbling over her shoulders.

"So where's this drawer full of lube?" she joked.

"We won't need it," I promised, and my T-shirt joined hers on the floor.

We started kissing again. Cassidy was on top, straddling me. Her hair swished against my cheek, and she bit my bottom lip a bit as we kissed, and I pretty much wanted to die, it was so sexy. I reached for her bra and waged a brief but unsuccessful battle against the clasp, managing to get it thoroughly stuck in the Velcro of my wrist brace.

"Um," I said. "We have a problem."

"Did you, you know . . . finish?" Cassidy asked awkwardly.

"Nope, still good," I assured her. "But, um, I'm caught on your bra."

Caught was an understatement. My wrist was practically handcuffed to her back.

"Oh." Cassidy bit her lip. "Maybe I should—what if I— no, hold on, I'll pull it over my head."

"This is so humiliating," I muttered as Cassidy wiggled out of her bra.

"Well, it brings new meaning to the phrase 'booby trap,'" she teased, and we both laughed, a situation made infinitely more interesting due to the fact that she was topless.

"So, do you care where I put it?" I asked.

"*What?*" she spluttered.

"Oh wow, no. Your *bra*," I clarified, unsnagging it from my wrist brace. "Sorry."

"You're cute when you blush." Cassidy grinned mischievously. "And since you asked, how about I show you *exactly* where to put it?"

Cassidy slid down beneath the covers, and I tossed her bra onto the floor and closed my eyes and clenched my fists and let the delicious pressure of her warm, soft mouth take me back to our fireworks, all of them bursting at once.

Later—after I'd returned the favor, and we'd gotten dressed, and Cassidy had expressed her undying appreciation for the fact that I had an en suite bathroom—after we'd let Cooper back into the room and were innocently playing Mario Cars with the door open in case my parents came home, Cassidy asked if I was a virgin.

I paused the game, since I had the A controller.

"Um," I said, wondering if she'd guessed.

"Oh my God." Cassidy's lips twitched as she held back a smile. "You're not!"

"Hey, I used to be cool!" I tried to make a joke of it.

"I know, it's horrifying," Cassidy said wryly, and then fiddled with the controller, realizing what she'd started.

"Well, I'm saving myself," Cassidy announced, like it was the punch line to an untold joke, and then shrugged, embarrassed. "Why do they even call it that, 'saving yourself'? Like we need to be rescued from sex? It's not as though virgins spend their whole lives engaged in the sacred ceremony of 'being saved' from intercourse."

"Just so long as you're cool with outercourse, I guess I don't mind." I grinned.

"What the heck is outercourse?" Cassidy frowned.

I tried to make myself the picture of innocence.

"Well, I could show you again?"

21

I'M NOT CERTAIN I can pinpoint the exact moment when I became irreparably different. These days, I think it wasn't a moment at all, but a process. A chemical reaction, if you will. I was no longer Ezra Faulkner, golden boy, and maybe I hadn't been for a while, but the more time I spent with Cassidy, the more I was okay with it.

After Cassidy went home and my parents returned from their outing to various home décor warehouses, which we discussed at length over dinner, I put on my new leather jacket and looked at myself in the mirror. A real look, something I'd been avoiding for a long time.

Ever since the accident, I'd only seen the things that were wrong: my hair grown out from its athlete's cut, my muscles diminished, my tan replaced by an unhealthy pallor, my formerly fitted jeans hanging off my hipbones, even with the aid of a belt.

But when I looked in the mirror this time, I didn't see any

of those things. They were still there, of course, but not as flaws, just as facts: skinny, messy-haired, pale. Me, I guessed, just a different version from the one most people remembered.

In some sort of grand gesture, I took the books out from under my bed and put them on the shelves. Not that I was planning on reading many of them, but it was a nice feeling, being able to glance at my bookshelves and contemplate the possibility of it. To think that a small piece of my bedroom finally represented something of me.

I wondered what Cassidy's bedroom looked like, if it encapsulated her in a way that mine didn't. I wondered if it was anything like Charlotte's bedroom had been, with lady-bug figurines lining the windowsill and an entire desk just for her makeup collection, which apparently was called a vanity.

"How come we never go over to your house?" I asked Cassidy when I picked her up for school on Monday.

"Because we have a housekeeper," she said, sighing. "And she'd tell my parents I have boys over when they're not around."

"Technically, I'm singular," I said, nodding at the security guard as we drove past.

"All the more disastrous," Cassidy assured me. "Trust me, it's easier if you don't come over. You're not missing anything."

"I guess," I said, sensing that Cassidy wanted to drop the subject.

Cassidy took a sip of the coffee I'd brought.

"Have you ever tried a French press?" she asked. "I think you'd like it better."

CASSIDY AND I went out to the movies on Friday night—a real date, at the Prism Center. She wore a nice dress, and I wore my new clothes, and we saw this awful comedy starring the same actors who always star in awful comedies.

Going to the movies always makes me strangely exhilarated when I exit the theater, surrounded by the smell of popcorn and everyone talking about the film. It's as though everything is more vivid, and the line between the probable and the cinematic becomes blurred. You think big thoughts, like maybe it's possible to move someplace exciting, or risk everything for a chance at your dreams or whatever, but then you never do. It's more the *feeling* that you could turn your life into a movie if you wanted to.

I've never been able to explain to anyone what's so holy about the moments after you exit a movie theater, so it surprised me when Cassidy smiled and said nothing until we reached the bottom of the escalator, leaving me to the perfect silence of my moment.

"It's creepy," she observed, slipping her hand into mine, "overhearing a hundred identical conversations."

"Then we'll be the one conversation that's different," I promised. "Tell me something that happened when you were a kid."

Cassidy smiled, pleased.

"When I was seven, my best friend blew out the candles on my birthday cake. I cried because I thought my birthday wish wouldn't come true. Now you tell me something."

"Um," I said, thinking. "In the second grade, Toby and I borrowed a bunch of plastic jewelry from his little sister and buried it in his mother's flower bed. We wanted to dig up buried treasure, I guess, but we got in so much trouble. I had to sleep over in a different room, like the world's longest time out."

"I didn't realize you'd been friends for such a long time."

"Since kindergarten," I said. "Alphabetical order. We had to share a cubby and everything."

A couple of guys from school interrupted us then, to say hi. We stopped to chat about which movie we'd seen—it turned out to be the same one—and how it had sucked.

By the time we got away, we passed half of the girls' water polo team, hanging out by one of the fountains. They waved, and I nodded back.

I didn't really have a big romantic evening planned, but neither of us wanted to head home, so I offered to show her the castle park. It's this great old playground with a huge concrete fortress built way back in the eighties, where I used to play when I was little.

On the drive over, Cassidy discovered that I'd never tried a Toblerone bar, which she deemed totally unacceptable, so we stopped off at the grocery store to buy some. While we were waiting to pay, what might possibly have been the entire varsity football team crowded into the checkout line behind us. They were buying two dozen cans of nonstick cooking spray.

It was so entirely magnificent that I was too stunned to laugh. Cassidy nudged me, grinning.

"Hey," I said, turning around.

Connor, the quarterback, seemed surprised to see me—although not as surprised as I was to see the entire starting lineup dropping what had to be a cool fifty on cooking spray.

"Faulkner," he acknowledged, and then nodded at Cassidy. "Lady friend."

Connor was plastered, the stench of liquor radiating off him in waves. I hoped someone else was the designated driver.

"They make different flavors," Cassidy said politely, nodding toward the cooking spray. "I don't know if you're aware."

I stifled a laugh. It was all too bizarre. And the worst of it was that the cashier was some kid from school, possibly a junior. He looked terrified at the prospect of ringing up the football team's purchase, and I didn't blame him.

"Got it, thanks," Connor said sheepishly, as though we'd caught him buying a bulk pack of tiny condoms. Honestly? That would have been less surprising.

I paid quickly and ushered Cassidy into the parking lot,

where we laughed our faces off.

"What *was* that?" Cassidy asked, gasping.

"I'm not certain," I said, "but I believe it may have been the starting lineup of our school's football team purchasing twenty-four cans of PAM."

"Oh my God," Cassidy spluttered. "I'm dying."

We were still laughing when I pulled into the empty lot in the castle park.

"Maybe it's some sort of ritual," Cassidy said, speculating. "Like, they have to cover themselves with PAM and play tackle football."

"Believe me, if that was going on, I'd know about it. The tennis guys would give football so much crap." As if we didn't already. We played a country-club sport; they put on protective padding and slammed into each other.

"Maybe they're pranking someone."

"It's probably a drinking game. PAM shots with beer."

We stared up at the enormous concrete castle, this bizarre combination sandbox and jungle gym with a tire swing I used to love as a kid. Cassidy held the candy and drinks we'd bought from the market, the plastic bag knotted around her wrist like a corsage.

"So we just climb up?" she asked doubtfully, taking hold of the rock wall that led up the side of the fortress.

I winced, realizing her doubt was focused in *my* direction.

"Well, there *are* stairs." I disappeared around the other side of the castle, trying to make a joke of it, of how I couldn't even handle a freaking jungle gym.

We claimed the castle's lookout tower, the highest point of the playground, and it was sad how triumphant I felt at getting up there. A little plastic steering wheel was bolted to the balcony, which made Cassidy laugh.

"It's like that castle from Monty Python!" she said, taking the helm. "Let's take it out for a spin."

"I thought you didn't have a license," I teased, sitting down on the rubberized floor of our little fort.

A full moon was shining high and white over the skeletons of the birch trees, and I could hear someone still on the tennis courts beyond the cookout area, even though it was nearly curfew. I wondered if it was anyone I knew.

Cassidy sat down next to me, her dress teasing me as it fluttered in the breeze. She broke the chocolate bar in half and waited for me to taste it with this I-told-you-so grin.

We finished the candy in an embarrassingly short time, and I watched as she absently licked the chocolate off her fingers. She blushed when she noticed my reaction.

"I bet you taste like chocolate," Cassidy said.

"I bet you're right," I told her, and then we were very busy in our private little turret, Cassidy sitting on my lap in her little dress, driving me crazy with her bare legs against my jeans. I was kissing her neck, and her hands were under my shirt, and I didn't know how far I was getting, but I didn't care, because the magnificent possibility of kissing Cassidy Thorpe had turned into an indisputable fact of my daily existence, and I could hardly believe my good fortune.

I ran my hand up her thigh, half expecting her to push it away, but she didn't. Instead, she sat up as though we'd been caught by her dear, sweet grandmother, and for all I knew, we had.

"Someone's here," Cassidy said, smoothing her hair. She scooted over to the edge of the lookout and peered through the crenellations. I hoped desperately that she'd imagined it, but then I heard laughter. Laughter and aerosol cans being shaken.

"You're not going to believe this." Cassidy motioned me over to take a look.

The football team had arrived, their trucks and Blazers lined up in the lot. With cans of cooking spray in hand, they advanced on the swing set and monkey bars.

"Are you kidding me?" I whispered as they began to PAM the monkey bars.

"That's horrible." Cassidy whispered back. "We should do something."

"I'll handle it," I told her. After all, nothing kills the mood quicker than bearing witness to mass vandalism.

They didn't notice me until I was right there, standing at the edge of the sandbox. I took out my car keys and hit the panic button, making everyone jump.

"Hey!" I said, killing the alarm. "Connor MacLeary, get

your drunk ass over here!"

Connor stumbled toward me, kicking up sand. He was barefoot, wearing his jersey with a pair of jean shorts, and he looked strangely vulnerable without shoes on. I'd known him since kindergarten, and what I was thinking about then wasn't how I was a cane-wielding member of my high school's debate team, about to face off against the varsity quarterback, but how Connor had refused to put on his construction paper pilgrim hat during our kindergarten's Thanksgiving party. He'd thrown a tantrum over it until Ms. Lardner had picked him up and sat him on top of the cubby nook to calm down.

He was the kid who'd refused to give fat girls Valentines even though you were supposed to bring enough for everyone, who'd always forgotten part of his Cub Scout uniform and who'd made dioramas on lined paper the morning they were due. And he was committing playground vandalism with cooking spray, which was so ridiculous that the vast difference between our respective lunch tables didn't even factor into my decision to confront him.

"Faulkner!" Connor shouted, spreading his arms as though literally embracing my appearance in the castle park. "Perfect timing! Grab a can!"

"You're an asshole," I told him. "Also an idiot, but mostly an asshole."

His smile disappeared and he scratched his head like he couldn't believe I was actually angry, as though he was probably misunderstanding.

"What? It's a *joke*," he explained laughingly.

I shook my head, disgusted.

"This is the furthest thing from a joke I've ever seen. We're on a *playground*. It's for *little kids*, you douchenozzle. Call off your goons before some second grader breaks an arm."

It finally got through to him that I was seriously pissed off. He cocked his head, sizing me up, and for a moment, I thought he might actually take a swing at me. But we both knew he wouldn't get away with it. Not at school on Monday; the entire football team against a kid with a cane.

I sighed impatiently and hit the alarm on my car again.

"Call it off," I threatened. *"Now."*

"All right, Faulkner. *Jesus.*" Connor shook his head and ambled back toward his team.

"Hey, assholes," I heard him call. "Drop your cans. This was a dumb idea. Let's get that beer from my garage."

I felt invincible as I swaggered back toward the castle, as though I'd actually accomplished something good. I grinned when I saw Cassidy. She was sitting on the stairs, solemnly watching the football team slink off in defeat. I sat down next to her and pulled her close.

"I have completed my quest, fair maiden," I joked, "and returned to yon castle to share tales of my triumph."

But Cassidy wasn't laughing.

"I can't believe you did that," she said. "I thought he was

going to jump you."

"I have bested the ogre," I insisted. "I am the king of castle park."

"Ezra, be serious."

"Connor wouldn't have done anything. I've known him since we were five."

I tilted Cassidy's face toward mine, trying to resume where we'd broken off, but clearly I'd used up my allotment of successes for that evening, because Cassidy wasn't having it.

"I don't want anything to happen to you," she said, twisting her hair up into a bun. "Just—don't scare me like that, okay?"

"No more questing," I promised, and then drove Cassidy home because it was getting late.

22

SCHOOL ON MONDAY was unbearable. I hadn't thought anyone would know what had happened, but it was pretty evident that *everyone* did. A junior from JV tennis named Tommy Yang (the younger brother of notable pantsless sake bomber Kenneth Yang) had been on the courts that night and seen the whole thing.

"I wish I was invisible," I moaned, putting my head down on the lunch table.

"Yeah, well *I* wish the turkey in this sandwich wasn't sweating more than a fat kid in a Jacuzzi," Toby said philosophically, peeling two pieces of incredibly clammy deli meat apart and jiggling them for emphasis.

I laughed, feeling slightly better about all of the unwanted attention. And then Luke grinned and leaned back in his seat.

"So I heard a pretty good joke," he said. "I heard Faulkner fought the entire football team on Friday night."

"What's funny about that?" I asked, in no mood for Luke's crap.

"It's true?" Toby let the halves of his sandwich drop onto the plastic wrap.

"Mostly true," I admitted. "Depending which version you heard."

"I'd rather hear your version," Phoebe said, leaning forward in her seat and reminding me strongly that she ran the school paper.

Cassidy joined us at the table then, unwrapping a pack of vending-machine granola bars.

"Hey," she said, quickly kissing me on the cheek. "I didn't say anything. I promise."

"I know." I sighed. "Tommy Yang was on the tennis courts."

And so I told everyone what had really happened, leaving out the part about my having a half-staff the entire time thanks to Cassidy's and my, uh, fortress play. Toby laughed so hard that he snorted, which I hadn't heard him do since we were kids.

"I hate to say it"—Austin shrugged helplessly—"but it's pretty genius, using cooking spray like that."

"The sort of genius that falls into the exclusive realm of pedophiles and psychopaths," Phoebe noted.

"I can't believe you didn't get your ass handed to you," Sam said.

"Well, I don't know if you can tell, but I'm limping," I deadpanned.

Toby laughed.

"I would have shit my pants," he told me. "If I was sitting in the park and those goons showed up drunk and spray happy, I'm not even kidding, I would've had a bodily misfunction."

"It's just Connor MacLeary," I said. "He's like a big drunk puppy. Honestly."

"Maybe to *you*," Toby said. "But he made my life hell in middle school. Who do you think dared Tug Mason to piss in my Gatorade?"

Actually, now that Toby mentioned it, the mystery of Tug Mason's sports-drink-pissing proclivity resolved itself. I mean, people don't just do that sort of thing without prompting.

"Toby's right," Phoebe said. "Football's a bunch of drunk rednecks. They haven't won a game in how long?"

"Well, they tied with Beth Shalom once last season," I offered. "Although that doesn't really count, since half of the other team was missing due to Rosh Hashanah."

"I'm so glad Faulkner's here to give us last year's *football* statistics," Luke grumbled.

"Screw you," I said.

"Screw your girlfriend," he retorted. "If you can get your crippled dick to work."

Our table went quiet, and the white noise of the quad seemed to drop away until it was just me and Luke Sheppard, with his slacker glasses and nasty smirk and unforgivable insult.

I always thought it wouldn't get to me, someone calling me crippled like I should be ashamed of myself. I suppose I'd only pictured it broadly, the word by itself, like when Charlotte called the debate team nerds, or the orchestra losers. But what Luke said wasn't some generalized insult. It was genuinely offensive, and he wasn't getting away with it.

"You are such an asshole," Phoebe said, slapping Luke across the face. The slap echoed—or maybe the word is reverberated—and in its aftermath, the whole world roared back into place.

Phoebe got up, taking her backpack with her. The poltergeist of her unfinished lunch sat on the table, half of a chocolate cookie and a peanut butter sandwich missing two neat bites.

"I'm going to see if she's all right," Cassidy said.

"No." I shook my head. "I'll go."

I found Phoebe sitting on the metal bench outside of the swim complex, at the very edge of the parking lot. There weren't any lunch tables over there, so it was a decent place to sulk, if you didn't mind the tang of chlorine.

Her eyes were red, and she cradled her right hand as though it still stung. She scooted down on the bench to make room for me, and I sat, and we said nothing.

"He's such a jerk," Phoebe mumbled after a while, wiping her eyes on the sleeve of her sweater.

"I know." I reached into my backpack for a packet of tissues.

"You have tissues." She shook her head as though I'd just offered her an embroidered handkerchief.

"My mom buys them in bulk. I've got hand sanitizer, too, if you want to cleanse Luke's face from your fist."

"You don't have to be so nice to me," she muttered.

"Well, you sort of defended my honor back there."

"I slapped *Luke Sheppard*."

She said his name as though it meant something. As though she didn't even have the right to expect him to say hello to her in the hallways, and he really was as big a deal as he made himself out to be. It killed me, Phoebe sitting there in her ponytail and glasses, a year younger than me and so tiny that her toes barely touched the concrete, appalled at herself for being the only one of us brave enough to call Luke out on his bullshit.

"He was being a *backpfeifen*—whatever. His was the face that launched a thousand fists," I said. "So don't worry about it. You didn't give him anything he didn't deserve."

"Now I sort of wish I'd slapped him harder," Phoebe said thoughtfully.

I snorted.

"God, I can't believe he said that." Phoebe winced, like she was replaying it in her head. "No one thinks of you like that. With pity, or whatever. Luke always used to compare himself to you, how you both ran things. He'd complain about it constantly, how you were this smug, brainless jock who did nothing but took all the credit. And now you're on the same side, and you're actually pretty cool, and it's killing him. I mean, if there's anyone who doesn't belong at our lunch table, it's me."

It had never struck me that Phoebe was insecure about sitting with us. Maybe it was because I'd always seen our table as co-ed, rather than a group of boys with their girl-friends, or maybe it was because Phoebe got along so well with everyone. But I couldn't stand to see her awash in self-doubt like that.

"Hey," I said sternly, the way I did back when I had to give pep talks to the team. "Listen. Everyone at our lunch table loves you."

Phoebe regarded me like she wasn't sure if I was telling the truth.

"But what if they stop?" she asked, wincing.

"If you and Luke break up?"

Phoebe shook her head. "It's hard to explain," she said. "It's like . . . I'm paranoid about people borrowing my laptop because I'm convinced they'll find some secret document on there that would make the whole world think I'm a terrible person—something I don't even remember writing. And it doesn't matter that there's no document like that. I'm still terrified, you know?"

"Everyone feels like that," I said. "Even Luke."

"You're wrong. Luke doesn't care if everyone thinks he's a horrible person, so long as they do what he says."

I realized then that Phoebe knew him infinitely better than I ever would. That Luke had put his arm around her at the movies and his tongue down her throat at debate tournaments, and not once had she ever seemed happy about it, about them.

"Just once I want someone to be afraid of losing me," Phoebe said. "But the only thing Luke's afraid of losing is power."

I shrugged, not knowing what to say, so I didn't say anything for a while. I stared out at the gym across from the swim complex, and after a few minutes, I put my arm around Phoebe, because she was small and crying, and it seemed like the thing to do. And we sat like that until the bell rang.

WE HAD VOTING for homecoming court that week, the glitter-encrusted ballot box mocking me as it sat in the front of my homeroom. We were supposed to nominate one boy and one girl for the court, and I was never good at that. It felt weird voting for myself, even in things like student government elections where I'd had to take the initiative to run, and I always felt like my votes were disingenuous when I wrote down my friends. In the end I left my ballot sheet blank.

When I sat down at my lunch table, it was oddly empty.

Luke and Sam had driven off campus, to Burger King or somewhere, and we didn't talk about it—where they'd gone, or if they'd be back.

Phoebe had swiped half a bag of candy corn from the journalism room, and we each took a handful. Cassidy showed us how to pinch off the bottom parts so they looked like teeth. Well, she didn't so much show us as pretend she'd knocked a tooth out, and then laugh when we realized what had happened. But our laughter felt too small, as though we were in a theater with an overwhelming number of open seats, and nothing we did could make the space less empty.

Our lunch table stayed like that for two days, until Luke and Sam reappeared as though they'd never been away. There was a smug cast to Luke's shoulders, and when he unpacked his sandwich, a flash of silver glinted on his finger. A purity ring. At first I thought it was meant to be ironic, so I didn't understand why everyone was laughing. But it turned out Luke meant it—or wanted us to think he did.

"What can I say?" he shrugged humbly. "I've seen the error of my ways."

Phoebe snorted and whispered in a way that suggested she wanted Luke to overhear her: "More likely he's hooking up with a girl from his church."

It was fantastic. Instead of Luke reappearing at our table in a massive cloud of awkwardness, the way these things usually went, his holier-than-thou attitude and Sacred Gift Ring gave us all an opportunity to poke fun at him, an opportunity

Toby seized with glee. It was as though the fault in our lunch table had resolved itself into a jagged crack, with Luke and Sam on one side, and the rest of us on the other, wondering how we'd missed the earthquake in the first place.

23

FRIDAY MORNING BROUGHT with it the second pep rally of the year. The balloon arches over each section of the bleachers were in fall colors. God, brown and orange balloons. It was like the world's most cheerless carnival.

I joined Toby and Cassidy in the third row of the senior section; Toby had saved me the end.

"Sure you don't want to switch to the teacher bleacher?" he joked.

"Screw you," I said, not really meaning it.

"Screw your girlfriend," Cassidy added, laughing. It was something we did now; the phrase had become a joke among our group of friends, and I was glad of it.

We settled into the bleachers, waiting for the pep rally to begin. In the row below us, Staci Guffin's hot pink thong rose magnificently out the back of her jeans in a neon whale tail.

Toby pointed it out with a disapproving frown that sent

Cassidy into muffled hysterics, and I felt sort of bad that they were laughing, even if Staci *was* one of my ex-girlfriends. The pep rally started then, with SGA coming out in plaid shirts to dance to some hideous Katy Perry number. I glanced at Toby, who shook his head as though embarrassed for them.

"SENIORS! SHOW SOME SPIRIT!" called Jill, putting her hand on her hip.

The noise was deafening.

It went on like that for a good five minutes, with the requisite *I can't hear you*'s and *That's more like it*'s.

Tiffany Wells, our hopelessly blonde social events chair, took the microphone. She'd written notes at SGA meetings the year before with a pen topped by a cloud of pink feathers. You got the impression that her friends made fun of her to her face, and she didn't quite understand why they were laughing.

We all paid attention as Tiffany announced the theme for the homecoming dance: Monte Carlo. She said it as though it was particularly thrilling that we'd have cardboard backdrops featuring casino motifs and "real live blackjack tables."

Toby almost died.

"Sober, fake gambling," he whispered. "In the *gym*."

I had to admit, it *was* terrible.

And then Jill handed Tiffany an envelope.

"Okay," she said, drawing out her vowels in that particularly Californian way, "we're going to announce the homecoming court nominees, and I'm, like, super excited about this, you guys!"

She squealed into the microphone, making everyone wince from the reverb.

"If I call your name, you should come down here and take a Royal Rose!"

"Dear God," Toby whispered. "It's like being at a reality television taping."

I laughed.

Cassidy shushed us, enthralled.

"The nominees for queen." Tiffany went on, naming Jill Nakamura; Charlotte Hyde; Sara Sumner, who ran that obnoxious clique of Charity League girls who pretended they lived in beachfront mansions in Back Bay; and Anamica Patel.

I winced when she called Anamica; it was one of those cruel games Charlotte liked to play, telling everyone to nominate someone as a joke, and Anamica was undoubtedly that year's target. Anamica was a bit too focused on earning straight As, but she didn't deserve to have her name hooted laughingly by the assholes sitting in the back of the senior section.

"That's awful," Cassidy whispered as Anamica accepted her Royal Rose, her face bright red.

"And now, the nominees for king," Tiffany continued, once the hooting had died down. "Evan McMillan."

Evan sauntered up there and hoisted the rose over his

head like it was a prize.

"Jimmy Fuller."

Jimmy fist pumped.

"Luke Sheppard."

Luke tried to act as though he was too cool for it, although you could see the triumph on his face.

"And Ezra Faulkner."

I froze. The gym seemed to go silent, and all I could think was, *Oh God, I'm Anamica Patel. I'm the joke vote.*

I have no idea how I got from my seat to the center of the gym, but suddenly there was a rose in my hand and the whole school was rising up around me like I was some doomed gladiator.

When I sat back down, Toby was laughing.

"Good thing you already own a suit," he said.

"Shut up," I whispered wretchedly, wishing that everyone would stop staring.

BY THE TIME lunch rolled around, I was thoroughly confused by what had happened: whether it was a joke, or residual pity, or something else entirely. Whatever it was, nearly half of my math class congratulated me as though the nomination was something to be proud of, rather than embarrassed about.

It felt strange, like all of those party invitations I'd turned down had been genuine, as though it didn't matter that I could barely handle stairs and was dating a girl on the debate team and spent my weekends studying for AP classes with Toby Ellicott.

"Congrats," I told Anamica after math class, since it seemed like the thing to do, the both of us sitting there with roses wilting on our desks.

"Not *you*, too." Anamica glared at me, like she suspected I was making fun of her.

"What?" I asked, confused.

"I *get* it, Faulkner. Your evil popular crowd voted for me as a joke. You don't have to rub it in."

"*My* evil popular crowd?" I wondered if she'd somehow missed the memo that the throne had been usurped months ago. I'd thought we were in the same situation, Anamica and me, awkwardly navigating through a day that had showered us both with unwanted and embarrassing attention. But clearly she didn't see it that way.

"Just leave me alone," she warned, tossing her rose into the trash.

THERE WAS A strange but unmistakable tension at our lunch table that afternoon. I'd never been in direct competition with Luke before, and I had the distinct sense that he didn't like it, that he felt as though we were adversaries who had finally been pitted against each other.

Toby was oblivious to the tension as he gleefully explained our school dances to Cassidy: the way we all had to pose for a photographer who set up his backdrop in the weight-training room, how our teachers stood awkwardly against the walls of the gym, appalled at the music and the dancing.

"It's hilarious," Toby assured her. "All of the girls wear tacky satin dresses covered in rhinestones, and all of the guys come up behind them and freak dance."

"Freak dance?" Cassidy raised an eyebrow.

"You know, rub their junk on them trunks?" Toby explained in an attempt to be gangster that made me choke on my iced tea.

"Can we please do that?" Cassidy asked me. "And you have to take me out to dinner somewhere awful, with unlimited breadsticks or a soda machine."

"I think the guy's supposed to ask the girl to the dance," I told her.

"Oh." Cassidy's face fell as she considered this. "Well, don't worry, I'll act surprised when you ask me."

I laughed.

"It's a plan," I promised.

"Ugh, hide!" Toby muttered, and it took me a moment, but then I saw what he was talking about. Charlotte Hyde was heading straight for our table—alone. Her ponytail was golden in the sun, and she smiled like she knew everyone was watching.

"Ezra," she purred. "Come over to the table for a sec."

The table. As though there was only one in the entire quad.

"Why?" I asked suspiciously.

Charlotte examined the end of her ponytail, annoyed.

"It's a homecoming thing. We need you."

I sighed and got up, figuring it was best to get it over with quickly. Luke stood as well, presuming the invitation had included him. Charlotte raised an eyebrow.

"Not you," she told him, grabbing my arm and steering me away.

Charlotte popped her gum and smirked up at me, stroking my sleeve. She smelled the way she always did—a combination of scented lotion and lip-gloss and fruity gum that gave the overwhelming impression of artificial strawberries.

"Your jacket's cute," she said as we walked toward my old lunch table. "I can hardly keep my hands off it."

"Cassidy picked it out."

Charlotte abruptly took her hand away.

"You're taking her to the dance, aren't you?"

"She's my girlfriend, Charlotte."

We arrived at the table then, everyone looking up.

"Dude," Evan said, grinning. "The badass trio on the homecoming court. We're fuckin' *kings*."

I didn't have the heart to tell him that the point of a homecoming court was that there would only be *one* king. So I smiled and said, "Yeah, totally."

"Oh my God." Jill rolled her eyes. "I lol'ed so hard when they called Anamica. And then *Luke*, what a joke."

"I know." Charlotte giggled. "He still has *braces*."

I stood there uncomfortably, wondering if anyone would dare to admit that I'd only been nominated out of pity, until Evan pulled me aside and explained that they were all getting a hotel suite after the dance. There would be Beer Pong, and afterward, a party in the hot tub. He wanted to know if I was in.

"For what?" I asked, figuring he couldn't really mean that they were inviting me—and my date—to get plastered with them at the Four Seasons.

"A couple hundred bucks. Maybe more if we get a Hummer limo."

Evidently, he really did mean it. Evan actually thought I wanted to pay for the prestige of co-hosting what would no doubt be a hot-tub mess of a party.

Somehow, I managed to make my excuses and extract myself from their lunch table.

"Hey," I said sheepishly when I sat back down with my friends.

"What did they want?" Luke asked, narrowing his eyes.

"Nothing. Limo share."

But I could tell that he didn't believe me.

I ASKED CASSIDY to the dance while we were studying with Toby in the Barnes and Noble café the next afternoon. I had the barista write it on her coffee.

When Cassidy saw it, she grinned.

"Why, deary me," she drawled in an overwrought

southern accent, "a gentleman caller wantin' to escort me to the dance."

"We'll have dinner at Fiesta Palace," I promised. "You can order chips in a sombrero and there's a guy who comes around and makes balloon hats with the mariachi band."

"Why, Mr. Faulkner," she said, still using that ridiculous accent, "that sounds positively delightful."

And then Toby acted disgusted when we kissed.

Cassidy's phone rang with some secretary confirming an appointment ("The dentist's office," she whispered, making a face), and when she went outside to deal with it, I asked Toby whom he was taking to the dance.

"I thought Phoebe and I might go as friends," he admitted. "And Austin's determined to take this girl from his SAT class. He thinks he's found his soul mate."

"Oh, so you guys aren't . . ." I trailed off, embarrassed.

"No, Faulkner, we're not," he said drily.

I shrugged, wishing Cassidy would come back and rescue us. But she didn't.

"Um, that's cool," I said. "I mean, either way. If you're going with Phoebe or if, whatever—"

"This is painful, dude," Toby informed me. Surprisingly, he looked as though he was trying not to laugh. "I'm not gay. I mean, I *think* I am, but I'll figure it out in college. You have to really *know* to be out in high school. And I'm hopelessly single, never been kissed, no prospects on the horizon, dating my left hand and a stack of *hentai* DVDs."

"Hentai?" I asked, trying to keep a straight face. *"Really?"*

"Major nerd points for knowing what that is, but yes."

"Huh." I considered this. "Good to know."

"Well don't worry, you're not my type," Toby said drily.

"I figured, if you're into hentai."

"Shut up about the hentai," he begged. "I never should have mentioned that."

We laughed, since admitting to enjoying naked Japanese anime was pretty shameful, and we both knew I was going to give him hell about that one until the end of time.

"Listen," Toby said, taking a sip of his frappuccino, "thanks for being cool. I was a little worried."

"Seriously?" I wondered for a moment if I gave the impression of being the sort of guy who would disown his best friend over something like that. It wasn't a nice thought.

"Your old friends would have called me a faggot," Toby said.

I winced. "They would not!"

"Let me clarify," Toby said bitterly, "they would have called me a faggot *again*."

He shook his head and wouldn't tell me when it had happened, and I wanted to press him on it, but Cassidy came back from her phone call then, and Toby made her pull up a silly website featuring awkward formal photos, and we laughed so hard that the barista came over and pointedly cleared our table.

24

EVERYONE AGREED THAT dining at Fiesta Palace was a deeply ironic stroke of genius, so I made a reservation for six. Or, I called and attempted to make a reservation, only to be laughed at by the woman who answered the phone.

Austin went on and on about the girl from his SAT class who went to the arts academy and did special-effects makeup, and Phoebe and Cassidy went shopping for dresses three days in a row after school, and the whole thing became such a big production that I couldn't tell if we were actually taking it seriously.

But then, that's how we always were. Outwardly mocking, but never quite to the point of not wanting to participate. Of course my mom was ecstatic over my asking Cassidy to the dance. She kept asking what color Cassidy's dress was (for all I knew, Cassidy was wearing a tuxedo and a top hat), and if we were going to the game (no), and where we were going for dinner (I lied and named the Italian place she and my father liked), and what we were doing afterward (having a Doctor Who marathon at Austin's).

We had voting for king and queen in homeroom on Monday, Scantron sheets this time. It reminded me of the student government elections, the way you had to bubble in A for this candidate, or B for that one. I passed forward my blank ballot and tried not to think about it, about how I'd been in the hospital during class-president elections last year. Instead, I thought about Cassidy, and how she pronounced "vitamin" the British way and hated when people took too many napkins in restaurants. It was as though I was collecting memories of her; as though I knew, or suspected, what was coming.

There was a huge line at the florist's the afternoon of the dance, and I tried to entertain myself by watching the kids who'd come with their parents standing around pretending they weren't embarrassed. But that got boring after a while, so I jokingly texted Cassidy a picture of a hot pink lei along with the message, *they said I could have this for the same price as a corsage!*

You're not serious?! she texted back immediately.

I laughed over it and let her wonder while I paid for her wrist corsage.

My phone rang as I was walking back to my car.

"Please tell me you didn't," Cassidy said.

"I didn't," I admitted. "Note to self: girlfriend does not want to get leid."

"Oh, very funny."

Tony Masters screeched into the parking lot then, the windows of his Blazer rolled down and shedding rap music. He honked his horn at me to say hey, and I only jumped a mile.

"Jesus," I swore, half panicked even though I was still on the sidewalk.

"What *was* that?"

"Nothing. Just this guy from school being an ass."

"Okay," Cassidy said. "Well, try not to die before tonight."

"If I see a big black SUV that looks like it's going to blow through a stop sign, I'll hit reverse," I promised.

"What?"

"The accident," I told her. "Last May?"

"You never told me that part. You always just called it the accident."

"Oh, I thought I had." I reached into my pocket for my keys. "I was leaving this kid Jonas's lakehouse party back when I still had my cool car, before I drove Voldemort."

Silence, and a bit of scuffling on Cassidy's end.

"Did I tell you I've decided to name the Volvo?" I pressed, wondering why she wasn't laughing. Probably she was just impressed by the amazingly clever name I'd given my car.

"Sorry," Cassidy said. She sounded distracted, like she

was at the salon or something. "I have to go."

"Yeah, me too. See you tonight."

I GOT DRESSED slightly early and put some product in my hair that I never bothered with for school and stood there adjusting my tie in the mirror forever.

It wasn't that I was nervous about taking Cassidy to a dance—I was certain we'd goof around and have a good time with our friends like we always did—but more than anything, the homecoming nomination made me feel as though I was being pushed back into a world I was happy to leave behind.

I didn't expect to win homecoming king. It would have been flattering, but useless, since it was the kind of thing that was over the moment it began. Still, I set the alarm on my phone for the time Ms. Reed, the student government advisor, had told us nominees to head to the green room. The "green room," as though it was someplace fancier than the little annex with the unisex handicapped toilet off the back of the gym.

I picked up my copy of *The Great Gatsby* while I waited for Cassidy to arrive and reread the parts about Gatsby's parties since they seemed festive enough. I got so engrossed in the book that I failed to realize it was getting late, and it startled me when my mom knocked on the door of my room.

"Maybe you should check with Cassidy, sweetie," Mom

said worriedly. She was carrying this camera my father had bought her for Hanukkah maybe five years ago, bulky and outdated.

"Yeah, I'll text her," I promised, pulling out my phone. When she didn't answer back, I called. It went to voice mail, and I didn't much see a point in leaving a message.

But when she was a half hour late and still hadn't returned my call, or either of my texts, I started to get worried. Mom stuck her head back into my bedroom and asked what was going on. She was all false cheer, clutching that sad old camera, and I don't know what made me do it, but I looked down at my phone and acted like Cassidy had just texted me back.

"She's running late," I lied, reaching for my keys. "And it's easier if I just pick her up. You don't mind, right?"

The gate guard at Terrace Bluffs was used to me picking up Cassidy; he waved me through without a second glance. Some little kids had done chalk drawings in the street again, of ghosts and pumpkins. A few of the houses on Summit Terrace already had Halloween decorations up, orange lights glowing from the trees and fake cobwebs over their hedges.

I grabbed the corsage and rang the bell, wondering if I'd finally meet her parents. No one answered, so I knocked louder, and rang the bell again, trying not to be too rude about it.

"Hello? It's Ezra," I called, in case they thought I was one of those kids on the bicycles who went door to door preaching the joys of the Church of Latter-day Saints. I mean, I *was* wearing a tie. A limo drove past, with Tommy Yang from JV tennis sticking his head out the sunroof. He hooted at me, and I waved back. It wasn't until the limo disappeared around the corner that I started to panic.

I gave Cassidy another call. Her phone rang five times before I got voice mail.

"Hey," she said laughingly. "Leave me a message in a hundred forty characters or less and—oh my God, Owen, stop, I'm trying to record a voice-mail greeting—sorry, well, leave a message. Or send a telegram if it's urgent."

"Um," I said. "Hi. It's me, Ezra. I'm staring at your front door, and your corsage is sweating. Wait, no, that sounds gross. It's moist. Sorry, that's worse. Anyway, you should come open the door soon because I'm leaving fingerprints all over your doorbell."

Some people have a fear of public speaking; I have a fear of leaving voice mails. Something about talking into a void, about having your voice *recorded*, unrehearsed and with no warning, has always made me hopeless at getting the point across.

I was fairly certain that no one was home, so I climbed back into my car, trying not to panic. Cassidy was, well, *gone*, and I was totally confused by what was happening. And then, because I didn't know what else to do, I called Toby.

"Hey!" he said, answering after the first ring. "You two

on your way?"

"Cassidy's missing," I said hollowly.

"What do you mean, she's missing?" He sounded amused, as though he expected the explanation to be hilarious.

"She never came over, and she hasn't returned my texts, and I'm outside her house but no one is answering the door. Put Phoebe on."

Toby told me to wait, and then I heard a muffled conversation, and finally Phoebe got the phone and asked me what was going on.

"I don't know," I said, my voice cracking. "Cassidy isn't home and she isn't answering her phone. Didn't you two get your hair done together or something?"

"No," Phoebe said. I could hear the frown in her voice. "I haven't talked to her since yesterday."

"I talked to her this afternoon," I said doubtfully. "Can you call her? Maybe she's just avoiding *me*."

"Sure," Phoebe said. "Hold on, I'll use my phone."

I heard the noise of the restaurant, and the faraway sound of a cell phone ringing, and then a faint beep and "Hey, leave me a message in a hundred forty characters or less . . ."

"Sorry." It was Phoebe again. "She didn't pick up."

"So I heard."

We studied each other's silence.

"Maybe her hair appointment went late?" Phoebe suggested.

"Maybe." I didn't sound very optimistic.

"Well, Austin just got here and oh my God, his date is full-on goth, I'm not kidding. She's wearing black lipstick and everything."

There was a bit of noise as Toby grabbed the phone back.

"We have to go make fun of Austin now. Let me know when you're on your way, okay?"

"I will," I promised. "Go ahead and order without us."

I hung up and put on the playlist I'd made for tonight, listening to the Kooks croon about the seaside while I waited for a car to pull into the driveway, or a light to flicker on, or my phone to buzz. But none of those things happened.

After a couple songs, I put on my seat belt and pulled away from the curb. Something felt wrong. She was always waiting for me. Always there, with her flashlight in her bedroom window, always hurrying down the front walk with a smile on her face, never late or missing.

More than anything, I was worried. I pictured her in a ditch on the hiking trails, a car accident on the side of the freeway, lying in one of those patient annexes surrounded by a flimsy curtain in the ER. I pictured her tragically; it never once occurred to me to picture her as the tragedy.

Since I didn't know what to do, I wound up driving around Eastwood. Driving always calmed me, especially at night, with the streetlights wavering slightly out of focus and the empty roads and the dark stretches of the old ranch lands.

And then I passed the castle park, and something made

me stop. One figure atop the highest turret, the one with the steering wheel. A girl.

I pulled into the lot, my heart pounding in my ears, not wanting to know but unable to stop myself from finding out.

There were stadium lights trained on the tennis courts, the overflow casting a soft glow against the concrete castle. As soon as I stepped out of my car, I could see it; the unmistakable green of Cassidy's favorite sweater.

I crossed the grass, calling out to her. She jumped down from the turret easily, vaulting over the castle's sandbox terraces and walking across the playground.

As she came toward me, I took in her jeans and plaid shirt, her sneakers, her hair in its ponytail. She looked like a girl who had no intention of attending a formal dance, and whatever this was about, it wasn't going to be good.

"What are you doing here?" Her expression was dark and cold, like I was the last person she wanted to see, and the anger in her voice confused me.

"The dance," I said, forcing myself to smile, to make a joke of it. "Remember?"

Cassidy opened her mouth as if to say something, but then she stopped herself.

"I'm not going," she informed me, as though it should have been obvious.

"Okay. Well, maybe you should have told me that before?" I shrugged helplessly.

The stadium lights seemed harsh all of a sudden, like the

lights they use in operating rooms.

"Go away, Ezra," Cassidy pleaded. "Please, just go."

"No," I said stubbornly.

Cassidy glared at me, her eyes not so much filling with tears as lacking the capacity to hold any more of them.

"God, can't you see that you're the last person I want to talk to right now?" she asked.

"Yeah, actually," I said. "And I have no idea why."

"It's complicated." Cassidy wrapped her arms around herself as though she was cold, and my first instinct was to offer her my jacket, but of course I didn't. Not with the two of us standing on top of that grassy hill in the castle park, a corsage going limp in the passenger seat of my car while our friends ate their entrees at a table with empty seats.

"Maybe you can explain it to me anyway?"

"Oh, honey." She'd never called me that before, and I didn't like it. "Isn't it obvious? You. Me. Dating. I was amusing myself. And then my boyfriend drove down from San Francisco to surprise me. He just ran to the gas station to buy cigarettes. You probably don't want to be here when he gets back."

Cassidy nodded toward the neon lights of the gas station, which was just across the street. I thought about going in there and punching that asscanoe right in the face. But then Cassidy sniffled, and asked me again to leave.

We stood there, coolly regarding each other. The castle park was behind her, like a photograph of a night we'd shared a million years and two weeks ago.

"I—just—the whole time, it's been someone else?" I said numbly.

She cocked her head slightly, her hand on her hip, as though it pained her to have to explain it to me.

"How could it have been you? My God, Ezra, look at yourself. You're a washed-up prom king who lost his virginity to some cheerleader in a hot tub. You take me out for burgers and Friday-night movies at the multiplex. You're everything I make fun of about small hick towns like this one, and you're still going to be here in twenty years, coaching the high-school tennis team so you can relive your glory days."

Back when they'd reset the broken bone in my wrist, I'd woken up on the operating table. It was just for a moment, before the doctors upped the anesthesia, but in those seconds when the lights were bright and hot and the surgeons were bent over me with my blood dripping from their scalpels, I'd felt as though I'd woken into a nightmare.

Hearing Cassidy say those things was worse. Because I hadn't been broken when I'd left my house an hour earlier, with a wrist corsage of white roses still cold from the refrigerator, but I was certainly broken now.

I stared at her, horrified. Her chin jutted stubbornly and her eyes were a hurricane, and there was nowhere for me to seek cover.

"Okay," I said hollowly. "Sorry. I just—sorry."

I turned and walked away.

"Ezra!" she called desperately, as though I was the one who was being unreasonable.

I paused, considering it, but what more was there to say? And then I continued my funeral march toward the parking lot.

The death of a relationship. At least I was dressed for the wake.

My phone was a grocery list of missed calls, but I didn't feel like dealing with them. Instead, I drove home in the cooling darkness, past the ghostly stretch of white birch trees and around the loop that encircled Eastwood like a noose.

I jammed my brakes at a stop sign that had gone up recently, and the corsage flew forward, landing on the floor. I left it there, sliding back and forth, its petals bruising with each curve of the road.

"Ezra?" my mom called when I came in.

"Yeah, hi."

She could see it in my face that something was deeply, horribly wrong. And that I didn't want to talk about it.

"Aren't you going to the dance, honey?" she asked.

"No."

I went upstairs, Cooper following worriedly, and slammed the door, barricading the two of us inside. I lay down on top of the bed in my suit and closed my eyes.

This is how they bury you, I thought. In your best suit,

the one you wear to weddings and funerals, a suit that girls have draped over their shoulders on cold nights and dry cleaners have absolved of all stains.

Suddenly, I couldn't stand wearing the thing. She'd picked it out for me, and I felt sick at the thought.

Cooper whined nervously, his tail thumping against the duvet as I stripped down to my boxers. I stared up at the ceiling fan, but the propellers reminded me of my old car, the BMW logo, so I turned over, burying my face in my pillow.

That was when I heard it: the alarm on my phone. Homecoming court. The results. And I couldn't have cared less.

The alarm continued to trill in two-minute intervals as I lay there undressed and miserable in the darkness. I cried for my brokenness, for the way her words had crippled me, and for the three unspoken words I'd been carrying with me for a while now, and how quickly one of them had changed.

"I hate you, Cassidy Thorpe," I whispered. "I hate you."

25

THERE'S A CLOCK in Mr. Choi's calculus classroom that has sixty-two seconds in each minute. I've counted it before, fascinated with the discrepancy, but not really believing in it. There was something wrong with the clock, not with time itself.

That weekend, there was something wrong with time. It passed in an agony of drawn-out minutes and lost hours. I neglected my phone and shut the blinds and endured my misery until it was time for school and I slunk out the door with two days' stubble and unfinished homework.

It felt strange driving to school alone, as though I was forgetting something. I stared out at the migrant workers in the strawberry fields, breaking their backs to harvest off-season fruit, and I thought about how I'd rather do that today. Feel the sun baking the back of my neck while I engaged in the sort of activity that occupied my mind just enough to push back the pain of what had happened. But no, I had a test in Calculus.

I flunked the test, badly. It was as though my brain didn't want to solve for the rate of acceleration, as though it just wanted to hit the brakes and not accelerate at all. Decelerate. Whatever.

When I handed in my answer sheet at the bell, Anamica looked up from her desk and glared at me.

"Well, well," she said, sliding her calculator into its case with unnecessary force. "If it isn't the homecoming king."

I'm fairly certain that the correct response to that isn't, "Uh, what?" but that's what I said.

Anamica sighed and thrust a copy of the school paper at me. Sure enough, the front page featured the picture from the pep rally, with all of us holding our Royal Roses and none of us looking at the camera. I supposed they'd wanted to take a shot of us at the dance, dressed formally and all, but I'd wrecked that.

Ezra Faulkner and Jillian Nakamura Named Homecoming King and Queen. *Article and photos by Phoebe Chang,* the subhead read.

"Right," I said, still in shock. "Wow. Yeah, so apparently that happened."

"You were supposed to escort me," Anamica accused. "When all the nominees walked to the stage. I had to go alone because you ditched."

"Sorry," I muttered as Justin Wong clapped me on the shoulder.

"Yo, Faulkner! Congrats," he called, already halfway out the door to break.

"Thanks." I stood there, sort of dazed, while a few more of my classmates added their well wishes. I'd gotten ready for school that morning in a fog of low-hanging misery, hoping I could muddle through the day largely unnoticed, but clearly that wasn't going to happen.

Tony Masters walked past and yanked the strap of Anamica's backpack. "Don't worry, Joke Vote, you'll win teacher's pet in the Senior Shout-outs for sure."

Anamica shot me a dirty look, like she blamed me for that as well, and suddenly I just needed to get out of there. The last thing I wanted to talk about was why I'd missed the homecoming court announcement, and the last person I wanted to talk about it with was Anamica Patel.

"I'm sorry," I said, and then fled the classroom, taking a back staircase to avoid the quad.

Homecoming king. And I'd been lying facedown on my bed in a pair of boxer shorts and a heap of despair when they'd announced it.

You'd think I would have been able to sense the entire school standing there, confused, as my name was called and I was nowhere to be found. You'd think someone—Toby, Phoebe, even Austin—would have texted. But of course my phone had been off, and still was. I'd extracted a disturbing amount of pleasure from watching it die on my bedside table, denying it a charge.

I wasn't headed anywhere in particular, just avoiding seeing anyone, so I wound up sitting in my car, wishing I had the courage to drive off but knowing the security guard would harass me.

When the bell rang, I decided I wasn't going to class. Instead, I disappeared inside my hoodie at one of the back tables in the library, listening to my old Dylan playlist from the summer and remembering when I'd first heard this music, in the waiting room of Dr. Cohen's office, the perfect sound track for my personal hell. By the time I looked up, the quad was already filled for lunch and the librarian was staring at me like she didn't know if I should be allowed to sit there all day.

I got up, trying to mentally prepare myself for the ordeal of going out there and facing the whole school as their homecoming king. I looked terrible; my hair was a mess and I hadn't bothered to shave all weekend. The dark circles under my eyes were turning into parabola, and I'd thrown on a T-shirt that had definitely seen better days.

My eyes went automatically to Toby's table: Phoebe spotted me and waved, but I hesitated, not feeling up to it. And then Evan McMillan's booming voice cut above the tension in the quad: "Yo, Faulkner! Get your royal ass over here!"

Suddenly, I knew what I had to do. And maybe I'd known it all along. So I nodded at Evan and walked over there with the whole school watching, to that choice lunch table next to the wall that separates the upper and lower quads, like I'd never been gone.

I endured the tennis team's backslapping and clowning with a good-natured grimace and waited for someone to offer me a seat at the already crowded table.

"Trevor, get up," Evan grunted at one of the juniors.

"Fuck you, I'm on crutches," Trevor grumbled.

He was, too. One of those superficial sports injuries, the kind that takes you out for a game. Trevor reached questioningly for a crutch, but I shook my head.

"Save it for me," I said. "I have to buy lunch."

But I made no move toward the lunch line. For one thing, I had no appetite, and for another, I didn't trust myself to come back. But it didn't matter, since I couldn't have gotten away if I'd wanted to—half the song squad wanted to give me hugs, because omigod, wasn't it like soooo epic that I'd won homecoming king and where had I been during the announcement?

I mumbled something about having a fight with Cassidy, and they all cooed in the way that girls do, as though sad things and cute puppies are interchangeable.

"Nah, it's fine," I said, uncomfortable from all of the attention. "Honestly."

Charlotte sat there on top of the wall, swinging her long, tanned legs back and forth as she watched everything.

"Just to be clear," she said, hopping down from the wall and tossing her hair in one fluid motion, "you had a fight, or you broke up?"

I allowed myself to say it.

"We broke up."

"It's about time." Charlotte rested her hand on my arm for the briefest of moments. "Oh, and welcome back."

The homecoming king's homecoming. The ridiculous phrase lodged itself in my head and stayed there for the rest of the lunch period, when finally Aaron Hersh got up so I could have a seat, and Charlotte went off to the lunch line with Jill and Emma Rosen, the three of them returning, giggling, with a turkey sandwich and a yellow Gatorade and extra mustard packets, insisting that I didn't have to pay them back.

I glanced over toward Toby's lunch table while I unwrapped the sandwich, and it was as though the past six weeks had never happened. Cassidy had vanished, leaving just Phoebe and the boys and too much room between them on the benches.

Luke caught me staring and gave an arrogant toss of his chin as if to say, *You stay on your side, and I'll stay on mine.*

"Faulkner? Whaddaya say?" Jimmy threw a curly fry at me, trying to get my attention.

I scooped the fry off my jeans and tossed it back into his container. "Have fun eating it, now that it's been on my crotch."

Everyone laughed. Jimmy shrugged before tilting the container of fries up to his face, emptying it.

"Don't care," he said. "So you coming or not?"

"Where?" I asked.

"Practice, yo."

For a moment, I thought he was joking.

"Someone's gotta keep Trev here company on the benches," Evan insisted.

I guessed there was no half-assing a descent into hell, so I said I'd show. And really, what was the alternative? Sit in my bedroom trying to pretend my mom wasn't hovering worriedly outside my door and that Cassidy's presence wasn't haunting me from across the park?

When the bell rang, launching me toward sixth-period physics, I passed the bike rack and something made me look for Cassidy's red Cannondale. But it wasn't there. Of course it wasn't. And neither was Cassidy Thorpe.

TREVOR AND I took opposite ends of the bench by the water fountain and nodded at each other. I didn't know him too well; he was a junior, and I thought I remembered him hawking Abercrombie and Fitch's official fragrance with his shirt off when Charlotte used to drag me to the mall, but that wasn't exactly a topic of conversation, so I didn't bring it up.

A group of tennis team girlfriends came by and sat around the picnic table by the water fountain. They chatted among themselves, none of them particularly interested in watching the courts.

"Hey Ezra," Emma called teasingly, holding up a bottle of nail polish. "Want me to do yours?"

"Absolutely," I deadpanned, dropping into the seat next to hers with a grin.

For a moment, she thought I was serious.

"Faulkner!" Evan called from the courts. "Hit some volleys with Trev, would you?"

I glanced up from my table of other people's girlfriends. "Can't!" I yelled. "My nails are wet."

"They are *not!*" Emma squealed. "I haven't even started!"

"Rain check, then," I promised, winking.

"So, uh, want me to grab some racquets?" Trevor asked nervously.

"Go for it," I said. I mean, why not?

We shared a court with Evan and Jimmy, using the crappy loaner racquets Coach kept in the locker room. Trevor, who only had a minor ankle sprain, tossed his crutches to the side, and hopped up to the volley line. I'd seen him play on JV, but hadn't expected him to move up to varsity before his senior year.

I put down my cane and stepped onto the court. And it hit me then that Trevor would be fine next week, but I'd still be sitting on the sidelines. I'd always be sitting on the sidelines, and this whole thing was just an elaborately cruel reminder that I could never go back to the way things had been, no matter where I sat during lunch.

I sent Trevor a couple of easy volleys and then some harder ones. It felt great to hold a racquet again; I'd taken off my brace about a week earlier, and the doctors were right, my wrist had healed up fine. But of course I couldn't really play—not a full game, not ever—and there was no use in kidding myself.

Unfortunately, Coach Anthony caught us coming off the court.

"Faulkner," he said coldly.

"Yeah, hey Coach," I said, realizing I was holding a racquet and a cane.

"Are you on my team, Faulkner?" Coach demanded.

"No, Coach."

"Then why are you on my court?"

I winced.

"Um," I said.

"We were just foolin' around, Coach," Trevor said, shifting on his crutches.

"Fooling around?" Coach's mouth twisted sourly. "Isn't that how you got injured in the first place, Barnes?"

Trevor mumbled that it was.

"Keep off my courts, gentlemen," Coach demanded, "until you can run three field laps with a racquet above your head. I'll require a demonstration, of course."

"Yes, Coach," we muttered, and then slunk back to the benches.

"Three racquet laps, damn." Trevor whistled at the punishment.

Three racquet laps, I thought. What I wouldn't give to be able to run even one. But of course I didn't say anything. Instead, I stretched out on the bench like I was enjoying myself but secretly wishing I'd never come back.

"Omigod!" Emma shrieked, sounding scared. "What's that?"

She pointed toward the far side of the tennis courts where some large animal was slinking through the bushes that rimmed the foothills, its fur coppery in the sun.

"Yo, that's a coyote," Trevor muttered, nervous.

But as soon as we spotted it, the bushes stopped rustling; the animal was heading back into the hills.

"That's weird," I said, "you don't usually see them during the day."

"Maybe it wasn't really a coyote," Emma teased, making her voice spooky. "Or maybe, it was looking for you."

MY MOM CORNERED me when I got home from school. She'd called twice, apparently. I hadn't picked up my phone.

"Where were you?" she demanded, more worried than upset.

"Tennis practice," I said, and she thought I was joking.

"Ezra." She glared that mom glare. Cooper, who was dozing on the rug under the kitchen sink, woke up and whined guiltily. "Sit down."

I sat. Lifted my eyes from the place mat as though it was an ordeal. Waited.

"Did you get that girl pregnant? Is that what's going on here?"

Out of all the things I expected my mom to say, that was so far down the list that it was practically on the waiting list.

"Yeah, and you can plan the *bris*," I muttered, which wasn't my finest moment. "No, Mom. *God*."

We stared at each other, and she softened, sensing exactly why I'd been moping in my room all weekend.

"Ezra, honey," she cooed. "Girls change their minds. It happens. Lord knows I broke enough hearts in my day."

"Mom," I moaned, putting my head down.

"I'm just saying, honey. A shower and shave wouldn't hurt. You can still be miserable *and clean*."

"That," I said sarcastically, "is *awesome* advice."

"Tone," she cautioned, pouring us each a glass of unsweetened juice. "How's school?"

"I won homecoming king." I said it in the way Toby's friends used to when they made serious announcements—a hint of a smirk, like maybe it wasn't true, but wouldn't it be hilarious if it were?

"Really?" She raised an eyebrow.

"Really."

"Well, that's wonderful," Mom said, all false cheer. "I bet that girl's kicking herself for throwing you over now."

I didn't have the heart to tell her otherwise.

26

CASSIDY STILL WASN'T back in school on Tuesday. Mrs. Martin, who clearly thought she was being very astute, singled me out during roll to ask if I knew where Senorita Thorpe had gone. The class laughed in this uncomfortable, knowing way while I muttered, "*No se, Señora,*" and wished I could disappear.

I had PT that afternoon, so I conjured some flimsy excuse to get out of hanging around the tennis courts that I doubt anyone believed, and I drove over to the UC Eastwood Medical Complex with my windows down.

The weather was gorgeous, and as the warmth streamed through my car, I replayed a conversation from lunch that day, when Jimmy had announced that outie bellybuttons looked like nipples. Evan had laughed so hard that he'd snorted Sprite, and the whole thing had been hilarious if you didn't think about it for too long, in which case it became incredibly depressing. The truth was, I didn't understand how it had suddenly turned so painful to be around Evan and Jimmy when we'd been teammates since the ninth grade.

The three of us had been the only freshmen to make varsity tennis. But sitting there at the lunch table we'd inherited, thinking back to the first upperclassmen party we'd attended, the three of us nervously wearing our letter jackets like they proved we were cool, it made me wonder whether we'd ever had anything in common besides taking crap from the seniors a year longer than the rest of our teammates.

It frustrated me, listening to conversations that consisted mostly of gossip and unfunny jokes told at someone's expense, holding back my clever remarks and pretending to enjoy myself. It was as though I'd gone off on epic adventures, chased down fireworks and buried treasure, danced to music that only I could hear, and had returned to find that nothing had changed except for me. But maybe it was better this way, remembering those few months at the beginning of the year as this wonderful thing that was over now, rather than living in Cassidy's world without her.

Dr. Levine had me go through the usual exercises and do a couple of sets on the elliptical. We chatted about how I was doing, and if I'd been to see Dr. Cohen lately, and I don't know what made me say it, but I asked if it was possible to ditch the cane.

Dr. Levine regarded me thoughtfully for a moment, and then looked down at my chart.

"I think we could try that for a week or so to see how

you get on," he said, "so long as you understand that you'll be working with your current range of motion, which really is on the borderline."

I said that I understood, and he went on to depress me with a list of cautions and don'ts and definite don'ts that came along with a stack of pamphlets.

I zipped the pamphlets into my backpack and stepped into the hallway, thinking it was lucky I'd kept that stupid elevator key after all. The bathroom where I usually changed out of my sweaty exercise clothes was out of order, so I used the one at the other end of the hall, near the north elevator.

I had to pass by Dr. Cohen's office, and I hesitated outside for a moment. I hadn't been there since the summer, when I'd quickly figured out what to say to get out of the weekly trauma of trauma counseling. It was strange, passing a door and knowing exactly where it led, and how lousy my life had been when I'd last used it, a sort of anti-nostalgia.

The door to the waiting room opened and a girl stepped out. She was wearing a red and yellow Rancho cheer uniform, and she caught my eye with an embarrassed smile before heading toward the stairs.

I didn't feel like going home, so I wound up crossing the pedestrian bridge and wandering around UCE's campus. The campus was smaller than I remembered, and with my backpack and leather jacket, I disappeared instantly into the crowd of students. It was a welcome relief, feeling as though I was invisible after the last few days, when staring at me had become an extracurricular activity the whole school had apparently signed up for.

Being there reminded me of the day Cassidy and I had pretended to be students here, but then, I'd known it would. I thought about how she'd made that crown of flowers by the creek, laughing at me when I told her I'd probably wind up at some nearby state school, that I didn't really have any plans to leave Orange County. She was right, though. I didn't belong here, in a dorm room ten miles from home, falling asleep every night to the only slightly more distant thud of the Disneyland fireworks.

I guess I half hoped to see Cassidy exiting a building, wearing jeans and sneakers, her disguise. I pictured her looking up, secretly glad that I'd found her. We'd sit down on one of those wooden benches and she'd tell me how she was sorry, and it had all been a mistake. But things like that never happen, except in really awful movies.

I wandered into the library, where the girl at the desk waved me through without looking up from the book she was reading. I hadn't really expected her to let me in, or thought about what I would do once I was inside. But I had a backpack full of textbooks, and there was this comfortable-looking lounge area, so I sat down and took out my homework and put on my headphones. But I'd chosen a sofa with a view of the entrance, stupidly hoping Cassidy would walk in.

Of course she never did, and after a while, I stopped

looking up every time the door opened. It was incredibly peaceful sitting there, listening to an old Frank Turner album and puzzling through my physics worksheets over a surprisingly good cup of campus coffee. By the time I packed up, I wondered if I'd really been looking for Cassidy after all, or if I'd been hoping to find myself.

I DON'T KNOW what I expected when I slunk into Speech and Debate on Wednesday. Certainly not for Cassidy to glance up from some thick book she was reading, this terrible sadness in her eyes.

"You're back," I said, a statement that only served to multiply the awkwardness between us.

"What happened to your cane?"

"I'm fine without it." I slid clumsily into my chair, unfortunately proving the exact opposite. The coffee I was holding splattered across our shared desk.

"Sorry," I said, fishing some tissues out of my backpack to mop up the table. "Overfilled it."

Cassidy closed her eyes and took a deep breath, like she was holding herself back from saying and doing a million things at once.

She picked up her book, angling it like a shield. The desk dried slowly between us, smelling faintly of French roast.

Ms. Weng didn't even notice that I'd been absent. She'd come down with a cold and was determined not to waste her sick days, so she put on some documentary about the history of public speaking and dimmed the lights.

Cassidy squinted at her book in the dim glow from the television, and I tried and failed to pay attention to the DVD. The air around us crackled with tension, the tension of an accusation I wasn't going to make, a relationship we'd once had, and an explanation I was fairly certain neither of us believed.

If she thought I was such a joke, if she'd had another boyfriend all along, then she should have been laughing in the aftermath of our breakup, not acting like she wanted to disappear entirely. Something had happened. Something important. Even though the signs all pointed to a mundane explanation: the way Cassidy sometimes wore boys' clothes, the background photo on her phone with the boy she claimed was her brother, the way she'd never had me over to her house, like I'd needed to be hidden or kept away, I couldn't bring myself to believe it. Any of it.

I BECAME A regular in the UC Eastwood library that week, driving there every day after school to get my homework done. I was used to my afternoons being filled with activities—tennis, student government committee meetings, even that horrible SAT prep class I'd taken with like half of the AP kids in my year. And then there had been the debate team, and Toby and Cassidy to fill my afternoons. It was disarming having endless swaths of free time, and I was oddly thankful my advisor had signed me up for so many advanced courses, since I could stretch out my homework for hours if I did it thoroughly enough.

I could tell my mom was worried about me, because when I got home from the library on Thursday, she'd taken my cane out of the closet and propped it against the door of my bedroom like she thought maybe I'd just forgotten I had one, instead of decided to stop using it altogether.

But there was something comforting about the pain of getting around without it. Something reassuring about having a physical ache to hold on to, this pain that was a part of me independent of Cassidy. I thought about the metal in my knee, replacing this piece of me that was missing, that no longer worked. And it wasn't my heart, I kept telling myself. It wasn't my heart.

27

WHEN I CAUGHT up with Toby and Phoebe at the coffee cart on Friday, they seemed surprised, and not entirely pleased, to see me.

"Hi," I said sheepishly, stepping into line behind them.

"Oh, am I allowed to talk to you?" Toby faked concern. "Or will your grunty jock friends shove me up against the lockers?"

I snickered at the joke. Our school didn't have lockers, since we each got a personal set of textbooks to keep at home.

"Well, you look miserable," Toby said.

"Cassidy and I broke up." Like the whole school hadn't known for days.

"I said miserable, not heartbroken, you asscanoe," Toby corrected. "And you could have at least returned my texts after I took care of your absence on Monday."

I'd been wondering about that.

"Yeah, thanks," I said. "The lack of detention was awesome."

It was so easy to slip back into the way I used to be around them that standing together in the coffee line made me miss them even more than I'd thought possible.

"I've been sort of avoiding my phone lately," I explained lamely.

Phoebe smiled hesitantly and started to say something, but then changed her mind.

"No cane," she said instead.

"I traded it for some magic beans and the dictatorship of a small Middle Eastern country."

"An unfortunately arid climate in which magic beans don't exactly thrive," Toby pointed out drily.

"Knew I was getting screwed on that deal somehow." I faked disappointment.

Phoebe laughed, and Toby started talking about how, in the event my magic beans did grow, I should order my subjects to go gleaning, and the three of us standing there making ridiculous jokes was the happiest I'd felt in a long time.

"Listen," I said, "I wanted to—"

"Ezra! Hiii!" Charlotte squealed, hugging me with an intimacy that she'd conjured out of nowhere. Jill and Emma materialized next to her, and the three of them joined our place at the front of the line like they knew exactly what they were doing and were confident they'd get away with it.

"You don't mind, do you?" Charlotte asked sweetly, cutting in front of Phoebe to give her coffee order.

Phoebe's expression darkened, and she mumbled something at her shoes. Toby coughed meaningfully.

"Ezra was saving our spot, weren't you, sweetie?" Jill patted me on the arm.

"Yeah, of course," I said hollowly, wincing as I heard the words come out of my mouth.

Toby looked disgusted, and I didn't blame him.

CASSIDY WAS CURLED in her seat in Speech and Debate, two-thirds of the way through the novel from Wednesday. I sat down quietly and took out a book of my own. She glanced over and sighed, shifting away from me in her chair, my presence actually making her recoil.

"Seriously?" I whispered.

"What?" Cassidy frowned, apparently unaware.

"You can't even stand to sit next to me now?"

Cassidy put down her book and studied me for a moment, and whatever she was looking for, she obviously didn't find it. "Well, we don't *really* need to keep sitting next to each other."

"Fine," I said stiffly, standing up.

I moved to an empty table a few down from the one where we usually sat, and Ms. Weng came in and put on that awful documentary, and Cassidy and I glared at our respective books and occasionally each other in the thin light from the tinted windows.

After a while, I felt a tap on my shoulder, and I nearly jumped a mile.

"Come with me," Toby said.

I hadn't even heard him come in.

Ms. Weng had abandoned us to the DVD, so I grabbed my bag and followed Toby into the Annex.

"Don't do this," Toby said, leaning against the center table. It was covered with a mess of papers he'd been grading and the world's most outdated iPod, which was leaking what sounded suspiciously like opera through its headphones.

"Do what?" I asked.

"You're severed head-ing me!" Toby accused angrily.

"I have no idea what that means!" I honestly didn't. But Toby was serious.

"Really?" His voice dripped scorn. "Remember my twelfth birthday? The severed head? How all of a sudden, we weren't friends anymore."

"Are you calling Cassidy a *severed head*?"

"No, Faulkner. I'm calling *you* an idiot. You're pushing me away, exactly like you did in the seventh grade."

Toby glared at me, and I crossed my arms, glaring back.

"In case you forgot, you were the one who caught that head," I said. "It was nothing to do with me."

"I'm not talking about that stupid head, Faulkner! I'm talking about you. *I* was the fat kid who drew comic books. I was going to be bullied no matter what. You act like that day at Disneyland was my big tragedy, but *you're* the one who lost your best friend. You're the one who started eating lunch with the popular jocks and forgot how to be awesome because you were too busy being cool. We could have still hung out after school if you'd asked, if you'd wanted to. But you just dropped me because everyone expected you to. And you're doing it again, and it sucks."

I stared at Toby in horror, realizing that he was right. I had pushed him away. To be fair, we'd been twelve, and I'd considered it a miracle that I'd looked and dressed and hit a ball well enough to be spared the brunt of that hell. But it had honestly never occurred to me that I didn't have to lose my best friend that year. That I had a choice.

"So I'm an asshole," I said.

"Well yeah. Insert gay joke about my liking assholes here." Toby shrugged, trying not to grin.

"Well, I would. But then that would make me a dick."

Toby snorted. "Touché."

"I'm sorry I severed-headed you. I just, I don't know. The whole Cassidy debacle."

I sighed and glanced toward the door to Ms. Weng's room.

"Yeah, thanks for texting. We waited for you two at the Fiesta Palace *forever*," Toby complained.

"Sorry," I muttered, feeling awful.

"How'd she do it, anyhow? Make you stop at some coffee place and then break your heart at the table?"

"No," I said bitterly, "because that would have been somewhat decent of her. As it happens, she just never showed up. I found her in the castle park, on a date with another guy."

Toby dropped the pen he'd been fiddling with. "You're joking," he said. "On the night of the dance?"

"What does it matter? She wasn't really planning to go." I shrugged gloomily.

"Of course she was!" Toby insisted. "She texted me pictures of this five-hundred-dollar dress asking if you'd like it and dragged Phoebe to every shoe store in Eastwood."

"You're serious?" I asked.

"Here, Faulkner. Behold the girly texts," Toby said, holding out his phone. "And note that I put up with them solely due to our friendship."

"I believe you," I said, but Toby was determined. I stared down at the picture Cassidy had sent him, a mirror snap in some fancy dressing room. She was making a silly face as she posed barefoot in a gold dress. I could see Phoebe in the background, trying to edge out of the picture.

"Okay," Toby said gingerly, prying the phone away from me. "Showing you that was a bad idea, dude. Your hands are shaking."

But I was barely listening. What I was thinking about was how these texts, this picture, proved it. Cassidy had meant to go to the dance with me after all. More importantly, it meant she'd lied that night in the park.

"Here's what you're going to do," Toby told me. "You're going to start at the beginning. Use of the introduction 'Once upon a time, my awesome best friend warned me about a girl, but I didn't listen' is optional."

He probably meant that I should start at the beginning of Saturday night, but there were so many parts I'd left out that I couldn't. I needed to go back further. So I told him everything: how Cassidy had made me cheat for her at the debate tournament, how we'd kissed during the Disneyland fireworks and communicated by flashlights, how perfect it all was, and the terrible things she'd said the night of the dance, about my being a small-town joke destined to coach the tennis team in a pathetic attempt to relive my glory days.

"It's like she wanted to make you hate her." Toby frowned. "That's the sort of untrue but awful thing you say to ensure that someone never speaks to you again."

"She can't even stand to be around me, and I didn't *do* anything," I said despairingly.

"You really know how to pick 'em, don't you?" Toby joked.

"I think I'm cursed."

"I wouldn't say cursed," Toby mused. "More like suffering the aftermath of a personal tragedy."

The aftermath of a personal tragedy. I liked that. It sounded appropriately gloomy.

"Yeah, probably," I said. And I felt unspeakably grateful to him. For putting up with me, for pulling me out of class and forcing me to talk about what had happened, even though I'd been kind of a dick lately. For being an actual friend, and not just someone with whom I'd shared a lunch table, or competed for the same team. Because if there was anyone who could help me find the answers I was looking for, it was Toby.

"Listen," I said. "I know it's crazy, but I have this feeling that I'm missing this massive piece of what happened. And I have to know. I have to find out the truth about Cassidy Thorpe, and I need your help."

Of course he'd help. Whatever I needed, because that's how it worked, the whole best friends thing. Toby was staring at me like he couldn't believe I'd half expected them to refuse. And I thought: Toby, Phoebe, Austin, they would have visited me in the hospital, not just sent some cheesy card. They wouldn't have asked me to come to tennis practice and pick up a racquet just to win some stupid bet.

Because Cassidy had been wrong about one thing in that desperate lie she'd delivered that night in the park. It wasn't me that would still be here in twenty years, coaching the high-school tennis team in a frantic bid to relive my glory days: it was Evan.

28

MY MOM WAS waiting for me with two enormous Halloween pumpkins and a set of carving knives when I got home, evidently harboring the delusion that I'd find such an activity fun.

"I thought you could use some cheering up," she said, gesturing toward the kitchen table, which was blanketed in at least a dozen layers of newsprint and guilt. So I sat and we carved smiling faces into our pumpkins and chatted until I was reasonably certain she wouldn't make me participate in any more cheering-up activities in the foreseeable future.

"I made you an appointment with Dr. Cohen," Mom said when she put our finished jack-o'-lanterns by the front door.

I stopped clicking the little LED on and off and stared at her in horror, realizing that this had been her itinerary all along. The pumpkins were just the first stop on her all-expenses-paid guilt trip.

"Mom, no."

Cooper, who was investigating the pumpkins, stared up at me, wondering why I was so upset.

"One appointment," Mom said firmly. "You're supposed to check in, you know this. Can you hand me that light?"

I scowled and handed her the LED I'd been playing with.

"I don't need to see a therapist."

Mom sighed. Adjusted the jack-o'-lantern. Made it clear we weren't discussing this on the front steps because, God forbid, the neighbors might overhear. Finally, she closed the front door and pursed her lips at my attitude.

"I'm *fine*," I insisted. "I got dumped, that's all."

"This isn't negotiable," Mom said. "I'm sorry, honey, but your father and I agree on this one. I made you an appointment after school on Wednesday."

"What if I'm not exactly jumping at the chance to drive myself over there and talk to a doctor about my personal life?" I asked.

I knew I was being an ass, but I didn't care. She couldn't just spring this on me. Expect me to go back to that office where the last time Dr. Cohen had seen me, I'd been on crutches, my pocket rattling with a bottle of prescription painkillers, trying to get over the news that I'd never play college sports. To have to catch him up on all of the things he'd never understand, about Cassidy and Toby and my old friends. To discuss my life like it was the plot of some novel

I'd read but hadn't really understood.

"You can sulk about it all you want," Mom warned, "but if you miss that appointment, you're losing your car privileges for the month. Even for school. I don't mind driving you, you know."

"Great," I said, wandering into the kitchen so I could glare at the pantry because of course she wouldn't have bought any Halloween candy. At least I wasn't in danger of suffering from *kummerspeck*, or emotion-related overeating, in our house.

LUKE HELD ANOTHER floating movie theater on Saturday night, some sort of classic fright fest in the gym, and of course I wasn't invited. Toby insisted that I should just come anyhow, but I didn't think it would go over well. In the end, I wound up attending Jill's big Halloween party, which I'd halfway been planning to back out of at the last minute.

I just wanted to stay home, since I'd been sort of exhausted lately. But it turned out I couldn't spend Halloween watching my mom hand out those little boxes of raisins to dismayed trick-or-treaters while my dad typed up some important document in his home office, sighing every time the doorbell rang. So I picked up some plastic fangs and body glitter on my way over to Jill's. It was pretty pathetic, and I doubted anyone at the party would get that I meant it ironically, but it was all I could manage on short notice.

Jill lived in one of the older subdivisions on the lake, where most of the homes had been purchased for their lots and then rebuilt. Her backyard had a private dock, and her parents kept a sailboat there. Every year for her Halloween party, Jill decorated it as a ghost ship, complete with cobwebs and a Jolly Roger flag and a hull filled with beer.

Junior year, the entire tennis team had come dressed in bedsheet togas and played so many rounds of flip cup that I was still drunk when I woke up the next morning, something I hadn't even known was possible.

The party was going strong when I got there. All of the girls seemed to be in costumes that consisted largely of lingerie and high heels, not that I was complaining. The football team had claimed a keg in the living room and some guys were attempting keg stands through a Hillary Clinton mask, which was just baffling enough to be plausible, since Connor MacLeary was involved. I walked past two girls in the kitchen in the same stripper Dorothy costume, who were screaming at each other while their friend tried to break it up by saying, "You guys! It's not like you're wearing the same prom dress!"

I tried not to laugh as I opened the screen door and stepped through into the backyard. I was starting to get the unfortunate impression that I'd arrived at the party too late. Some sophomores, whom I doubted had been invited, were already sick in the bushes, and cups littered the grass.

"Ezra!" Charlotte said, launching herself at me. She was a bit unsteady in her high heels, and seemed to be dressed as a Disney princess with a penchant for pole-dancing. "You came!"

"Of course," I said. "Who could miss a pirate ship full of beer?"

"How come you're not wearing a costume?" Charlotte asked. I couldn't tell if she was teasing me.

"I'm a vampire," I insisted, popping in the plastic fangs.

"Hmmm." Charlotte considered this. "It's more realistic without the fangs. Come on."

She giggled and dragged me over to a picnic table crowded with our friends. I'd missed the theme, apparently. The girls were all sexy Disney princesses, and the guys were in zombie makeup, convincingly slack-jawed by the girls' revealing costumes.

"Dude, you made it!" Jimmy enthused, sloshing beer out of his Solo cup. It was as though he thought I was actually the life of the party, or maybe he always got too drunk to remember that I wasn't.

The party was a mess, filled with the kinds of things you regretted doing when they spilled out into the schoolwide rumor mill on Monday. After flirting heavily, Trevor and Jill wandered away to hook up, and apparently Trevor threw up in the middle of it. To his credit, he gallantly avoided her shoes—and they say chivalry's dead. Evan and Charlotte got into a fight over nothing, which ended with Charlotte glaring at him from a circle of pissed-off Disney princesses while Evan broke into the off-limits liquor cabinet and downed half a bottle of whiskey despite Jill screaming that her parents would kill her if they found out.

I figured it was only a matter of time until the cops showed up and shut it down, and I didn't want to be there when they did. I left my unfinished beer and plastic fangs on the table and was considering how best to step over the kid passed out across the sliding door to the kitchen when Charlotte caught up with me.

"You're leaving?" she asked.

And I don't know what made me say it, except that I was tired from sitting there and watching the sloppy falling action of the party, but I shrugged and told her, "Well, yeah. I mean, it's a terrible party."

"It really is," she agreed. "But no one's going to remember that on Monday."

"All anyone's going to remember is the pirate ship filled with beer."

"And that Ezra Faulkner showed up without a costume," she teased.

"Screw you, I'm a vampire!" I insisted.

"Really?" Charlotte grinned, leaning toward me. "Should I be afraid?"

She stared up at me through her eyelashes, and I realized that the conversation had turned uncomfortable, and we were at one of those parties no good ever comes from, and she wasn't wearing all that much, and I was covered in body glitter.

"So, uh, Happy Halloween, Char," I said, awkwardly stepping around the kid who'd passed out in the doorway.

"Ezra, wait," Charlotte said. "Before you go—can we talk?"

I told her okay and led her into the laundry room. Charlotte sat on top of the dryer, and I sat on top of the washer, watching her examine the ruins of her manicure.

"I miss us," she said, still staring at her nails.

I hadn't been expecting that, and it threw me.

"Charlotte, you're drunk," I pointed out. "And you're dating Evan."

"Evan and I had another fight," she blurted. "You and me were so good together, Ezra. I wish we hadn't broken up."

She put her hand on my leg, and I was surprised to see that she was serious.

"Well, we did," I said matter-of-factly.

"I know. But, like, we could get back together."

She squeezed my leg and tilted her face toward mine, daring me to kiss her. For a moment, I let myself imagine it. The taste of her lips, the curve of her back, the breasts that were so obviously spilling out of her gold bra-top. And then I imagined Evan opening the door and finding us there. Except it wasn't Evan, it was me, five months ago, at a different party, because this was the way things were with

Charlotte: so impulsive, and so meaningless.

"No," I said, removing her hand from my leg. "We can't. It's not a good idea."

Charlotte's lips trembled for a moment, and then she composed herself, leaving me wondering if I'd imagined it.

"Why not?" she demanded. "You don't have a girlfriend, and Evan would get over it. I mean, don't you ever think about how we used to cuddle on my couch after school, and I'd bake cookies, and you'd get nervous that I might burn them when we kissed? Or the time we went to the OC Fair and you gave me ten dollars and told me to win you a stuffed animal? Or that time we double-dated with Jimmy and that freshman who spilled her Slurpee on his lap during the movie and we couldn't stop laughing?"

I did remember those things, and I couldn't help but smile at the memories of them. They seemed like part of my childhood; they seemed forever ago.

"See, you're smiling," Charlotte said, encouraged. "And I know you think I'm drunk, but I had like four beers, so I'm not even that bad. And this is different. Remember last year on the beach when you asked me to be your girlfriend and then on Monday the whole school wished they were us? We could *be* that couple again. It doesn't even matter that you were on the debate team for like two seconds, or that you dated that snotty redhead. Seriously, I don't even care about those things. We can pretend the last five months never happened."

Charlotte stopped babbling long enough to look up at me, her expression pleading.

"We could," I said gently, "but I don't want to."

"I'm sorry, did you just *reject* me?" Her eyes narrowed in disbelief.

But the thing with Charlotte was that she'd only mentioned the good parts of what we'd had. I wondered if she'd conveniently forgotten how she'd tormented me with her moodiness while we dated, picking fights over nothing. How she'd given me shopping lists for her birthday and Christmas, and I always still managed to get it wrong. How I never got to pick the movie, how she put her own presets in my car because I listened to "depressing hipster crap." The offensive grammar in her text messages, and the way she freaked out if I took too long to text back. How she always volunteered me to be the designated driver at parties, even for *her* friends, and how she always copied Jill's Spanish homework at break because I refused to let her have mine.

For a moment, I wondered if I should just tell her that she was a selfish, reckless girl who thought the world owed her something simply because she was pretty, and that I didn't want to be around when she discovered it didn't. But of course I couldn't. Around her, I found it impossible to conjure much of anything worth saying.

"Look, Char, I think you're great," I said. "You know that. But you don't want to date me. We're not even remotely compatible. I'm sort of a nerd. I have a limp and a lousy car and I hate it here so much that I sit in the UCE library after school pretending that I've already left."

"How can you hate Eastwood? It's perfect."

"You see perfection, I see panopticon."

"Oh my god, *why* do you use such big words?" she demanded in exasperation.

"Sorry," I apologized, realizing she was the sort of girl who got upset when someone used an unfamiliar word, rather than learning what it meant.

"You're really weird sometimes," Charlotte accused. "Like tonight, when everyone dressed as zombies, and you wore *that*. I mean, don't you want to be like everyone else?"

"Not particularly," I said, willing her to finally understand how much I had changed, and how very little she knew about me.

Charlotte considered this for a moment, and then her face broke into a sly smile.

"Very funny," she announced, and then she launched herself at me.

"Charlotte," I said, pushing her off and climbing to my feet. "I said no."

"How was I supposed to know that you meant it?" She seemed tremendously offended all of a sudden. "You can't agree to talk someplace private at a party and that's *it*."

"Oh. I didn't realize . . ." I winced as it dawned on me that she'd thought I'd wanted to be alone with her, too.

"You *never* do." Charlotte said with an exasperated sigh. "You can be a real jerk sometimes, and you don't even see how you are. I used to think you did it on purpose, so I flirted with other guys to make you jealous."

I laughed hollowly.

"That's what you call it? Flirting with other guys? My mistake. At Jonas's party, I should have realized you were just *flirting*."

"No, what you should have done was sucked it up and dealt with it on Monday and taken me to prom like everyone expected," Charlotte fumed.

"Prom?" I didn't think I'd heard her correctly. "Do you know where I was the night of *prom*, Charlotte? I was in the hospital, wondering if I'd ever *walk* again. And we both know how I got there."

It got really quiet for a second, and I think we both expected some drunken couple to stumble through the door and interrupt us, rescuing us from the uncomfortable silence, but none did.

"If we both know, then why does it feel like you blame me?" Charlotte demanded. "I wasn't even *there*."

"No, you *weren't* there," I said. "The paramedics found me all alone. And you just *left* me like that. You left me."

Charlotte's face had gone pale, and she couldn't quite bring herself to look at me.

"We were drunk," she said defensively. "I didn't have a ride, and everyone was shouting about the cops coming

because of the accident, and I'm terrible with blood, I probably would have fainted."

"'I'm sorry' would have been enough," I told her. "Look,
it's late, and I think we're done here. Why don't you go find
Evan or something?"

"Are you going to tell him what I said?" she asked nervously. "Because I only said I'd dump him if—"

"No, Charlotte, I'm not going to tell him," I said drily.
"The hymen of your integrity remains intact. Your precious
jewel of a reputation is un-besmirched."

I left Jill's party thinking that sometimes it isn't worth
confirming what we already know about people we understand so well. Because what Charlotte had wanted that night
wasn't me. It was some imaginary version of the boy she
used to date but had never bothered to really think about as
a person. And maybe the imaginary Ezra would have gone
back to her and tried to forget the last five months. Maybe
he would have convinced himself that he was happier for it,
that neither of them were terrible people in the end, that it
was possible to retreat into one's popularity and carelessness
and never have to acknowledge the harm they'd caused to
those around them, or the lies they believed to make their
happiness possible.

But it doesn't matter what the imaginary Ezra inside
Charlotte's head would have done, because he wasn't real,
and he certainly wasn't me. What *I* did was drive home, past
the egged stop signs and toilet-papered poplar trees, and

coax Cooper off the kitchen mat where he was still sulking over not being allowed to play with the trick-or-treaters, and fall into bed without even bothering to wash off that ridiculous body glitter.

29

COOPER WAS ACTING strange on Sunday night, his expression uneasy, his head cocked as though listening for something just beyond the mosaic tile of our leaf-strewn pool.

"It's all right, boy," I told him, absently patting the top of his head as I sat at my desk flipping through college catalogues.

They were filled with pictures of a world that reminded me of her, a place brimming with unknowable possibility and almost certain adventure. For a moment, I let myself imagine what it would be like to go East, where leaves turned golden and snow coated the rooftops, where libraries looked like castles and dining halls were straight out of the Harry Potter films. But the brochures all seemed to blend together with the same promise of New England, and I realized that there's a big difference between deciding to leave and knowing where to go.

◄-◄-►-►

THE COYOTES WERE back in Eastwood again, and somehow Cooper had sensed it. Two housecats were dragged off over the weekend, and a coyote had been spotted in Terrace Bluffs. The local newspaper's headline hinted that our town was being "terrorized"—as though the streets were filled with nocturnal wolves gliding through the shadows, preying on the old and the sick.

In the way that some places have a rash of burglaries or hubcap thefts, we have coyotes. It's not that surprising when small animals disappear, and every once in a while I would see something slink past the tennis courts while I was practicing after dark. Occasionally the neighbors' koi ponds were depleted overnight, or a jogger would spot a coyote watching him on one of the trails, but no one had ever been killed by coyotes. It was an absurd idea, like something out of those novels filled with vampires and witches.

Still, there was an Animal Control van parked by the side of the football field on Monday, and every day that week, we'd watch officers comb the trails through our classroom windows.

I sat at Toby's lunch table again, where little was said about my reappearance. Austin looked up from his iPad long enough to flick his bangs out of his eyes and announce that it was about time I was back, and had I seen the new Nintendo console?

"No, but did you know there's an eight-bit Great Gatsby game?" I asked.

"You're making that up." Austin furiously started typing.

I glanced over toward my former lunch table, where Jimmy had pulled a roll of Mentos out of his pocket and was threatening to dump them into Emma's soda bottle. Evan roared with laughter, and Trevor started a chant of "Do it and you're cool!" When Jimmy inevitably succumbed to the temptation, the boys backed away laughing as Emma's soda shot a geyser of fizz into the air.

"Oh *shit!*" they muttered gleefully.

The girls stood there, dripping and indignant as the fizz explosion turned to a trickle. The pavement under their lunch table was drenched, and the front of Charlotte's Song Squad uniform was soaked. Evan looked up and caught me watching. He flicked his chin, telling me to get over there, but I just shook my head.

"Emma's going to kill him," I said, breaking off a piece of Phoebe's Pop-Tart.

"Their relationship's *fizzed*," Phoebe said, belatedly swatting my hand away from her breakfast.

"Ten points to Chang," Toby said.

"He should probably keep that soda as a *mementos mori*." I smirked, and our table went totally silent.

"Get it?" I asked. "Mentos, like, memento—"

"We got it," Toby assured me. "Jesus, Faulkner. Was that *poetry*? In *Latin*?"

"That was fifty points," I told him. "Unless any of you can do better?"

"Pop-Tart sharing privileges activated," Phoebe said, offering me another piece.

"Dude!" Austin looked up from his iPad. "There really *is* an eight-bit Gatsby! Why are you guys looking at me like that? What'd I miss?"

ANIMAL CONTROL GAVE up their search on Wednesday, and our homeroom teachers distributed a safety precaution handout that culminated in a laughable series of true-false questions about coyote attacks. I rolled my eyes and turned it over on my desk, not caring that we were doing popcorn reading, since no one would dare to popcorn me.

My school was big on using recycled paper, and it took a moment before I recognized what was on the backs of our *Preventing Coyote Attacks!* handout: leftover fliers for last year's Junior-Senior Luau, complete with a poorly photocopied picture of the class council in sunglasses and leis. If you held the handout up to the light, the photo of us seeped through, creating this disturbing impression that it was a picture of attack victims, that we were the cautionary tale.

When I drove over to the medical center later that afternoon, the sun was just beginning to set, and these shafts of golden sunlight slanted through the magnolia trees that divided the rows of parking spaces. In that light, the leaves looked fake, like they were made of wax. Cassidy would have loved them.

I was slightly early when I pushed open the door of Suite 322 North: Cohen and Ford Group Mental Health Practice. The receptionurse smiled at me blankly, and asked which doctor I was there to see, and if I was a new patient. I told her Dr. Cohen and I'd been before, and she typed something into the oldest functioning computer I'd ever seen, and said the insurance stuff was taken care of and I should just sit and relax.

One thing I've noticed is that the only places people insist you relax are the least relaxing places on the planet. Airplanes, the dentist, psychiatric waiting rooms, those little curtained-off areas in the hospital where you have an IV put in. Anyway. I sat, waited, considered how incredibly *unrelaxed* I felt.

The whole place, and I really mean all of it, was decorated for Festivus. There were non-denominational snowmen, and seasonal snowflakes, and glittering garlands of enormous plastic peppermints. It was pretty terrible. Plus there was this older lady already sitting there, wearing a sari and an I'm-waiting-for-my-kid expression as she flipped through a decrepit magazine.

She coughed and shifted in her chair, making the peppermint garland rattle. A small avalanche of glitter sloughed off, and I wasn't lucky enough to avoid it. I made a face and tried to wipe it from my shoulders, but there was no use.

The receptionurse poked her head through the vestibule and let me know that Dr. Cohen was running about twenty minutes behind. I sighed and put on my headphones, taking out the college app I was working on. The lady with the magazine was being pretty nosy, and after about five minutes, she finally decided to come out with it.

"Are those college applications?"

I nodded.

"Where are you applying?" she asked shamelessly.

"Um, this one's for Duke," I said, "and this is for Dartmouth."

"You must be a smart boy." She said it like I was some three-year-old, which wasn't actually reassuring.

"Not really." I shrugged. "But it's worth trying."

"My daughter was a National Merit Scholar," she said, as though this fact was at all relevant to our conversation.

"That's great." I fiddled with my headphones, hoping she'd lose interest.

I'd just started back on my application when the door to Dr. Ford's office opened. I glanced up, figuring it was going to be the nosy lady's daughter and she'd make us awkwardly introduce ourselves, but it wasn't.

Cassidy Thorpe walked into the waiting room, something in the cast of her shoulders suggesting this visit was routine. Her eyes were slightly red, as though she'd been crying, and her white sweater slipped off one freckled shoulder. Her trench coat was bundled in her arms, the belt dangling.

When she saw me, she paled. Bit her lip. Looked like she wanted to disappear.

We stared at each other, totally embarrassed, since the waiting room in a mental health clinic isn't the best place to run into your ex, particularly when it's decorated with a thousand glittering pieces of fake candy. I had no idea what she was doing there, but I was damn well going to find out.

"Hi," I said, taking off my headphones.

The papers on my lap slipped onto the floor, and Cassidy and I stared at them like I'd carelessly broken a vase in someone else's house.

"What are you doing here?" she demanded.

"Selling Girl Scout cookies," I deadpanned.

Neither of us laughed.

"No, really."

"Well, I was in this accident." I was still trying to make a joke of it. "So I have to go through the hassle of convincing doctors that I'm not experiencing a crippling bout of clinical depression. Get it, *crippling*?"

"Stop," Cassidy insisted, like what I'd said made her feel even worse. It was strange, since she used to laugh at stupid puns like that.

She knelt and picked up my papers. I muttered my thanks and zipped them back into my bag.

"You'd hate Dartmouth, by the way," Cassidy said.

"Wow, really? We're talking about this right now?" It was out of my mouth before I could think it through, floating there sarcastically, and I instantly wanted to take it back.

"Okay, well, see you in school." Cassidy started to walk off, but I wasn't having it.

"No way," I said, standing up. "You don't want to sit next to me in class, fine. You want to sulk in the library, be my guest. But I run into you here, you're telling me what's going on."

I didn't care that the lady in the sari was spying on us from behind her magazine. I didn't care that my T-shirt was lousy with glitter. I just wanted her to trust me, for once, to tell me what it was that had turned our smooth-sailing relationship into a total shipwreck.

"Stay out of it, Ezra." Cassidy's eyes were pleading, but it sounded more like a warning than anything else. And that infuriated me.

"Make me."

"What do you think I've been *trying* to do?" Cassidy asked in exasperation.

Her expression was the one she'd worn a lot lately, full of this sadness that had lurked there for far longer than we'd been together. And I was tired of wondering why.

"I don't know? Screw with me?"

"Excuse me," the receptionurse said, poking her head through the vestibule. "Is there a problem?"

"We're fine," Cassidy and I said in unison, both of us sounding terrifically not fine.

"Hallway?" I suggested.

Cassidy glared but followed me anyway.

"What?" she demanded once the door had closed behind us.

"So, do you come here often?" I tried not to grin at how ridiculous it sounded.

"It's none of your business," Cassidy shot back, clearly not seeing any humor in this.

And if she wanted to play it that way, it was fine by me. Because I was tired of whatever we were doing, of whatever it was between us being this vast and unbreachable waste-land of misery.

"Of course not. But you know what I think?" I asked, not waiting for an answer. "I think you were alone that night in the park. That your 'boyfriend' didn't exist."

I'd been privately toying with that theory for a while and hadn't planned on making the accusation, but the moment I said it, I knew I was right.

"Why would I make something like that up?" Cassidy demanded, avoiding the question.

"Did you?" I pressed.

"What does it *matter*, Ezra? We broke up. Not all nice things have happy endings."

"I'm just trying to figure out what I did to make you act like this. Seriously, Cassidy, what tragedy occurred that made you wish we'd never met?"

Cassidy stared at the carpet. Tucked her hair behind her ears. Smiled sadly.

"*Life* is the tragedy," she said bitterly. "You know how they categorize Shakespeare's plays, right? If it ends with a wedding, it's a comedy. And if it ends with a funeral, it's a tragedy. So we're all living tragedies, because we all end the same way, and it isn't with a goddamned wedding."

"Well, thanks for that. That clears everything up nicely. We're all prisoners. Wait no—we're living tragedies, just passing time till our funerals."

Cassidy scowled at this, but I didn't care. I was furious with her for being there, for being miserable, for refusing to explain.

"No one's *dead*, Cassidy," I said harshly. "I can't decide whether you're just crazy, or a liar, or someone who likes hurting people. You're all riddles and quotes and you can't give me a straight answer about anything and I'm *tired* of waiting for you to realize that you owe me one."

I hadn't meant to go off like that, and I wasn't exactly using my indoor voice when I said any of those things. Cassidy studied the carpet for a long moment, and when she glanced up at me, a tropical storm was churning in her eyes. Two tears slid down her cheeks.

"I don't owe you anything," Cassidy sobbed, "and you're right, I do wish we'd never met."

She rushed past me, taking the stairs, where she knew I couldn't follow.

"Yeah, well, so do I!" I called after her, not meaning it but not caring.

The door to the stairwell banged shut in response.

I took a deep breath, and ran a hand through my hair, and kept my shit together long enough to go back into that doctor's office and calmly tell the receptionurse that it was probably best if I rescheduled.

30

THERE'D BEEN ANOTHER sighting on the hiking trail behind Meadowbridge Park, and the coyotes were all my parents talked about, eclipsing even the subject of whether or not they should return the new light fixture in the downstairs guest bathroom, which had arrived with a slight imperfection in the glass.

Even my friends made jokes about it, with Phoebe in particular relishing how, and I quote, "deeply ironic it is that our school mascot, a supposed emblem of pride, has become emblematic of our collective fear."

Some of the tennis guys at my old lunch table had taken to making fake wolf howls, and Connor MacLeary landed himself two days of in-school suspension for it, which we all found hilarious, because the school was literally forcing him to skip class.

There was a debate tournament that weekend up in Santa Barbara, and of course I wasn't going. Sign-ups had been weeks ago, back when we were all still obsessed with the homecoming dance, and Cassidy hadn't wanted to. I hadn't pressed her on it, since I figured we'd probably spend the weekend together. But one interesting thing Toby told me was that the Barrows School was on the tournament list. I assumed Cassidy had known that back when she'd suggested we both sit this one out, that the way she avoided certain things was another part of this maddening mystery.

Toby went all out, wearing his suit to school on Friday, swaggering through the quad with this purple pocket square and peacock-printed tie, and even Luke and Sam joined us sheepishly at lunch, sporting matching American flag pins in their lapels. It felt wrong, the six of us, like we were two groups that had never been a cohesive whole. And it was strange, thinking that Cassidy had been the glue connecting us.

"Still here, Faulkner?" Luke sneered.

"Still doing that terrible impression of Draco Malfoy?" I asked.

Everyone at the table cracked up, and even Sam was trying not to laugh. Luke muttered something under his breath, dragging Sam off to the breakfast line.

"It's sort of sad, when you think about it," Austin mused.

"What is?" I asked, figuring he was probably talking about some video game.

"How no one ever invites Luke to anything because his brother's a cop. Man, he takes it so personally."

"Whoa. Please be a human being more often," Phoebe begged.

"What's the point? I'm never going to make the leader boards." Austin shrugged philosophically, retrieved his phone from the pocket of his suit jacket, and returned to his game.

"So Faulkner," Toby said. "Anything specific you want me to ask the Barrows School when I see them at the tournament?"

"I guess about last year?" I suggested. "About what happened?"

"Well, it's your call." Toby put on his sunglasses and leaned back to catch the sun. "You know her better than anyone."

I didn't have the heart to tell him I was starting to think I didn't know her at all. And that maybe whatever Toby found out wouldn't help anything. Because the thing was, after what had happened at the medical center, I wasn't sure if we were worth fixing. And I didn't know what answers would make me know whether I even wanted to try.

I kept seeing it over and over again in my head, Cassidy's eyes filling with tears as she announced that she wished we'd never met. The way her hair streamed behind her as she ran away from me, confident I wouldn't follow. The stupid lie I'd shouted after her.

We'd been so good together once, and then we'd rotted, like some corpse with a delayed burial. I read somewhere that the hair and fingernails on dead bodies don't actually grow, it just looks like they do because the skin contracts as the body dries out. So it's possible to lie even in death, to deceive people from beyond the grave. I wondered if that's what this was. If I was staring at the rotting corpse of what Cassidy and I had once had, wrongly convinced there was still life in it, grasping onto an uninformed lie.

I watched my friends climb into the team van that afternoon, their luggage filled with baguettes and liquor and Fruit by the Foot, and then I went home and played this useless video game with the sound off so I wouldn't miss it if Toby called.

MY MOM MUST have felt sorry for me, because she let me sleep in on Saturday. I finally got up around noon, after having decided that, as far as monogamous relationships go, I could probably do worse than marrying my bed.

Since all of my friends were up in Santa Barbara, I wound up at the library again, halfheartedly working on college applications but mostly checking my phone like a madman.

There was no point in bothering Toby, since he'd have debate rounds all day, and I found myself wishing I'd gone to the tournament. I pictured Austin with his endless supply of entertaining YouTube videos, and Phoebe passing out contraband snack foods ("nineties nostalgia guaranteed") and even Sam rolling up his sleeves to mix massively intoxicating cocktails. And Toby, with his thrift-store suit and stubborn insistence that we call him "O Captain My Captain."

The girls next to me in the library had been talking loudly, so I'd resorted to headphones. Which is why, when my phone rang, I almost missed it.

"Yeah?" I said, lunging for it.

"Dude, you missed a sick party!" Toby sounded incredibly caffeinated, like someone should have pulled him away from the Red Bull two cans ago. "Ah! Faulkner! You should have come! Everyone wishes you were here. Except Luke, because last night he got so drunk that he peed the bed."

"How much pee are we talking?" I asked, gathering my things. The girls sitting nearby gave me an odd look, which I supposed was justified.

"If his bed was the gulf, this was an oil spill."

"You are a magnificent friend for telling me this." I passed through the turnstile, nodding to the girl who always let me through without ID.

It was cloudy outside, not so much overcast as overcome by fog. It happened sometimes. A huge beast of a cumulous would swallow Eastwood whole, and for a day or two we'd live in the belly of the cloud, unable to see more than five feet in front of us.

Toby drew out the story of Luke's hour of shame, and I stared at the fog and listened to him laughing over how Luke had not only peed the bed, he'd peed the bed in *another team's hotel room.* I laughed along once or twice, because I knew I was supposed to, but I was starting to get the feeling that Toby wasn't telling me something.

"How bad is it?" I blurted.

Toby paused. We knew each other too well, and I knew that silence. It was a serious one.

"I talked to some people on the Barrows team today," he said, trying to play it off.

"And?"

"Dude, are you sitting down?"

"Dude, tell me!" I pleaded.

"Christ, I'm trying!" Toby insisted. "Okay. Well, you know Cassidy's brother?"

"Six years older? Big-shot debate champion? Went to Yale, then med school at Hopkins?" I filled in, wondering what Toby knew that I didn't.

Toby sighed, his breath crackling through the phone.

"Cassidy's brother is dead."

"What?" I choked. Because whatever I'd been expecting Toby to say, it wasn't that.

"He passed away last year," Toby said. "That's when Cassidy dropped out of school—and debate."

I'd never heard Toby sound the way he did when he told me that. Not just sorry, but ashamed of himself, like he'd been too hard on Cassidy, misjudged her, misread her somehow in the worst possible way. That the big mystery of the legendary Cassidy Thorpe wasn't the sort of story anyone would want to tell.

"How did he die?" I asked, breaking the silence.

"Some heart condition, apparently? It was really sudden. There was a whole article about it in his school newspaper. It's—ah, hold on."

There was some scuffling, and then Toby came back on.

"Sorry," he said. "Listen, I have to get to the award ceremony, Ms. Weng is frog-marching me in as we speak. But I can still text—only kidding, Ms. Weng—"

"Go," I said. "It's fine. I'll come over later."

I hung up and stared down at my phone, at the little flashing time display of how long it had taken Toby to thoroughly wreck everything I thought I knew about Cassidy Thorpe. I saw now the way she'd talked about escaping the panopticon—what she'd really been doing was talking about everything besides the fact that her brother already had.

31

I DROVE HOME that evening with the strange impression that whatever had happened between Cassidy and myself wasn't about us at all. It was about her brother. His sudden death—the way she'd left school, moved home for senior year. It was like she was trying to find some place where she could escape from the fact that it had happened, or perhaps come to terms with it.

So many missing pieces of Cassidy Thorpe clicked into place. The boys' clothes she sometimes wore, the ghostly house, the concerned lady pulling her aside at the debate tournament, the desperate way she'd made sure to lose.

I knew what it was like to have people stare at you with pity. For everyone's gaze to follow you through the hallways as though you were marked by tragedy and no longer belonged. And I could understand why she hadn't wanted that. Why she would have kept her brother's death to herself. Why she would choose a town where she barely knew anyone, and a boyfriend who knew how broken felt.

Suddenly, I realized what an unforgiveable dick I'd been at the psychiatrist's. No one's dead, I'd told her. I couldn't have picked a more horrible thing to say if I'd tried.

And then it occurred to me: It wasn't that Cassidy didn't want to date me, she just didn't want to tell me. But now I knew. I knew why she seemed so deeply miserable sometimes, why she'd pleaded with me to just let it go.

It had all started the night of the homecoming dance. She'd been fine before then. Even on Friday, when Mrs. Martin had us plan an ideal vacation, and Cassidy had gotten carried away telling me about this art concept hotel where you slept in coffins. Actually, yeah, that was pretty morbid.

"But if we stayed there, we wouldn't be able to share a bed," I'd said. "A coffin. Whatever."

"Oh, we'd figure something out," Cassidy had assured me, putting her hand on my leg even though we were right there in Spanish class.

It was only the next day that everything had curdled.

So there Cassidy was, on the afternoon of the homecoming dance. Maybe she'd started to get ready. Painted her nails or whatever it is girls do. Cut the tags off her dress. Picked up the phone after I'd made that joke about getting her a lei. And then she'd remembered something. The anniversary of her brother's death? No, it hadn't been long enough for that. Maybe she'd forgotten something instead. His birthday? Some tradition they had? And suddenly the dance didn't matter anymore, nothing mattered except the fact that he was gone and he wasn't gone because she couldn't escape his death no matter what she did.

So she'd gone to the park, because Cassidy liked parks, because that was where she went when things needed to be said or thought through, and that was where I'd found her. It had gotten dark and she hadn't realized, and then it was too late to explain the truth that she'd been hiding from everyone for so long. She hadn't expected to get close to anyone at Eastwood, and now that I was there, what could she say so that I'd leave?

So she'd lied. Of course she'd lied. I'd caught her off guard and she didn't have time to make it good. So it was her boyfriend she was there with, and I was just an amusement. It was a lie inspired by the very story I'd told her about how Charlotte and I had ended, and she hadn't realized how completely it would shatter me. She'd tried to take it back—changed her mind—but I was already leaving. And when she'd finally had the courage to go back to class and face me, she hadn't been able to face me at all.

I played this explanation over in my head as I drove home against the purpling sky, past the endlessly pristine golf courses that lay between Eastwood and Back Bay. If I'd gotten it right, then Cassidy had pushed me away because it was easier than explaining that her brother was gone, and there was nowhere else to run to pretend that it hadn't happened. If I'd gotten it right, then we were never meant to break up that night in the park, and we were both hurting because of it.

MY FATHER STOPPED me when I got home.

"Come on in here a second, champ," he said, beckoning me into his home office with a schmoozy grin.

I shrugged out of my backpack and took a seat on his sofa. The scent of dinner cooking drifted in from the kitchen—it smelled suspiciously like Italian food, which couldn't be right.

"Is Mom making lasagna?" I asked hopefully as my father tabbed between multiple Excel files.

"Gluten free." He swiveled his chair around to face me and steepled his fingers.

"Maybe it tastes better." I somehow managed to keep a straight face.

"First step: lasagna; next step: pizza," my father said, winking. And then he crossed his ankle over his knee, and got down to business. "I hear you've been keeping busy these days."

"College applications," I said. "It's easier to get them done at the library."

He said he was happy to hear I was being proactive about my future, and I nodded and listened while he launched into one of those endless stories about his good old days as chapter president of Sigma Alpha Epsilon. When he finished, he beamed at me, waiting I suppose for me to confirm my ambitions to follow in his footsteps like we'd always planned. But I didn't.

Instead, I told him I was thinking of going East. I named a string of schools whose brochures I had stashed in my desk drawer. His eyebrows went up at a couple of them, and I didn't blame him. Mentioned history, English, chemistry. Mentioned that I thought I could do better than state college, and that I wanted to at least try.

"Well, I'm surprised," my father said, scrutinizing me. "You've grown up a lot this year, kiddo. You've had to, and I'm sorry about that. But I'm glad to see that you have a plan."

"You mean you're okay with it?" I asked, hardly daring to believe it.

"I don't presume to speak for your mother." He smiled wryly. "But *I* think it would be good for you. And of course my old fraternity has chapters at most schools."

I laughed, for once finding one of my father's pseudo-jokes funny. And when my mom called us in to dinner and stood beaming over a platter of only mildly healthy-tasting lasagna, we finally had something to discuss besides light fixtures.

AFTER DINNER, I drove over to Toby's house.

"Hey," he said, ushering me into his bedroom. He was wearing glasses and pajama pants, and it reminded me of when we were little, the two of us sneaking around the house at night when we were supposed to be asleep.

He passed me an old N64 controller, the see-through one we used to fight over, and put in a game without asking. It was some retro Mario I'd given him for an elementary-school birthday back when it was the cool new thing, and we sat there and played it, like we had a hundred times, secret levels and all, except this time felt different.

"Do you want to see the article?" Toby finally asked.

I told him I did, and he pulled it up on his computer.

Sure enough, Owen Alexander Thorpe. Graduated first in his class from the Barrows School, gone on to Yale, and then Johns Hopkins for medical school. He'd died at twenty-three, unexpectedly, from a sudden cardiac arrest caused by a thromboembolism. I'd picked up enough from my time in the hospital to know what that meant: Owen had died of a broken heart.

There was a picture, too, a cheesy tourist shot, taking up half of the screen. I could see the Eiffel Tower in the background, the ground slick with rain, some strangers still under their umbrellas. Owen was smiling in this embarrassed way, his blond hair flopping into his eyes, Cassidy's particular shade of blue that evidently ran in their family. A scarf was around his neck, and his arm was slung around someone who had been cropped from the picture. I could see the corner of a trench coat, the edge of a shopping bag.

To his credit, Toby let me sit there staring at his computer screen for a good long while. It was only when his neighbor's lights came on, splashing through his bedroom window, that I looked up, remembering where I was.

The house across the street had turned on their Christmas lights. Toby and I looked out the window horrorstruck by the pair of twelve-foot-tall glowing inflatable snowmen that had ballooned out of nowhere, bookending a neon nativity. Someone had climbed onto the roof and used dozens of strands of lights to spell out "HAPPY BDAY JESUS" in flashing red and green.

"It's not even *Thanksgiving*," I said.

"They could have at least gone to the effort to spell out 'birthday,'" Toby observed, shutting the blinds. "So, what are you going to do?"

I sighed and raked a hand through my hair.

"Um," I said. "Knock on her door with flowers?"

It sounded pathetic even as I said it. Like I was giving her some belated funeral bouquet.

"Yeah?" Toby asked doubtfully.

"Ugh, I don't *know*," I said wretchedly. "Look, I love her. Loved her, whatever. And if I can make things right between us—because I just really, completely miss her and think she misses me, too—then I'm going over there and knocking on her damned door."

"This is *Cassidy* we're talking about." Toby raised an eyebrow, trying to convey the full gravitas of the situation. "She called you a washed-up, podunk, unoriginal townie."

"I remember," I said drily, hoping Toby was going somewhere with this that didn't contribute solely to his own amusement.

"And you want to show up at her front door with *flowers*?"

I winced, catching Toby's point immediately.

"Okay, bad plan," I muttered.

"What you need is a lawnmower and a boom box," Toby suggested. "Or a TARDIS. You could build her a TARDIS, invite her to come away with you on an adventure."

I knew Toby wasn't serious, but something about that last part got to me. An adventure. Cassidy had given me one once, as an apology for the debate tournament.

"You're not even listening to me, are you?" Toby complained.

"Nope." Because a strange idea had started to take shape in my mind, something that certainly couldn't be considered ordinary. I knew how I was going to win her back.

THE NEXT MORNING, I woke up at dawn. I put on dark clothes and slipped out of the house while the whole world slept. Just as the first lights began to turn on in Terrace Bluffs, I crept back home.

It was too early to take a shower, and I was afraid I'd wake my parents, so I scrubbed off the dirt and paint as best I could with a damp washcloth and changed into something more presentable.

I waited, and I paced, and when the clock hit seven, I couldn't stand it any longer. I crept downstairs and was tying my shoes when Cooper padded into the foyer. He cocked his head at me and whined.

"Shhh," I told him.

What's this about, old sport? his eyes seemed to say.

"I'll be back. I'm just going to see Cassidy," I whispered.

At the mention of her name, Cooper perked up and whined louder.

"Stop that! You'll wake up everyone!"

But it was no use. Cooper followed me to the front door, letting out another insistent whine.

"Do you want to come with me, Cooper?" I asked in exasperation. "Is that it? Either you come, or I don't go?"

He started turning circles at the word "go," so I gave up and went to get his leash.

"You have to be good," I told him, clipping it onto his collar. "I'm serious. I'm not supposed to be walking you. You can't tug the leash or anything."

I had the impression that he understood, because when I let him out the front door, he stopped to wait for me, as though sensing that it was a special occasion.

The streets were empty, and gray with fog, which I'd been hoping would burn off, but no such luck. The pavement was damp, and the windshields of the cars we passed were beaded with condensation. Even the gate to Meadowbridge Park was slippery.

Cooper sniffed indignantly when he realized we were headed across the wet grass, but I told him that he was the one who'd insisted on coming along, and he dutifully pranced through it with his nose in the air, making me laugh.

I wasn't laughing when he shook the water out of his fur at the other side, though.

"Cooper!" I scolded.

You asked for it, old sport, his expression seemed to say.

I sighed and supposed he was right. And the more I thought about it, I was glad I'd brought him along, since Cassidy had always adored him.

When her house came into view, I breathed a sigh of relief. I'd half expected him to have disappeared, but he was still there, adorning her front lawn with magnificent irony: my tumbleweed snowman.

He was about five feet tall, with button eyes and a piece of licorice for a mouth. An old scarf around his neck fluttered in the breeze. He sat there, still slightly wet from the spray paint. A snowman in a town where it didn't snow, made by a boy who couldn't wait to leave, and given to a girl who had never belonged.

Toby had been right—now wasn't the time for flowers. Now was the time for grand gestures. The time to build a snowman out of tumbleweeds.

Cooper stared up at me, wondering why we'd suddenly stopped, and I whispered for him to wait. He cocked his head and then relieved himself on a neighbor's rosebush.

The fog was thinning, finally. We were across the street from Cassidy's house, and I pictured her coming out the front door in her pajamas, her hair mussed from sleep, grinning with delight when she caught sight of the snowman.

I took out my phone and dialed her number. Waited three rings. Four.

And then a sleepy, murmured hello.

"Come outside," I told her.

"Ezra, is that you?" she mumbled.

"If you're not standing on your front lawn in five minutes, I'm ringing the doorbell until you do."

"You're not serious," she protested.

"Doorbell," I threatened. "Outside. Five minutes."

And then I hung up.

"Time to hide," I told Cooper, but he wouldn't cooperate with me at all.

He was acting strangely, his ears perked, body rigid, hackles raised.

"Come on, Coop," I urged, tugging his leash. "You'll give us away."

Finally I managed to coax him across the street, behind a parked car, just as Cassidy slipped out of her house.

She'd thrown on jeans and that green sweater she always wore. She looked so beautiful—so vulnerable—hugging her arms across her chest in the gray light of early morning as she padded down the front walk.

She was frowning, and then she caught sight of the

snowman and laughed. It was the happiest I'd seen her in a long time.

"Ezra?" she called doubtfully.

"Yeah, hi," I said sheepishly, joining her on the lawn.

Cooper rubbed his nose against her leg, and she yawned, scratching him behind the ears.

"Hello, gorgeous," she cooed. "Did you make me this snowman?"

"He did," I said. "All by himself. He dragged me here so I could call you to come see it."

"It's wonderful," Cassidy said, and then she bit her lip, her expression serious. "Here, I'll help you take it down."

For a moment, I didn't think I'd heard her correctly.

"You'll help me take it *down*? I just spent all night *making* the freaking thing."

Cassidy sighed. Stared at the grass. Pulled her sleeves over her hands.

"I didn't ask you to," she muttered.

"No, you didn't," I said angrily. "God, I'm trying to apologize for what I said, okay? I'm trying to give you something interesting and weird and wonderful so that maybe you'll finally talk to me about your brother, and you want me to take it *down*?"

"I want you to take it down," Cassidy said coolly, her eyes darting up to meet mine. "And I told you to let it go. I told you it was better not knowing."

"Evidently I didn't listen."

"Yeah, *evidently*," she said, mocking me. "Now if you're not going to help get rid of this snowman, please, just—please *leave*."

"Fine," I said. "Come on, Cooper, we're going. Cassidy doesn't want to talk to us right now because she's mad I figured out why we broke up."

"You didn't," Cassidy called after me. "You just found the riddle."

But I was sick of riddles, and I was sick of Cassidy's unpredictable moods, and I was sick of never, ever being good enough for her.

I slammed open the gate to the park, and Cooper promptly sat down on the sidewalk, refusing to budge.

"This is the last thing I need," I told him. "I can't drag you. You have to walk."

Cooper glared at me, like maybe he thought I should go back there and help Cassidy wreck another thing I'd mistakenly thought she'd wanted. Finally, he got up and followed me into the park.

The haze still hadn't burned off, and it was almost impossible to make out the bright blue of the swing set, much less the other side of the park.

"Ezra!" Cassidy called, and I turned, squinting back at her across the park. She was at the gate. She hadn't let me walk away after all.

"Ezra, run!" she screamed, her voice tinged with panic. And then I saw the coyote.

It was enormous, five feet long at least, gliding sound-lessly through the fog.

"Run!" she screamed again, but I couldn't, and part of me knew that the coyote could sense it. I stood frozen in terror, watching that huge animal stalk toward me through the amorphous fog.

And then Cooper let out a ferocious bark and yanked his leash from my hand. He bounded toward the coyote, snarling and barking, his leash dragging behind him over the damp grass.

The two animals were scrabbling for purchase at each other's necks, locked in fierce combat at the lip of the sand-box, while we both watched helplessly.

I limped toward them, Cassidy's screams turning into choked sobs as she pressed her hands over her mouth. But what chance did Cooper have? A sixteen-year-old poodle against a wild coyote?

"Get out of here!" I screamed at the coyote, but there was already so much blood. The coyote's jaws were locked around Cooper's throat, and Cooper was bleating, making these horrible whining noises, and my heart was pounding, and all I could think was *no, this isn't possible, this can't be real.*

"Cooper, no!" Cassidy wailed. "Please, no."

Cooper went limp, and the coyote, apparently satisfied, released its grip on his neck and trotted off, slipping through the fence and disappearing into the hiking trail.

I didn't care that I was sitting in the middle of a park on a foggy Sunday morning. I didn't care that it had started to drizzle. Cooper's head was in my lap, and my hands were pressed over his wound, and his fur was already matted and wet with blood, and my hands were red and dripping.

"Oh God," I gasped. "I'm so sorry. I'm so sorry, boy. You're going to be okay. Just hold on. You're a hero, Coop. It's going to be okay."

I looked up at Cassidy, who had gone so white that I was worried she might faint.

"He needs help," I said. "Your parents are doctors."

"They're on call."

"We have to do something! We'll take him to the animal hospital. I need you to get my car keys out of my pocket."

I kept my hands pressed on Cooper's wound, and Cassidy reached her hand into my pocket and somehow managed to extract my keys.

"What you need to do is run straight to my car and pull it around." I was surprised at how calm I sounded.

"I don't drive," Cassidy said, her voice quivering.

"Bullshit you don't drive. Get the car."

Cassidy nodded numbly, and took off across the grass, her hair streaming behind her like it was a flame and the fog was smoke.

Cooper let out a heartbreaking whine, and I pressed my hands harder against the gash in his neck, trying to keep it, and us, together.

Cassidy honked the horn at me when she pulled into the parking lot.

"I can't lift him," I yelled, my voice cracking shamefully.

Cassidy came and helped, and we managed to wrangle Cooper into the backseat. She climbed in after him, placing her hands over mine on his wound.

"You drive," she insisted. "There's too much fog."

I turned on the low beams and drove, the car thick with silence, and the steering wheel slick with blood.

32

CASSIDY AND I sat staring straight ahead in the frigid air-conditioning of the animal hospital's waiting room. It was like a bad dream, and I was slightly hazy on the details, but this much I knew: it was seven thirty in the morning, and Cooper was in trouble, and I was terrified that they wouldn't be able to save him.

Cassidy shivered, pulling her hands inside the sleeves of her sweater. I shrugged out of my leather jacket and handed it to her.

"Thanks," she murmured, putting it on and curling her legs up under her, like she was trying to fit completely inside that jacket.

I was in shock, dazed by the vastness of what had just happened; we both were. The waiting room was empty. It was just us, and the animal scale that looked almost like a treadmill in the corner. The receptionist, whose presence I'd sort of forgotten about, cleared her throat and frowned in my direction.

"Excuse me, sir?" she called. "Why don't you use our bathroom to clean up?"

Her smile didn't quite match her eyes as she pointed out where she wanted me to go. Numbly, I drifted toward the bathroom and turned on the light.

A specter leered at me from the mirror. Gaunt cheeks, face too pale, button-down shirt streaked with blood. My hands were particularly gruesome. I thought bitterly that this was a far better Halloween costume than the one I'd attempted.

I hunched over the basin, watching the metallic orange water swirl down the drain, and even long after the water ran clear, I couldn't bring myself to turn off the tap and go out there again.

I kept replaying it in my head: that coyote ghosting toward me through the fog, and the way my heart had lurched when Cassidy called my name and screamed for me to run. The way Cooper had fought the coyote even when the ground was coated with his blood, and how it was all my fault, because I'd known about the coyotes and hadn't listened.

Eventually, there was a knock at the door.

"Ezra?" It was Cassidy, and she sounded concerned.

"Just a second." I splashed some water on my face and opened the door.

"Hi," she said. "It's been forever. I was worried about you."

I raised an eyebrow at this, and Cassidy looked away.

"Do they know anything yet?" I pressed.

Cassidy shook her head.

"Come on," she said, taking my hand in hers. My hands were icy from the sink, and I felt her flinch, but she didn't say anything about it. We sat back down in the waiting room, and she scooted up next to me so our jeans were touching. I didn't know how she meant it, but it gave me a small glimmer of hope, the feeling of her—of us—touching, like maybe the distance between us wasn't as permanent as I'd once despaired.

Cassidy pulled my jacket tighter around her shoulders.

"I remember the day we bought this thing," she said, half to herself. "We made out on top of your lost library. McEnroe and Fleming watched the whole thing. Your wrist brace got stuck on my bra."

"And here we are," I said, trying to make a joke of it. "You and me and Cooper. We're like a positively charged molecule, the rate we're attracting tragedy."

"Don't," Cassidy said. "Don't build me a snowman out of tumbleweeds and say things like that."

"I'm sorry?" I tried.

"I'm the one who should be sorry," Cassidy muttered.

Outside, a fire truck sped past, its siren wailing, on its way to someone else's disaster.

"How did you find out about my brother?" Cassidy asked, and I didn't blame her for being curious.

"Toby," I admitted. "The tournament last weekend."

"And now you know why I don't compete anymore," Cassidy said.

"I do, and I'm sorry," I said quietly, realizing how useless the word "sorry" had become.

"It's okay. I mean, it isn't. It's completely *not* okay about Owen, but I guess I don't mind anymore if you know about him."

"Well, if you'd decided that three weeks ago, it would have saved us both a lot of trouble," I said, and Cassidy's shoulders rose slightly as she stifled a laugh.

"It's just . . ." I said, and then started over. "I don't get why you had to lie about it that night in the park. I would have understood that you didn't want to go to that stupid dance for whatever reason, but you just pushed me away, and it hurt like hell."

"I had to," Cassidy whispered. "God, I can't believe I'm even talking to you right now."

"I want you to talk to me," I insisted. "I've been *trying* to get you to talk to me, hence the snowman, which you hated."

"I didn't *hate* it. I actually really loved it? I just didn't want my parents to see it and ask where it had come from." A look of anguish came over Cassidy's face once more. "Ezra, I can't do this. I'm sorry, but I can't. You're right, though—I *do* owe you an explanation. So I'll play Sherlock Holmes for you, just this once."

She toyed with the zipper on my jacket for a moment, and I listened to the nervous rhythm of it, like a heartbeat.

Zip-zip. Zip-zip. Zip-zip.

"The thing about Owen," Cassidy began, "isn't how we'd mess with the universe or talk about subversive graffiti artists or sneak me into college classes. It's how all that stopped when our parents forced him into medical school and it wrecked him. He'd call me, convinced his cadaver was someone he knew, an old teacher or someone. He'd break down on the phone over stuff like that, how he was trapped in that lab, expected to cut open human flesh and fill out charts before washing the blood off his clothes, and to tell people that they were dying, or their loved one was dead, or their insurance wouldn't cover it, or there was nothing more he could do to take away their pain, and he was just completely terrified that this was going to be the rest of his life. He started showering a lot, because he said that no matter how much he washed, there were bits of the dead and the dying and the sick that clung to him, and little by little he was turning into a ghost, but he couldn't take it back because he'd already wasted college studying the requirements for this, and he was too afraid of our parents to tell them that he wanted to quit."

Cassidy lapsed into silence again, and I didn't blame her. I reached for her hand, and we stared down at our hands clasped together. At mine, calloused from tennis but growing soft. At hers, small and freckled and trembling, with gold nail polish that had largely chipped off.

She pulled her hand away, wiping her eyes and sniffling

even though she wasn't quite crying.

"One night," she continued, "he snuck a scalpel out of his lab and into his dorm room. And he called to tell me he was so scared, and so sorry, and so stressed, and I told him to fly home. I told him I'd take the train down that weekend, and we'd talk to Mom and Dad together. But they were awful about it. We were at this stupid fancy restaurant out in Back Bay, and they kept ordering drinks and arguing low over our entrees, and finally Owen grabbed Mom's keys and just slammed out of there. And I didn't stop him. I didn't run after him and make him give me the keys."

Cassidy turned to me, choking to hold back her tears.

"But he died of a, um, heart thing," I said. "Not a car accident."

"Ezra," Cassidy said, begging me to understand. "When he left the restaurant, he took our mom's black Land Rover."

I felt my whole soul twist as I realized what she was telling me. The car. The one at Jonas Beidecker's party that hadn't stopped after it crashed into the side of my roadster.

"No," I said as the full weight of it hit me head on. I was slammed back into the memory of that night, the jolt of our collision, the sickening skid of everything I'd wanted and everything I'd had slipping through my outstretched hands. It was the answer to the wrong mystery—the mystery I didn't ever want to solve.

And so we sat there in the sickening sillage of the truth, neither of us angry, or upset, just muddling through this shared sorrow, this collective pity. And as much as I wanted to sound my tragic wail over the rooftops, and let go of the day, and crawl back toward that safe harbor, and give in to the dying of the light, and to do all of those unheroically injured things that people never write poems about, I didn't.

"How long have you known?" I managed.

"The afternoon of the dance," she said. "When you called me from the florist."

"Voldemort the Volvo," I said, remembering.

So that was what had happened. I'd supplied the missing details of the accident. And once I'd unknowingly told her, she'd wanted to get as far away from me as possible. She wasn't running from me, she was running from the obligation of having to look me in the eye and tell me exactly who'd driven that black SUV through the stop sign.

"You know, he told us that he hit a tree." Cassidy shook her head. "And my parents were furious, but they believed him. I went back to Barrows, and he stayed home since he wasn't feeling well, but I figured he was just avoiding school. He thought it was panic attacks, you know? Because there's this horrible joke that med students always think they have some fatal disease, and he didn't want to be laughed at. But he had this embolism from the accident, and the clot got into his heart. Four days later, my parents came home and found him dead."

Cassidy squeezed my hand and stared up at me, as though asking forgiveness. For what, I wasn't quite sure.

I was thinking about how her brother had died in that house. It made an odd sort of sense, the way it had always felt ghostly to me, haunted. No wonder she never wanted to go home.

"I'm so sorry," I mumbled.

Cassidy shrugged, because as far as I know, scientists have yet to discover the proper reaction to "I'm sorry."

"What I can't figure out," she persisted, "is why he didn't say he hit anyone. Maybe he was so out of it that he honestly thought you were a tree."

"Or maybe it wasn't him," I said, hardly daring to hope. "There are lots of black SUVs in Eastwood."

"Ezra," Cassidy chided, like I was being irrational. "The Friday night before prom, around ten? The roads between Terrace Bluffs and Back Bay? It was him. I couldn't tell my parents. I haven't told anyone, except you."

She smiled sadly, and squeezed my hand again, in a way that constricted my heart.

"Well, I'm glad you did," I said. "It's better this way. We're two sides of the same tragic coin. It's like we were tied together before we even met."

"No," Cassidy said fiercely. "It's *not* like that. Don't you see? We can't *ever* be together. When I look at you now, all I see is Owen. I see him dead in you. The way you're sitting with your leg out, I see him crashing that car into you. And I think, how can I introduce you to my parents? The boy their dead son cripp—injured, sorry. So we can't. Not ever."

I considered this. Stared at the industrial clock on the far wall without really seeing it. Ran a hand through my hair. And then I looked over at her, aching to hold her close to me but knowing not to. Maybe part of me had already started to understand that reaching for Cassidy was the same as pushing her away. Maybe I'd already guessed that the physics of us didn't defy any laws of gravity, and with her, there was always an equal and opposite reaction.

"I wish you'd let me decide what I want to do," I finally said. "Because I'm serious, none of this changes that I miss you and want you back. We're so good together, and it's a tragedy in its own right to throw that away because of something neither of us did. Because the way I figure it, everyone gets a tragedy. And all things considered, I'm glad that car accident was mine. Otherwise I wouldn't be applying to East Coast colleges, or on the debate team, or any of those things, because I wouldn't have met you."

"But I didn't *do* any of that," Cassidy insisted. "Ezra, the girl you're chasing after doesn't exist. I'm not some bohemian adventurer who takes you on treasure hunts and sends you secret messages. I'm this sad, lonely mess who studies too much and pushes people away and hides in her haunted house. You keep wanting to give *me* credit because *you* finally decided you weren't content with squeezing yourself into the narrow corridor of everyone's expectations, but you made that decision before we'd even met, back on the first day of school when you shot your mouth off in AP Euro."

I'd totally forgotten about that. About the day we'd met, when I'd already gotten kicked out of the pep rally, been a smartass toward my coach, and ditched my friends at lunch. In my memory, it had been her, always her, as the motivating force behind my actions.

"There," she said smugly, because my expression must have changed. "You see? You're just figuring it out now, but I discovered a long time ago that the smarter you are, the more tempting it is to just let people imagine you. We move through each other's lives like ghosts, leaving behind haunting memories of people who never existed. The popular jock. The mysterious new girl. But we're the ones who choose, in the end, how people see us. And I'd rather be misremembered. Please, Ezra, misremember me."

There was a pleading quality to Cassidy's eyes that I hadn't seen before, and I realized that it didn't matter whether any of what she said was true; she believed it so completely that there was no convincing her otherwise.

To Cassidy, the panopticon wasn't a metaphor. It was the greatest failing of everything she was, a prison she had built for herself out of an inability to appear anything less than perfect. And so she ghosted on, in relentless pursuit of escape, not from society, but from herself. She would always be confined by what everyone expected of her, because she was too afraid and too unwilling to correct our imperfect imaginings.

But I didn't tell her any of those things. Instead, I acted

as though I believed her, because what else could I do? It was that poem she'd given me that day at the creek, about everything dying at last, and too soon. It was both of us asking the unanswerable question of what else we might have done.

"I don't want us to be over." It wasn't a question.

"Ezra," Cassidy said, sounding tremendously sorry. "You're better off without me. And I don't want to be around when you realize it."

She shrugged out of my jacket and draped it over my shoulders. I watched her do this, not really comprehending until she stepped back and sniffled, trying to be brave. I could feel the good-bye hovering between us, heavy and final, and then the vet appeared in the doorway, his expression grim.

"Mr. Faulkner? Could you step back here for a moment?"

"Oh, good. He's fine, right? He's going to be fine?" I asked.

The vet looked down at his clipboard, not daring to meet my eyes, and in that moment, I knew. I followed him without looking back, and just like that, Cooper's tags were pressed into my trembling hand, as though asking me to mourn him as a hero, and Cassidy disappeared from my life.

33

FOR MORE THAN a week, the urn containing Cooper's ashes sat on my desk, and whenever my mother gingerly revived the subject of moving it somewhere more discreet, I glared at her and wordlessly left the room.

Eastwood was distorted for me, a picturesque place meant to lull its residents into believing that behind our gates and beyond our curfew, nothing bad could ever happen with any sort of permanence. It was a place so fatally flawed that it refused to acknowledge that any such imperfection was possible.

The impeccable rows of homes marched onward, little soldiers on the front lines of suburbia, hoping valiantly they would never meet a tragic end. But so many of them did. So many identical houses behind identical gates bore the marks of tragedy, and it was from those houses that the determined few left Eastwood and all its empty promises behind forever.

Toby and I scattered Cooper's ashes over the hiking trail

one afternoon in late November, even though it was illegal. In eulogy, I read from my dog-eared copy of Gatsby, reciting that famous line about the foul dust that floated in the wake of his dreams as I emptied the funerary urn into the wind.

As Toby and I walked back toward the park, my cane sinking into the freshly watered grass, the light was on in Cassidy's bedroom, and I remember glancing at it and wondering. I wondered what things became when you no longer needed them, and I wondered what the future would hold once we'd gotten past our personal tragedies and proven them ultimately survivable.

When Cassidy failed to show up at school for the spring semester, I wasn't particularly surprised. I'd been expecting for some time that she'd go back to boarding school, returning to the panopticon that she had never truly escaped, and it was just as well. The finality of her leaving allowed me to reclaim the places that had once been ours as mine, to say good-bye to my childhood parks and hiking trails rather than grasping for lost moments with a lost girl who refused to be found.

I'm at college now, and it's been some weeks since the leaves turned to memory beneath our feet and trays began disappearing from the dining hall, smuggled out under wool coats in anticipation of the first snow.

Incidentally, it's snowing again as I write this, the fat flakes drifting past the window of my dorm, which faces out onto a gothic quadrangle. Toby came down from Boston over the weekend, and my room still bears the unmistakable signs of his visit; some art book on Magritte his boyfriend insisted on sending along for me, even though I can't imagine where he got the idea that I'm a fan of surrealist art. An inflatable mattress, which I've meant to return to the girl down the hall for days, except our schedules never seem to match up. And this fantastic picture from my eighteenth birthday that Toby taped up over my desk when I went to rinse out the French press in our hall kitchen.

Phoebe took the picture, twisting around in her seat on the roller coaster at the last moment, even though the Disneyland cast member was yelling at her to face front. It's a blurry shot of Toby and me in the back row of the Thunder Mountain Railroad. Toby's laughing at something Austin just said, and I'm almost but not quite looking at the camera. I'm smiling at Phoebe, at the whispered promises of that last summer, and the profound reluctance I'd discovered for leaving good people behind. But we had plenty of time for youthful indecision, both apart and together, for limping into the future past the unforgettable ash heaps of our histories.

I often wonder what will become of Cassidy Thorpe. She was the first of us to leave Eastwood, returning to the Barrows School that senior spring with what I can only imagine to be tales in which we're all elaborately misrepresented. I can't say I forgive her for refusing to indulge the perhapsness of what we might have been, but I understand why she chose to do it, and she never asked for my forgiveness.

She was right, though, in the end. I never should have given her so much credit. It all got tangled together, her appearance and Toby coming back into my life and the first time I ever read a book that spoke to me, and the question of who I wanted to be in the aftermath of my personal tragedy. Because I made a decision that year, to start mattering in a way that had nothing to do with sports teams or plastic crowns, and the reality is, I might have made that decision without her, or if I'd never fallen in love with a girl who considered love to be the biggest disaster of all.

The truth of it was, I'd been running the wrong experiment my whole life, and while Cassidy was the first person to realize, she didn't add the elements that allowed me to proceed down a different path. She lent a spark, perhaps, or tendered the flame, but the arson was mine. Oscar Wilde once said that to live is the rarest thing in the world, because most people just exist, and that's all. I don't know if he's right, but I do know that I spent a long time existing, and now, I intend to live.

ACKNOWLEDGMENTS

If thank-yous were notes, I'd probably sing them off-key, so be glad I haven't awarded each of you a literal thank-you note. Instead, I have condensed you—like soup!—into this handy little list.

First, to my agent, the wonderful Merrilee Heifetz. Your unwavering faith in both me and this little book has quite honestly changed my life. Sorry for emailing you so many pictures of giraffes sticking their tongues out (although I still maintain that you enjoy it). To my editor, Katherine Tegen, for helping me to give this book a super-cool plot mohawk and for being the best thing on Facebook. Sarah Nagel, for being delighted by everything to do with this book and for conspiring to send me a stuffed sloth when I was in the hospital. Liane Graham, for sitting on Brooklyn rooftops with me and talking about love. If books can be written as presents for people, this one's for you. Kaleb Nation, pretty much the only reason I go on Skype.

Philo, the indirect inspiration for everything, but particularly Sam and Cris, for being consulting, Ezra-gendered people and letting me smash a piano with a hammer and joking that I'm a manic pixie dream girl—but obviously not meaning it, ahem. The YouTube crowd, Paige, Karen, Adorian, Kayley, and Alexa. My roommate, Jennifer, for editing it before you were an editor and before it was a book. And everyone at HarperCollins, I can't thank you enough. If I were allowed, I'd link a GIF here, but probably my acknowledgments shouldn't be quite so Tumblr-like, so I'll resist.